2

The Body in the Wetlands

Books by Judi Lynn

Mill Pond Romances
Cooking Up Trouble
Opposites Distract
Love on Tap
Spicing Things Up
First Kiss, on the House
Special Delivery

Jazzi Zanders Mysteries
The Body in the Attic
The Body in the Wetlands

Published by Kensington Publishing Corporation

The Body in the Wetlands

Judi Lynn

LYRICAL UNDERGROUND
Kensington Publishing Corp.
www.kensingtonbooks.com

LYRICAL UNDERGROUND BOOKS are published by

Kensington Publishing Corp.
119 West 40th Street
New York, NY 10018

First Electronic Edition: April 2019
eISBN-13: 978-1-5161-0837-4
eISBN-10: 1-5161-0837-X

First Print Edition: April 2019
ISBN-13: 978-1-5161-0840-4
ISBN-10: 1-5161-0840-X

Printed in the United States of America

Chapter 1

Sweat dripped in Jazzi's eyes. It stung. She swiped the rest off her forehead. When you roofed a house in Indiana in late August, being closer to the sun only made you cook faster. She glanced at Ansel and Jerod, her boyfriend and cousin, their T-shirts drenched and stuck to their skin, just like hers. Muscles rippled as Ansel spread another layer of shingles over the last row and hit them with his nail gun. Tat, tat, tat. The guns beat out steady rhythms. Usually the sight of her beautiful, blond Norseman in a tight shirt set her hormones atwitter, but not today. He looked just as salty as she felt.

She was keeping up with the guys, the three of them roofing as fast as they could while Thane—who'd bought this long, sprawling ranch-style house with Jazzi's sister, Olivia—had the unfun job of carrying shingles up the ladder to them. It was his house, after all, and they were doing him the favor. The shingles were so hot, they wore gloves to protect their hands.

Jazzi, Jerod, and Ansel had promised to help with renovations between their regular fixer-upper projects. They'd just finished the Victorian on Lake Avenue and sold it before they put a sign in the front yard. They could stall on starting the big, old house they'd bought off Anthony Boulevard. Since Thane's biggest worry had been the ranch's roof, they'd packed their gear on Thursday and shown up here early Friday morning.

The temperatures had been in the seventies when they'd made their promise. Now the heat had climbed into the high eighties, and it was only ten in the morning. They'd started work on the double garage at seven. It took more time than planned, because they had to strip three layers of old shingles and replace most of the plywood beneath them. It was finished now, but the house was so long and angled that they'd be lucky if they got half of its roof done today.

Jazzi smiled when she heard kids' voices, yelling and laughing, on a recess break. A private school bordered the end of Olivia's subdivision. Jazzi loved the sound of kids playing. How teachers could keep their attention on hot August days was beyond her.

She finished her row of shingles, and Thane dropped another stack for her to start on. They kept roofing for another hour before Thane called, "It's too darn hot. We need a couple of beers to cool off."

Finally. A break. They started down the ladder to go inside, the guys first, Jazzi last. When she reached the bottom and turned around, Jerod and Thane were already on their way into the cool air-conditioning, but Ansel was standing there, waiting for her.

"Was I that slow?" she asked.

"You can take all the time you want. I was just enjoying the view."

Her tall Norseman was nothing to snicker at, either. She'd noticed women coming outside to pick a weed here and there just to gape at him. She didn't blame them. Hooking her arm in his, she headed inside for a beer.

The smell of fresh paint smacked her. Voices came from the back rooms. Jazzi's mom and sister were painting the four bedrooms—the only rooms in the entire place that didn't need serious updates. But that's why Olivia and Thane had gotten the property for such a good price. It needed TLC.

They huddled around the kitchen island—a sturdy wooden worktable. Ansel's pug, George, who went everywhere with him, raised his head off the kitchen tile to look at them. The dog might pout if he was left at home, but he wasn't devoted enough to lie outside in the shade while they worked.

Ansel ran a critical gaze over the open floorplan for the kitchen, dining area, and living room—all carpeted. He shook his head. "Who carpets a kitchen?"

After the roof, that was their next project, to rip up all the worn, plush green pile and matching indoor/outdoor kitchen carpet and install wood floors. Jerod grimaced at the worn spots and stains. "I'd do the whole house and get it over with. That way, all the wood would match."

Thane reached for his second beer. "If I were swimming in greenbacks, I'd agree with you, but the bedroom carpets aren't as bad as these. We want to save money and do them later."

Jazzi had been lucky when she remodeled her house. When she and Jerod had bid on the stone cottage in the summer, they got it at a bargain price. They'd meant to sell it as a fixer-upper until she fell in love with the place. Its value was so high, she could borrow enough to redo everything she wanted and still have decent mortgage payments. And then she'd gotten the cherry on top of the cake—Ansel had moved in with her.

Ansel studied the carpet in Thane's hallway that led to the baths and bedrooms. "Jerod's right. All of that plush is going to need to be replaced, but no one wants you to be house poor."

Thane clinked his beer bottle against Ansel's in a salute. "I need enough fun money to go out with you every Thursday while Jazzi and Olivia do their sister supper thing."

Ansel glanced at Jazzi, a smirk on his lips. "Our girls need to bond once a week to be able to put up with us."

"You're lucky it's only once a week," Jazzi shot back. She was just blowing smoke, and he knew it. She didn't think she'd ever get tired of her Viking.

Jerod stood and patted the top of her head. He was almost as tall as Ansel, but bulkier. "You don't appreciate the fact that you're looking at three prime male specimens. All over six feet. All decent-looking. And all holding down good jobs. I hope you girls genuflect and say thank-you prayers every night of the week."

She snorted. Half of what her cousin said was only to bait people. "I'll be sure to mention that to your Franny. Maybe she'll want to light incense and build a shrine." Franny was pregnant with Jerod's third child and was hot and miserable. Worshiping him might not be high on her list of things to do.

Jerod threw back his head and laughed. "Maybe not right now. She'd be tempted to throw something at my head." He started to the door. "Let's hit the roof again. I want to reach the peak sometime today."

She drained the last of her beer. The guys had already finished theirs. The minute they stepped outside, the heat and humidity hit them. They went straight to the ladders. Time to sweat again.

Jazzi glanced at the street and noticed a man—gray-haired, with stooping shoulders—who'd been walking a chocolate Labrador, standing there watching them. He wore a blue, button-down, long-sleeved shirt and tan slacks. A brimmed cap perched on his head. "A neighbor?" she asked.

Ansel and Jerod followed her gaze. The old guy didn't look like he meant to move anytime soon. Ansel and Thane had plenty to say around friends but tended to be quiet around people they didn't know, so they both shrugged and started to the roof.

"Better see what he wants," Jerod told her.

Really? It wasn't her house, but the man was probably just curious. Jazzi walked toward him. "Hello? Can I help you with something?"

When she got close enough, he said, "I'm Leo. I live in the third house across the street, the dark blue ranch with the deep front porch. This is my dog, Cocoa."

She gave a brief smile. She'd like to hurry this along. "I'm Jazzi. My sister and her boyfriend just bought this house. My friends and I came to help them renovate it."

Leo nodded. He was her height, five-eight, and thin. "I always liked the deep red clapboards and the limestone at the double-entry doors. You're not going to change those, are you?"

"They're not in the plans."

"Good. The house needs some work. I understand that. It's in good shape, just dated, like ours. That's what happens when you get old."

Jazzi gave another smile and turned to walk away. "We have plenty to do, but it was nice to meet you." Leo didn't budge. She hesitated. "Is there something you wanted to ask?"

"No. I'm not nosy, you know. Some people accuse me of that, but I just like to keep an eye on things in the neighborhood. I take Cocoa for a walk every morning and late every afternoon."

"Dogs need exercise." She was running out of things to say to him and wanted to get back to work, but he looked sort of lonely and disoriented. She didn't want to brush him off. "How long have you lived here?"

"Fifty-some years. The school wasn't private back then. Our daughter went there. And I played golf every weekend."

When she was on the roof, she'd seen the golf course. It started behind the school and stretched the entire length of the connecting neighborhood. A chain-link fence separated it from the houses. The area's layout was a little odd. Olivia's small addition connected to another one by a narrow, one-lane patch of asphalt, and that neighborhood connected to another that connected to another until an open field stretched to businesses that faced Jefferson Street and heavy traffic. Somewhere, on the far side of the subdivision, Thane said there was a woods and a wetland that led to another busy street.

Jazzi studied Leo. "Do you walk very far?" He looked too frail. Cocoa could drag him behind her if she got too excited.

"Sometimes Cocoa and I make it to the field before we turn around." A decent distance. He must be more fit than he looked. "We both like to walk, and it's nice to get out of the house a bit. My wife's wheelchair-bound. She can stand but not walk. I take care of her, but we both like a little alone time a couple times a day."

It would be hard living with an invalid—for both of them. "I'm sorry to hear about your wife. Caring for her must be a huge responsibility."

He shrugged. "She was in a car accident four years ago. Louisa and I have led happy lives. We have plenty of wonderful memories, and we still have lots of interests."

"That's good." She glanced back at the guys on the roof, nailing down shingles.

He tipped his head, taking the hint. "Better start walking or Cocoa's not going to be happy with me. It's so hot, not many people will be out today."

She almost asked if he stopped to talk to each person on his route. "This is a nice neighborhood. I bet you meet a lot of friendly people on your way."

His expression grew serious. "We're all still a little shaken about Miles. You must have heard about it on the news."

Miles? She tried to remember, but failed.

He said, "Three weeks ago, Miles disappeared from a neighborhood two subdivisions down. Police knocked on everyone's doors. We all knew him, watched him ride by our houses a few times a week. He lived with his parents, and everyone tried to keep an eye on him."

Jazzi shook her head, confused. "How old was he?" She hadn't heard about a child going missing.

Leo pressed his lips together thoughtfully. "In his thirties, but an innocent. He'd suffered a head injury."

How awful. Jazzi had heard something about it. An attractive young man's face had been flashed across the TV screen for a few days, and the police were asking people to report any sightings of him. "He packed all of his things and just left without a good-bye?"

Leo shook his head. "Walked out the door and never came back."

Now she remembered. She hadn't paid much attention at the time. She'd had enough going on after finding Aunt Lynda's body in her attic and Noah Jacobs's body near the septic tank. She didn't realize that the guy who'd disappeared lived so close to Olivia. "Do the police suspect foul play?"

"Not sure, but folks around here think he has to be dead." The dog tugged on the leash, and Leo sighed. "I'd better get going."

She watched him walk away. What a sweet old man, but Olivia had better be careful. He'd try to snag her every time she left the house. Olivia had mad people skills. After all, she and Mom ran a hair salon together, but Leo was lonely. He'd corner her whenever he could.

Jazzi climbed the ladder, tugged on her work gloves, and started nailing her section of shingles. When they stopped to eat lunch, she told Thane what Leo had said about the missing man. She remembered how hard

Noah's parents had searched for him when he disappeared. How awful would it be to not know what happened to your child?

Olivia and Mom had already eaten and were painting another bedroom. Strong fumes hung in the air. Jazzi would have liked to tell her sister about the missing man, but it could wait.

Thane wasn't surprised when she told him. "People think he got in a car with the wrong person."

Jerod frowned. "The guy was in his thirties?"

"Not mentally. He'd be easy to talk into almost anything."

Jazzi meant to ask Thane more, but the guys were ready to get back to work. Every time they left the air-conditioning and walked outside, the heat felt more oppressive. It was sweltering in late afternoon, but they worked through it. Even with frequent breaks for water, they felt wrung-out by the time they reached the peak. Tomorrow they'd finish the other side.

The weather man predicted the same heat as today. Jazzi mopped the back of her neck. Saturday was usually their day off. Instead, they were going to melt again. But when they finished, the roof would be done.

When they gathered back in the house again, Olivia and Mom had finished their painting, and her sister offered to order food for everyone for supper. Jerod shook his head. "I'm going home to jump in our pond and cool off. I told Franny I'd grab something to eat on the way home."

Ansel and Jazzi both shook their heads.

"I feel like a limp dishrag," Jazzi said. "We're hitting our pond, too. Then we're going to throw steaks on the grill for supper."

Mom reached for her purse. "Your dad and I have plans for tonight."

"Thanks again for everything!" Thane called after them as they filed out the door. "See you tomorrow at nine."

"Not me," Mom yelled. "I love my girls, but the painting's finished. Doogie and I are meeting friends in Marshall, Michigan, for a historic house tour."

"We'll be here, on time." Jerod slid into his pickup.

Jerod, Ansel, and Jazzi never worked on flip houses on weekends, but for Olivia and Thane, they'd agreed to cram in as much work as possible until Thane had to go back to his job after the end of next week.

Jazzi loved her sister, and it was a good thing. This was a lot more work than they'd first signed up for. It had started with the roof. Then the floors. And then Olivia decided she wanted a new kitchen. And new bathrooms. But they might as well do it now. What was one more week of work here?

On the drive home, when they turned out of the subdivision onto Sycamore Drive, a tall, thin boy was walking on the edge of the street.

Jazzi's heart stopped. When they passed him, she craned her neck to get a better view of him. Not Miles. Too young and the wrong coloring. She thought about Noah, the son Aunt Lynda had given up for adoption, and how relieved his dad had been when he came to River Bluffs to claim his body.

Yes, his adopted son was dead. But at least the family knew what happened to him. They could begin closure instead of playing one horrible scenario after another in their minds. She leaned back against the van's seat and wished the same for Miles's family. She hoped they'd learn the truth...and soon.

Chapter 2

Saturday morning, Ansel rolled over and pressed his long body against hers. Mmm. *This* was the way to wake up! Jazzi snuggled closer. She felt him lift himself onto an elbow. He pushed her long hair aside and nuzzled her neck. Delicious tingles radiated through every nerve of her body.

He lowered his lips to her ear and whispered, "Get your fanny out of bed. We promised to finish your sister's roof today."

She opened an eye to glare at him. "You're a tease!"

Laughing, he swung his legs over the side of the sleigh bed. "It's better than waking up to the alarm, isn't it?"

"The alarm doesn't make promises it's not going to keep."

His voice dropped. "I *can* keep them." Jazzi's breath caught, and he shook his head. "I'm not going to, though. Move it, woman, or we're going to be late."

And Jerod would give them grief. Lots of it. She waved Ansel away. George stretched in his dog bed in the corner, not quite ready to get up. "Your pug's still sleepy. It's the weekend, and he's ready to chill."

With a chuckle, Ansel dug for some clothes. "When isn't he in relax mode?"

He had a point.

They'd showered last night after cooling off in the pond, so it only took a few minutes to get ready. They'd be drowned in sweat again when they finished work today. On a Saturday. Her day. Their house wouldn't get cleaned this week. Not the end of the world. Dust didn't kill you, right?

Jazzi grimaced at her reflection in the bedroom mirror. Her hair hadn't dried completely by the time they crawled into bed last night, and it looked a little funky this morning. She couldn't tame the waves, so pulled them into a thick ponytail. Ansel finished tying his work boots and came to stand behind her.

"I love you with bedhead, all mussed up and sexy."

"You're biased." She turned and wrapped her arms around him. "Morning, Norseman."

That had become their joke. Ansel looked every bit like the Norwegian he was. Tall and fair, he never had to worry about sunburn. He only tanned more golden.

He bent to kiss the top of her head. "I'll go down and pour us some coffee."

By the time Jazzi and George got to the kitchen, he had a pile of buttered pumpernickel toast on the kitchen island and two steaming mugs of coffee. She sank onto a stool and reached for a slice.

"We should finish the roof today," Ansel told her. "Then if it stays this hot, we can work on inside projects."

"I should have become a hairdresser like my mom and sister."

His blue eyes twinkled. "Yeah, I can see that—you all dolled up with lots of jewelry and wearing high heels to work."

She reached for another slice of toast. "I've been known to dress up."

"And I love it when you do, but every day? If I hid your hammer, you'd take it more personally than if I lost your earrings."

She smiled. "Yeah, I like what I do, just not on Saturday."

"You'd only do this for your sister. You two are tight." So were Ansel and his sister, Adda. She was the only person in his family he ever called. For good reason.

Jazzi decided to kick her grumpy mood to the curb. "Olivia's the best. I'll get myself in gear. The sooner we finish the roof, the sooner we can come home. My family's coming for the Sunday meal tomorrow."

"You promised to keep it simple." Ansel constantly gave her grief about overworking. The man could do heavy labor from morning to night, but he fussed when she put in long hours. In a way, it was nice to have someone think of her as a girl. But she was a lot more durable than he realized.

Her family got together at their house every Sunday, no matter what. They'd vowed to make it a priority so that they'd keep in touch. "I have four chuck roasts to throw in the oven with potatoes, onions, and carrots. I'm making sautéed green beans and a Waldorf salad for sides and setting up an ice cream sundae bar for dessert. You can't get any easier than that."

He finished his coffee and went to put his cup in the dishwasher. "Only you would call that simple. Your mom and sister don't even cook. Neither does my sister since she works."

"I wouldn't either if I didn't like doing it. Cooking relaxes me. It's fun."

He laughed at her. "Even your hobbies are work, but I'm not complaining. I love home-cooked meals."

So did she. They were healthier than eating out all the time. She finished her breakfast and carried her plate and cup to the dishwasher. "I'm ready. Let's go melt."

She remembered those words when they were installing shingles with Thane and Jerod a half hour later. When they stopped at noon for lunch, she was drenched in sweat. Stepping into the house, the air-conditioning felt chilly until she adjusted to it. After lunch, just like yesterday, when they walked outside, Leo happened to be waiting with Cocoa. The guys left her to trot over and talk to him. He didn't stay long, and soon she was picking up her nail gun to join them.

"He's lonely, isn't he?" Jerod asked.

"He's retired and takes care of his wife, who's stuck in a wheelchair. A car accident."

Jerod pulled up the hem of his soaked T-shirt to wipe sweat off his forehead. "I feel sorry for both of them. Franny's nephew's in a wheelchair for life. Afghanistan. It sucks. The world is made for healthy people."

Jazzi remembered Franny talking about her nephew when he returned. He had a wife and two kids. Everyone worried, but he worked a job at a factory now and didn't let his handicap slow him down. It sure as heck made things more difficult, though. "Leo and his wife put a positive spin on it, just like Brady. He says they're pretty happy."

Jerod took another bundle of shingles to spread. "What are your options? You can sit around and feel sorry for yourself, or you can try to make the best of it. I gotta give 'em credit. Talk about getting lemons and making lemonade."

Jazzi felt guilty for griping this morning about having to get up early to work. She was strong and healthy. Life was good to her. What did she have to complain about?

They were up high enough that she had a decent view of the houses that made up Olivia and Thane's neighborhood. It only encompassed three main streets lined with ranch-style houses. In the distance, she saw Leo and Cocoa at the narrow strip of asphalt that connected this subdivision to the next—another small pocket of mostly Cape Cod–style houses. Leo kept going. The man and his dog went farther than she expected.

Ansel rubbed his back. He stood to stretch and yank off his soggy T-shirt. Muscles flexed, and a group of young women tumbled out of a house two doors down. One of them looked up and waved at him. "Want some lemonade? I came home for the weekend, and Mom told me Mrs. Neilsen had sold her place."

More like her mom called and told her to come over to see the hottie working on the roof two doors down. Jazzi couldn't help but smile. Ansel didn't realize he could compete with Thor. He grinned, and the girls' knees wobbled.

"Thanks," he called down. "But Thane and Olivia have stocked up on beer for us. We're fine."

The girls turned away, disappointed.

"That was nice of them," Ansel said.

Jerod rolled his eyes. "You're such an innocent, buddy. They didn't offer Jazzi or me anything to drink."

Ansel *was* an innocent compared to her cousin. Jerod had been a player before he met Franny and willingly wrapped himself around her little finger.

Biceps bulging, Ansel took another bundle of shingles from Thane. The girls gathered under an umbrella table and settled in to watch. Looking was fine. Jazzi could see how Ansel might make for great public entertainment... and fantasies. As long as no touching was involved.

By five, the roof was finished. The girls had gotten too hot, consumed way too much lemonade, and moved inside. Ansel had gotten even more golden than before, while Jazzi's hair turned into a frizzy mop and she felt like a salt lick. She, Jerod, and Ansel followed Thane into the house for one last beer before they headed home.

On the drive, Jazzi shot a dirty glance at Ansel. How could he still look good after hot, heavy work? "You could make a lot of money as a male stripper."

"Always a dream of mine." He grinned. "You meet such nice girls that way."

The man might be quiet, but he had a wicked sense of humor. When they got home, he grabbed her hand and pulled her to the pond behind the house. George followed at a sedate pace. Ansel dropped his wallet on the gazebo's bench. "Ready?" He tugged her to the end of the pier, and they jumped in, feet first, clothes and all. The cool water encircled her, and Ansel surfaced with a smile. "Boy, this feels good."

George stretched on the pier, content to watch them. The pug was so solid and heavy that swimming wasn't his thing.

Jazzi swam a little closer to shore and dipped her head back to get her hair out of her face. The water wasn't deep here. Ansel had angled the banks so that the water was shallow for a long time and the bottom gradually dropped deeper. They treaded water until they cooled off, and then Ansel said, "I'm starving."

"Me, too." Jazzi started for shore. Her gym shoes squeaked when she walked through the grass, but she'd kick them off at the house and let them dry on the back patio. No neighbors were close, so she stripped out of her clothes before going inside. So did Ansel. When the air-conditioning hit them, they both shivered. George, however, sprawled on the cool wood floors and closed his eyes.

They ran upstairs, took quick showers, and changed. Jazzi had planned ahead. She brought out a pork tenderloin for Ansel to throw on the grill, some baked beans she'd made ahead that only needed reheating, and a tossed salad.

He wrapped her in a bear hug. "You think of everything."

The man loved food. If Emily—his old girlfriend—had cooked for him, they might still be together, even though she was a super control freak.

The meal was cooked, eaten, and cleaned up an hour later. Ready for some R&R, they each headed to their favorite couch, plopped down, and watched some mindless TV. Two hours after that, Ansel yawned, picked up George, and started upstairs. He called, "You coming?"

When the dog went upstairs, there was no hanky-panky. The dog was too pure and innocent to hear or see. Jazzi turned off the TV and pushed to her feet to follow them. She and Ansel hadn't hit their first-month anniversary yet, but it was close. They'd had more than enough sex to skip tonight, though. And she was dead on her feet.

Chapter 3

Sunday, at one, everyone settled in the kitchen for the family meal—Jazzi's parents, Gran and her roommate Samantha, Jerod's parents, and Jerod and his family, along with Olivia and Thane. The room was plenty big enough to seat twenty, and the time might come when they needed to. For now, fourteen of them lined the two tables they'd pushed together, but if Olivia and Thane had kids, and she and Ansel had a couple, they'd need bigger tables. *If* she and Ansel stayed together, that was. Sure, everything was great now, but they were still in the honeymoon stage, weren't they?

She and Chad had started out great, too. They'd seemed to have a lot in common until she moved in with him. He owned a landscaping company and liked running his own business as much as she did. But once they lived together and she wore his ring, he wanted to move to marriage and starting a family right away. He badgered her to stop working with Jerod. He didn't like it when she visited her family. When she gave his ring back and moved out, it wasn't a friendly parting. Things got better over time, especially when he married and was happy, but it was a bitter experience for Jazzi.

As if reading her thoughts, Ansel came to wrap an arm around her. They arranged the food on the kitchen island, buffet style, and for the hundredth time, Jazzi admired how easy it was to entertain here. She glanced at the beam she and Ansel had installed so that they could knock out a wall to make a space this big. The white tin ceiling tiles added an Old World flavor, and the stainless-steel counters made cooking functional. Finally, she glanced at the refinished, wooden floors. This was the kitchen of her dreams.

It was hard to get a word in edge-wise when her family got together. Mom and Dad talked about their trip to Michigan. They'd taken the house tour, then eaten at Schuler's restaurant, known for its schnitzel. Jerod's parents, Eli and Eleanore, had spent Friday and Saturday at their lake cottage, and Eli was complaining that he had to spend most of Friday working on his boat's engine.

Eleanore glanced at her husband and snorted. "That man is never happier than when he's getting his hands greasy, but he finally got the boat running in time for our evening cruise."

When there was a small slice of silence, Jazzi told them about Leo and what he'd said about someone disappearing from a neighborhood close to Olivia's.

Thane shook his head. "It was all over the news for a while. I asked my friend about it. He works with me on the heating and cooling crew and lives in the neighborhood where it happened. He's the guy who told us about our house before the realtor put a sign in the yard. Knew the family and heard the kids were going to sell it when they put their mom in a nursing home. He told me the area is nice and we could probably get it at a good price."

Jerod loaded his plate with a second helping of chuck roast and vegetables. "Houses are going so fast right now, someone makes an offer before you actually put your place on the market. Our last fixer-upper sold like that."

Jazzi hoped the trend lasted, but she wanted to hear more about the disappearing neighbor. She turned to Thane. "Did your friend hear anything about the guy who never came home? Leo said the police knocked on doors all up and down Sycamore Drive."

Olivia scrunched her face. "The cops think someone snatched him, right?"

Why would someone grab a thirty-year-old man? "It makes you wonder what they did to him."

"Ich! Don't say that. I don't want to think about it." Olivia drained the last of her wine.

She and Thane were sitting next to each other, and Jazzi had to smile. Her sister, as usual, looked trendy and chic. She wore canary-yellow short-shorts to show off her long legs and a cherry-red spandex top. Her dark blond hair was twisted into a spiky do, held in place by what looked like chopsticks. Thane's longish auburn hair looked disheveled, and he wore old jeans with an oversized T-shirt, emblazoned with an air-conditioner on the front and the slogan KEEP YOUR COOL. The two didn't seem to match, but they complemented each other really well.

Thane reached to put his hand over Olivia's. "Something happened to the kid. And I know he was grown, but he had had a head injury. After that, he was nervous, a little paranoid. He had anger issues. He had to move back home to have his parents take care of him. He rode his bike to work at a pet shop close by. Couldn't handle any stress."

Jazzi's dad stared. "They let him drive a motorcycle?"

"Not a motorcycle, a bike—the kind with pedals." Thane tipped his plate to move the last of the roast's sauce into a spoon, then pushed his empty plate away. He licked his spoon before glancing at the jars of hot fudge, caramel, and marshmallow toppings on the kitchen island. Stacks of bowls sat next to nuts, sliced strawberries, and maraschino cherries.

"What's for dessert?" Thane waggled his eyebrows.

"Ice cream. I bought four kinds." Jazzi stood, and Ansel joined her to gather dirty plates. They could do the washing up after everyone left. The farmhouse sink was deep enough to hide them from view.

Jerod stabbed his last potato before Jazzi took his plate. "I remember reading about a kid who went out partying and disappeared. They pulled his car out of the subdivision's pond a few days later."

Olivia grimaced. She stood to go get a bowl and dessert. "That's happened a few times. The run-off ponds are close to the houses, and the kids are so drunk, they drive right into them."

Thane followed her to the kitchen island while Ansel carried over the last two containers of ice cream. Thane went for the double chocolate. "There's no pond close to us, and even if the kid rode his bicycle into one, it's not like he'd be trapped inside."

Gran laid her hands on the table, wringing her fingers. She'd been having a good day, so far, her mind sharp with clarity, but stress could change that. "Have they found him yet? Did he disappear for good, like Lynda did?"

Oh crap, Jazzi hadn't connected the kid and Lynda. When they'd bought the house, they'd found her aunt's skeleton in a trunk in the attic. Every time they talked about Gran's missing daughter, Gran slipped back in time to better days, when she was a young girl.

Jazzi's mom hurried to make Gran feel better. "They'll find him, Mom. Maybe he got lost or confused. Someone will bring him back home."

"He never went far, according to my friend," Thane added. "And he was on a bike. Someone will notice him and help him."

Gran quit fidgeting, and Samantha—who shared the big, old farmhouse with her—said, "I love ice cream sundaes. What do you want on yours, roomie?"

A good distraction. Gran's expression cleared, and she grinned. "A little bit of everything." The two of them went to fill their bowls.

Jazzi walked to the end of the line to wait her turn, more worried than she'd been before. How long had the *kid* been missing? The longer, the worse his odds. She thought about the man's parents, and that made her think about Noah Jacobs. His adoptive parents had worried, too, when he didn't come home. And then she, Jerod, and Ansel found him, buried by the septic tank.

Ansel came to stand behind her and wrapped his arms around her. "Don't worry until you have to."

Right. A good rule to live by. Impossible to follow, but he was right. There was nothing she could do about it, so she shook her gloom away. No one should be dreary when they ate ice cream on a Sunday. Another rule to embrace.

Chapter 4

Everyone started for the door at about five. When the last person left, Ansel helped Jazzi with cleanup and then they hit their favorite couches in front of the TV. Sunday was the only day Ansel immersed himself in sports, and Jazzi was happy to read a book and listen to his occasional comments as his favorite teams won and lost. George, as usual, lay on Ansel's feet at the end of the sofa.

A few hours later, they were getting a little hungry again, so Ansel made them popcorn. The smell filled the house, and Jazzi went to pour herself a glass of wine to go with it. She carried a beer in for Ansel. He plopped the two bowls on the coffee table when his cell phone buzzed. As he glanced at the ID, his whole face looked like a gathering thunderstorm.

Jazzi stared, surprised. What could make him change moods so fast? "Who is it?"

"My brother." He stalked out of the room.

Ansel was usually pretty easygoing, but he wasn't on good terms with his family right now. Feeling no shame whatsoever, Jazzi turned down the volume on the TV so that she could listen to his side of the conversation. He went to the kitchen, sitting in the small grouping of armchairs near the big front window. A bathroom and coat closet divided the kitchen from the living room area, so she couldn't see him, but she could hear plenty.

"And you thought this would concern me—how?" His tone was blistering.

There was some more back-and-forth before he ended the conversation with "Forget it. You wanted me out of the family business. I'm out. Don't expect me to jump in to help now."

Uh-oh, not good. Something drastic must have happened to his family. When he started back toward her, she sat up. He dropped onto the couch opposite her, leaned forward, his elbows on his knees, his hands balled into fists.

"Want to talk about it?"

"That was my brother Radley."

"The younger one?" From comments he'd made, Jazzi thought Ansel liked Radley more than his oldest brother or his dad.

George moved down the couch to stretch next to Ansel's leg. Ansel's shoulders relaxed a little while he scratched the top of the pug's head. If ever a man loved a dog, Ansel was devoted to his George. "There's Bain, Radley, Adda, then me. Bain was trying to patch Mom and Dad's roof three days ago, fell, and broke his leg. He won't be out of a cast for months. Dad just went in to have knee-replacement surgery, so he's no help in the barn either. Both the house and barn need new roofs, Radley said. They've been leaking for a while, but now they're worse. They can't really afford to hire someone to fix them or to help with the dairy right now, so they thought I might want to come back and help with things until Dad and Bain are better."

"You're kidding."

"Nothing about my family's funny."

"Your mom can't milk?" Jazzi thought farm wives could manage almost everything.

It was pretty nervy of them to ask Ansel. They'd kicked him out the minute he graduated from high school so he wouldn't get any ideas about working on the farm and living off his share of the profits.

"Mom's always been on the frail side. She can't do heavy work."

Jazzi hesitated, unwilling to state an opinion. His family had treated him shabbily, but they were family. Jazzi didn't want Ansel to regret not helping them if he wanted to. "Jerod and I can manage without you if you want..."

"I don't. Not one of them thought a thing about kicking me out."

Jazzi took a deep breath. "I know that, but won't it bother you if they go under? What if your mother..."

"She had a vote, too. She voted against me."

Jazzi couldn't imagine turning out one of your kids, especially one as nice as Ansel.

"The only person I care about is my sister, but this won't affect her. She has a great husband. She'll be fine."

Jazzi let it go. Ansel wasn't in the mood to forgive his parents and brothers, and she didn't blame him. But she hated to see him so upset. She reached for her popcorn and gave him a sideways glance. "Know what I'm in the mood for?"

His blond brows furrowed into a scowl. He was big and broad-shouldered, but he didn't intimidate her. "What?"

"A scary movie. You always say they work off negative energy. And I won't watch one unless I'm plastered next to you. And that always puts us in the mood for..." It was a private joke between them.

He grinned. "Strenuous exercise. Let me find a movie that will scare the crap out of you. Then you'll need lots and lots of reassurance, and I'll have to work hard to make you feel better."

Scare the crap out of her? Not exactly what she'd had in mind, but the lots of reassurance sounded like a winner. She drew the line at too much blood and gore, so they chose one of his old favorites—*Scream*—and when it was over, she was more than ready to hold his hand and head upstairs. As an added bonus, he'd moved past being upset by his brother.

Chapter 5

The temperature dipped to the low eighties on Monday. Even better, the humidity was low, too. When Jazzi and Ansel got to Olivia and Thane's, Thane decided to take advantage of the nice weather and replace the gutters. George sprawled on the grass under a tree to watch them and stay close to Ansel—so devoted, as long as he was comfortable.

Each of them took a side of the house to work on. They'd hardly gotten started when Jerod gave a yell. "All the wood under the gutters is rotted on my side. We'll have to replace it."

Crap. Jerod was working on the front of the house. They went to study it. Ansel glanced at the beautiful sugar maple halfway between the house and the road, then tugged off the metal downspout at the corner. "Completely clogged. No one cleaned the gutters. Any rain or snow backed up and spilled over."

Thane glanced at Jazzi and Ansel. "How were your sides?"

"Fine." Jazzi thought a minute. "But it wouldn't hurt to repaint all the wood fascia boards before we install the new gutters."

Thane nodded toward the two-car garage. "I bought exterior paint to touch up the trim. It's in there. We can use that. Olivia and I bought this place from a widow who had to go to a nursing home. Some things got neglected at the end. That's to be expected. An old woman can't keep up with a house and yard this size. The new gutters will be bigger and wider. That should help move more water."

Jerod pointed to Jazzi. "Why don't you paint while we install new boards across the front of the house?"

Fine with her. She went to the garage and came back with a gallon of crisp white.

Once they'd tossed all the old gutters into the back of Jerod's pickup, Jazzi started painting the fascia boards while the guys ripped out the rotted wood and put up new. By the time they'd finished that, Jazzi had finished painting the boards at the back of the house and on both sides, so they could install the new gutters and guards. Hopefully, she could stay ahead of them.

She was halfway through the long front board when Thane called for a break. The men started into the house when Jazzi noticed Leo and Cocoa waiting for her. She glanced at Ansel, but he grinned and gave her a thumbs-up before leaving her. Why was it her job to talk to Leo? He wasn't even her neighbor. But he stood there, looking so ready for company that she trotted toward him.

"I hope you had a nice Sunday," she said.

He grimaced, clearly upset. He was wearing plaid pants today and a lightweight sweater. It must be true that people's circulation slowed down with age and they were always cold. She couldn't imagine wearing long sleeves in this weather. "I had a bit of unpleasantness. A neighbor two subdivisions down yelled at Cocoa and me."

"Yelled at you?" Why would anyone scream at an old man and his dog?

"We stopped in front of his yard while he was arguing with his wife, and he got mad."

"You just stood there and watched them?" Jazzi could see how that might annoy someone. If she and Ansel ever had an argument, she wouldn't want an audience. "How mad was he?"

"Out of control. I wanted to make sure no one got hurt."

"Was the man going to hit his wife?"

"His hands were balled into fists. It bothered Cocoa and me." Leo reached down to scratch the chocolate Lab behind her ears. "He yelled for us to move on, that the argument was none of our business. So we walked in front of his neighbor's yard so we were off his property."

Good grief! It was a good thing Leo didn't get punched. "Do you carry your cell phone on your walks?"

Leo patted his pant pocket. "I could have reported him."

For arguing with his wife? Did police respond to that? If he'd hit her... yes. But couples fought. Chad had spewed plenty of vitriol when she left him. Leo didn't need to provoke someone who was already on the brink of losing control. "Did you ever think the man might fight with his wife, but hit you? That you were pushing your luck?"

"Cocoa wouldn't like that. She's a wonderful dog, but she can be protective."

Jazzi bit her bottom lip. She didn't think Leo understood what he could have gotten himself into. "Husbands and wives get mad at each other. Don't you and Louisa ever argue?"

"I don't make fists," Leo said. "I've watched the news. I know how many women suffer domestic abuse. It won't happen on my watch."

His watch. Leo the Enforcer. That wouldn't go over well. "Did the wife look afraid?"

Leo tilted his head, thinking about that. "No, she talked back to everything he said, just kept cranking him up more."

"Then I doubt she's abused." Didn't most women who got pounded flinch and cower? Try not to say the wrong thing? Try to become invisible until things settled down or their guy slept it off? She couldn't imagine living in constant fear. "It sounds like the wife has a temper, too, just kept goading him on. But you took a real risk, Leo."

"I was only trying to do the right thing."

"You might have cranked him up more."

His shoulders slumped. "I see that now. I didn't think it through. I used to warn Miles about that."

"About arguing with people?"

"He didn't understand. He was awfully gullible. His whole life revolved around how far he could ride his bicycle and watch people."

"Watch people?"

Leo looked embarrassed. "He didn't have a life of his own. He worked at the pet shop and lived with his parents. So if people had a barbecue and invited lots of company, it was an event to him. He'd climb a tree and watch them. And he liked to park his bike at night and look in people's windows."

"A voyeur?"

Leo looked away, bent to pet Cocoa's head. "A bit of one."

Jazzi wondered what else Miles had seen. Something he shouldn't have? The kid lived through other people. "When he disappeared, did anyone find his bicycle, or did he take off on it?"

"That's the thing." Leo's voice sounded sad. "A sheriff found it on Highway 114, close to Manchester. Miles would never have gone that far."

"Even if he saw something that really excited or interested him?"

Leo shook his head. "Miles felt safe here, but after the accident, he was almost paranoid. He had so many fears, he could hardly function. He'd never go that far unless he was with a friend."

"Did he have a friend?"

"Not that I know of. He talked a lot about some woman who was kind to him, but it was out of pity, I could tell. When I first heard that he'd disappeared, I thought maybe he'd met someone and was ready to spread his wings. But after I talked to you, I thought about it more. And now I think someone stuck his bicycle in their trunk and dumped it on 114."

"And Miles?"

"I think Miles got dumped somewhere else."

Jazzi shivered. It was eighty degrees, but Leo made the boy's disappearance sound sinister. The sad truth was, she agreed with him.

Chapter 6

Upset, Jazzi went in the house to join the guys on their break. She told them what Leo had told her.

Jerod leaned back on the kitchen stool and stretched his long legs. "Sounds like Miles might have been in the wrong place at the wrong time."

Thane shook his head and spread out his hands. "Around here? What's to see? Not much happens."

Ansel finished his second beer while she started her first. "If the kid was a voyeur, hiding in the shadows to peep in houses, he might have seen plenty."

Olivia came out to join them. She must have heard Jazzi's voice. "Like what?"

At first, Jazzi was surprised to see her, but this was a Monday, after all—her day off from the salon. Her trendy sister wore her blond hair scraped back in a ponytail, like Jazzi. Leggings hugged her long legs, and an oversized, faded, button-down shirt hung over them. Work clothes.

Ansel shrugged. "The kid might have watched people undress, couples getting it on, things that are private."

Olivia rubbed at a drip of white semigloss splattered on the front of her shirt, smearing it more. "And you think someone would kill him for that?"

Jazzi frowned. "I thought you and Mom got all of the bedrooms painted."

"The ceilings and walls. I'm working on trim today."

"That's always fun." Painting was one of the jobs Jazzi dreaded, especially trim, but it was a cheap way to make a big difference in how a house looked. And what was she doing today? Painting fascia boards for gutters. Still easier than crown moldings and baseboards—you could just slap it on without worrying about tape and drips.

Olivia laughed. "I'd rather paint than put up gutters, so no complaints from me."

Jerod sipped his beer, wearing his brooding face. Jazzi pursed her lips. "You okay?"

"I can't help but think about Miles's parents. They thought they had their kid raised, in good shape, and then a head injury sent him home. You have to feel sorry for them. And now? They have no idea what happened to him. That's every parents' nightmare."

Her cousin adored his brood. He was a good daddy, through and through. Having a kid go missing would drive him crazy.

Ansel's good mood vanished, too. "My parents sent me away and didn't much care what happened after that."

Jerod tossed him a sympathetic look. "Jazzi said your brother called you last night."

"Yeah, can you believe that?" Ansel's fingers tightened on his empty beer can, crushing it. "To come home, because they need my help for a while."

Jerod glanced at Jazzi and Olivia. "We're all so close, it's hard for us to wrap our heads around your family. But Aunt Lynda didn't mind using anyone and everyone to get what she wanted. Your brothers must be like that."

"My parents, too."

How had Ansel and Adda turned out so nice? How did one or two people in most families turn out so differently from everyone else? Genes?

Olivia went to the cupboards for a box of fat-free crackers. She took a few and offered the box to the others. When they declined, she left it on the counter close to her. She reached to touch Ansel's arm. "What did you tell your brother?"

"I told him not to call me again."

"Good!" She finished a cracker and washed it down with water. She kept close track of calories during the day, not so much when she went out to eat. "You guys make it sound like you think this kid who disappeared is dead."

"That's what I think," Thane said, "or he'd have come home by now."

Olivia narrowed her eyes. "We're not talking another murder, are we? We had enough of that when Jazzi renovated *her* house."

Jerod brought the recycle can over for everyone to toss their empty cans in. "I didn't think foul play until Leo said the bike was miles out on 114. That worries me."

"Why?" Olivia closed the cracker box and put it away.

Jazzi answered. "Because Miles wouldn't have ridden that far. We're guessing someone dumped it there, far away from the crime."

"Crime? So you think someone killed him?" Olivia went to stand next to Thane.

He put his arm around her waist. "This time, at least, we're not involved. That's the good news."

"The silver lining," Jazzi agreed. They'd had enough of missing people and murder.

And with that, they all dropped the subject and returned to work. No more investigations for them. By late afternoon, they were finished. The fresh paint on the fascia boards and the new white gutters made the whole house look better.

Thane stood back to admire their work. "You guys are the best. It looks great. We've done enough for today. There's no reason to start on the floors. We can do them tomorrow." He motioned to Ansel and Jazzi. "You're meeting friends for supper tonight. Why don't the three of you take off, and I'll go help Olivia finish painting the woodwork?"

Jerod started across the yard toward his pickup. "I'll dump the old gutters and head home. The kids are back from preschool by now. I'll jump in the pond with them and give Franny some time to herself."

Thane gave him an odd look. "If the kids are in preschool, doesn't she have more time off than you do?"

Jerod chuckled. "It always sounds good, dropping the kids off and getting them out of your hair, but by the time Franny drives them to school and drives home, she loses time. Then she gets busy in her shop, refinishing furniture. And before she turns around twice, it's time to pick them up. Believe me, kids gobble up time like black holes, and when the baby comes along, God help Franny."

Thane scratched his head. "Maybe Olivia and I will wait before we start a family."

"If you want kids, you have to do it before too long." Jerod gave them a wave and went to his truck.

Jazzi started toward Ansel's van. She liked the idea of a little extra time to get ready to meet their friend Reuben and his girlfriend, Isabelle. She'd never been to Club Soda but knew it attracted a high-class clientele. Reuben had chosen it to celebrate. He and Isabelle had finished work on the Victorian where Jazzi had rented the first floor and Reuben the second until Jazzi moved out to buy Cal's place. Cal had been engaged to her Aunt Lynda, and her mom and grandmother had fond memories of his house. Once Jazzi had decided to renovate it, Reuben and Isabelle had bought the beautiful old Victorian and restored it to a single-family home.

She and Ansel were climbing into his work van, along with George, when Leo called to them. Ansel winced but forced a smile on his face and followed Jazzi over to talk to him.

"You're taking your evening walk a little early, aren't you?" Jazzi asked.

George and Cocoa sniffed each other, then George lay down. Cocoa tried to make friends with him, but he closed his eyes. Not even a pretty young female could motivate the pug.

Leo motioned to a car in his driveway. "Seth, my wife's nephew, comes to visit her once a week. I'm not a fan, so I take Cocoa for a long walk to avoid him."

Ansel glanced at the black SUV with tinted windows in Leo's drive. "Not many nephews drop in once a week to check on their aunts. That's pretty nice. The guy must be doing all right. That's a Cadillac he's driving."

"Looks like a gangster's car to me."

Jazzi laughed. "He must like your wife. Are they close?"

"I guess. He owns a bar on Jefferson Street. We could walk there. He used to visit his mom once a week, but when she moved to Arizona, he started dropping by to see Louisa. I don't approve of bartenders. They offer people drinks and watch them get stupid."

Ansel looked surprised. "I think that's the patron's call, not the bartender's."

"Our country should never have given up Prohibition. Some people have no control."

Jazzi hadn't realized Leo could be so opinionated. "I like my beer and wine. I wouldn't appreciate someone telling me that I couldn't have any."

"It's poison. You know that, don't you?" Leo's fingers tightened on Cocoa's leash. Drinking obviously upset him.

"You never drink?" Jazzi asked.

"My father was an alcoholic. I swore I'd never touch the stuff. Every time he drank too much, he'd pick fights with Mom."

That explained it. Jazzi reached out to touch his hand. "Does your nephew drink too much?"

"Never, but he tolerates it when other people do."

"Does your wife enjoy his visits?"

Leo glanced back at his house. "She gets lonely for family. I'm glad he comes. I just don't want to make small talk with him."

Ansel smiled and reached for Jazzi's hand. "Then enjoy your walk. It's a beautiful day."

"Indeed, it is." Leo regained some of his joviality and tugged on Cocoa's leash. "You two enjoy your evening." And he and his Lab set off.

Chapter 7

They were crossing town at a little after four. That meant long lines of traffic on Jefferson Boulevard and Hillegas Road. Ansel kept glancing at the dashboard clock. Finally, Jazzi asked, "Is there something you want to do before we meet Reuben and Isabelle?"

"I was hoping to mow the yard if we had enough time."

"The grass isn't that long yet." It was late August. They hadn't had rain for a while.

"I didn't get a chance to mow on the weekend."

"So? It still looks okay." But not perfect. And Jazzi hadn't known how seriously Ansel took grass until he'd moved in with her. He and Emily had rented an apartment, so his obsession didn't surface until he had a yard to tend. "You grew up on a dairy farm. Did your parents keep their yard perfect?"

"My mom didn't care about the fields or barns, but she liked everything around the house to be taken care of. I was the youngest boy. It was my job to mow and weed her flower beds. If I didn't mow at least once a week, I heard about it."

"I'm not as strict as your mom."

He frowned, obviously torn. "It's uneven and taller than I like it."

"It hasn't hit my knees yet."

"Your *knees*?" He sounded shocked.

She couldn't help it. She laughed, and he gave her a dirty look. She liked to give him a hard time once in a while. She glanced at the clock. "I don't think we're going to make it home in time."

"If we hadn't stopped to talk to Leo, we would have missed most of this traffic."

"But he looked upset."

They drove past the apple orchard on Huguenard, and Ansel pointed to a sign near the barn. "The peaches are ready."

Peaches were a new crop there. Jazzi kept saying she wanted to stop and buy some to see how good they were. They were Red Havens, her favorites. Ansel kept driving.

"You're not going to stop?" she asked.

"On Friday. We're busy this week." And he wanted to get home to his lawn.

When they finally reached their house, they had two hours before they had to meet Reuben and Isabelle. The two hours went fast. Ansel started straight to the garage and their riding lawn mower.

"I can mow everything to the hedge," he told her. "I can wait to do around the pond until I mow the whole thing again on Saturday."

The man was nuts, but everyone had their own kind of crazy. She waved him off, and George followed her into the house. The pug walked to his dog bed. She went to the refrigerator for a glass of wine. If Ansel wanted to work right up until they left, that was his problem. She ran upstairs to take a shower, then pulled on her sleep shorts and a tee to relax on the sofa. She sipped her zinfandel while she read her latest Savannah Martin mystery. Rafe, the bad boy love interest, was tall, dark, and sexy. But he couldn't outdo Ansel, her blond, gorgeous Viking.

An hour and a half later, Ansel hustled into the house and hurried upstairs to take his shower. While he cleaned up, she closed her book and went to get dressed and ready. She took her cues from Savannah and reached for a flirty dress and some heels. Not three-inch wonders like Savannah wore, but better than the usual gym shoes or flip-flops she favored. She even wore eyeliner. Then she went downstairs to wait for Mr. Lawn Obsessed to join her.

He stopped and stared when he saw her. "Doggone, you look good."

Ha! She'd surprised him. "I clean up once in a while, you know."

"We never have shopped at Victoria's Secret. My treat. You keep putting it off."

"It's sort of a waste of money. I wore those when I first started dating. I'd put on cute undies for guys, and before I knew it, they took them off me."

He stared. "I think you miss the point. That's the fun of it—taking them off."

"Then why bother in the first place?"

He shook his head. "It's sort of like lighting candles on a birthday cake. You blow them out right away, but they set the mood."

"Oh." She'd never thought of it that way.

He laughed at her. "Let's go, or we're going to be late."

George followed them to the door and pouted when they left without him, but the minute the door shut, Jazzi looked through the window to watch him pad to his dog bed in the kitchen. Ansel peeked over her head. "George loves it here."

Traffic wasn't bad on their drive back into town. The TinCaps were playing a baseball game tonight, but the traffic didn't come as far as Superior Street. There must be a festival in Headwaters Park because a girl in a lawn chair greeted them when they pulled into the parking lot to make sure they were dining at Club Soda. Reuben and Isabelle pulled in right behind them, and they walked into the restaurant together.

Jazzi liked the restaurant's vibe right away. Old brick walls gave it a cozy feel, and a row of windows let in light. She liked the menu even more. Four bacon-wrapped diver scallops were listed as an appetizer, enough to satisfy her as almost a meal, so she ordered a spinach salad and a baked potato on the side. Ansel decided on the walleye, and both Reuben and Isabelle chose the salmon.

Isabelle had an intensity about her tonight that made Jazzi think there was more going on than just celebrating their finished house. And Isabelle had gone to more bother than usual with her hair and makeup, which were always perfect. Tonight Isabelle's sleek black hair was pulled up in a knotted chignon, her eyes were rimmed with black liner, and her lips were painted cherry red. Isabelle was so striking, she could pull off the severe look. If Jazzi tried that, she'd get laughed at.

Jazzi's dear friend Reuben—equally elegant with his mocha skin, slight build, and trimmed goatee—radiated excitement. He ordered martinis for Isabelle and him, wine for Jazzi, and beer for Ansel.

Once the waiter came with their drinks, Jazzi quirked an eyebrow at him. "Okay, what's up? You two are practically humming with happy energy."

Isabelle held her hand out to them, displaying the huge diamond on her finger. "We wanted to personally invite you to our wedding."

"Oh my God!" Jazzi put a hand to her throat. "I'm so happy for you!"

Isabelle deserved a happy ever after. She'd worked with Cal to expand his businesses for years, waiting for him to get over Jazzi's Aunt Lynda and notice and love her, and it had never happened. Cal thought of her as his best, most trusted friend—nothing more. The man was rich and a wonderful person, but he'd never gotten over Lynda walking out of his life to spend time in New York, ostensibly to think things over before she married him, then disappearing without a word to anyone. Not to him. Not to Jazzi's mom, her sister. And not to Gran, her mother.

Disappearing. Jazzi pushed thoughts of Miles out of her mind.

"Congratulations!" Ansel raised his glass and clinked it against theirs in a toast.

"When's the wedding?" Jazzi beamed at Reuben. "You wanted to marry Isabelle the minute you met her. You're not rushing things and eloping, are you?"

He laughed. "No, Isabelle deserves a ceremony, something to celebrate how wonderful she is."

Yes, she did. Jazzi turned to Isabelle. "When's the big day?"

"September twenty-ninth, my parents' anniversary. They're both gone, so this is my way of including them in our day." She glanced at Reuben. "We want to keep it small, but memorable. The Oyster Bar is closed on Sundays, but the chef has agreed to open it for us and make appetizers and lots of shrimp. A retired minister will perform our vows, and we've invited a few of our dearest friends to join us. We'd love for you to come."

A lump closed Jazzi's throat for a minute. She swallowed how honored she felt. "Are you kidding? I'll even buy a new dress."

Reuben smiled and turned to Isabelle. "You have no idea what a compliment that is. Jazzi thinks of shopping as torture."

"Not true." The waiter came with their food, and she waited for him to leave. "I like to shop for kitchen things and tools."

Isabelle laughed. "Between your sister and me, maybe we'll convert you to love clothes. We should go to Chicago and hit some of the shops there."

She made a face. Shopping overload. She glanced at Ansel. He liked it when she dressed up. She might have to put more effort into her appearance. "Have you picked out a dress?"

The conversation veered to flower arrangements, dress shopping, and honeymoon destinations. Both men volunteered plenty of opinions. But when the meal was finished, the topic changed to the Victorian Reuben and Isabelle had renovated.

"Just wait till you see it," Reuben told them. "It's fabulous."

"You're an interior designer," Jazzi said. "You'd have to have a wonderful house, wouldn't you?"

"Let's hope. We'll meet you there." Reuben held out a hand for Isabelle. "You won't recognize your old apartment."

He hadn't exaggerated. When she and Ansel pulled to the curb in front of the house, Jazzi blinked at her former home. No longer pink, it was painted lavender with cream trim and deep purple details. The wraparound porch had dark purple floorboards. It was stunning.

Reuben and Isabelle opened the gleaming mahogany front door and motioned them inside.

Jazzi stopped and took a deep breath. Ansel stared. Reuben had turned Jazzi's old bedroom into an office with floor-to-ceiling bookcases and pocket doors. The walls and high ceilings were painted charcoal, set off by white crown molding and woodwork. Two golden, overstuffed sofas faced each other in the front room, covered with red and cobalt-blue throw pillows. A square, glass coffee table sat between them, and two flowered armchairs finished the grouping. In the dining room, a modern glass light with huge dangling bulbs hung over a long, sleek wooden table with straight metal legs. Three crimson, slip-covered chairs were arranged on each side. Nothing she'd ever choose, but they sang with dramatic flair.

"It's amazing." Jazzi circled the dining room table and stepped into the kitchen and stopped to gape again. Reuben had designed it to be galley style with white and gray marble counter tops and a V-patterned marble backsplash. Black cupboards stretched to a mustard-gold ceiling. Stainless-steel appliances gleamed. "Wow."

Reuben smiled, happy with her response. "Not your style, I know, but it suits Isabelle and me, don't you think?"

She nodded. "Sophisticated, but not pretentious."

He hugged her. "Exactly what I was trying for."

Isabelle led them upstairs to the two bedrooms and baths they'd designed. Everything could have come out of *Architectural Digest*. Ansel shook his head, trying to take in all of the elegance. Jazzi looked at the deep, clawfoot tub in the master bath and grinned.

Isabelle laughed. "You know how I love those."

The bed had a high, custom-made, plush headboard and a monstrous round mirror hung over the chest of drawers. By the time Jazzi and Ansel had oohed and aahed at one special piece after another, it was time for them to go home.

She stopped on the sidewalk to turn and wave good-bye. Isabelle and Reuben were silhouetted in the window, waving too. She could see through the entire first floor. Beauty and elegance. And that's when it hit her. Ansel was right. If you rode your bike to peoples' houses and parked to watch them, you could see a lot. Had Miles seen something that got him killed? And what in the world would it be?

She pushed Miles out of her mind and settled on the front seat next to Ansel. The air had cooled down, and they rolled down the van's windows to enjoy the breeze. Ansel pulled away from the curb, and his lips curved into a smile.

Jazzi loved seeing him so happy and smiled, too. "You look like you enjoyed tonight."

"Reuben and Isabelle haven't wasted any time. They finished their house, and now they're getting married. Do you ever think about that?"

They turned away from town onto Main Street. Jazzi turned to study his profile. "Getting married? Not much. It's too soon."

"I'm twenty-five and you're...?" He frowned. "How old are you?"

"Twenty-seven. You're just a kid."

"Lots of people are married by our age. When you know you have the right person, why wait?"

"We just moved in together."

"But we've known each other a while now. We've worked together almost every day for two and a half years."

"It's different than being a couple. Somewhere down the line, you'll fuss about me squeezing the toothpaste tube in the middle. I'll growl because you never fold the bath towels right."

"I think we can work past those. Small potatoes, but I'm patient. I can wait another few months if you still have cold feet."

She turned to stare at him. "You call a few months being patient?"

"Sure do. I'd take you to the courthouse tomorrow if you'd let me."

She shook her head. "Didn't you learn anything with Emily? The glow might fade. Let's see what happens."

"We could have a Christmas wedding."

"Will you stop it?" She crossed her arms over her chest, and he laughed.

"I've never met a girl I could threaten with marriage before. Most women hint at it."

"Then find one of those."

They came to their turn, and Ansel glanced down the road toward their house. He shook his head. "I can't find someone else. George is fond of you."

She rolled her eyes. "George *would* get a vote."

"George didn't like Emily. I should have listened to him."

She laughed. "I'll remember to always be extra nice to your dog."

When they reached the house, Ansel punched in the numbers for the security code, and they walked in, arm in arm. He tugged her closer in the foyer for a long, thorough kiss, then he glanced at the stairs. They were headed toward their bedroom when his cell phone buzzed. He glanced at caller ID and frowned.

"Who is it?" Jazzi could feel his good mood drain away.

"My sister."

"Then answer it. It will hurt her feelings if you ignore her."

He walked to the kitchen to talk to her. Jazzi sat on the step and stayed where she was to listen. The conversation got straight to the reason for the call.

Ansel's voice sounded stern. "You don't owe them anything. How much did you give them?" After a short pause, he said, "That must have been everything you've saved so far."

Jazzi could see his reflection in the front windows. His shoulders stiffened, and he said, "I'm not driving there to help them, and I'm not sending money. I've made a life here. I'm happy."

He listened more, then sighed in exasperation. "I understand how you feel, too. And I'm glad you still love me, but I'm not changing my mind. They can figure this out on their own."

When he hung up, he called, "I'm getting a beer. Want to sit out on the back patio with me?"

She looked at the clock. It was getting late. She'd been in the mood to have her way with him, but it wasn't going to happen. Adda had crushed his libido before Jazzi could get him upstairs. She heaved a long-suffering sigh and traipsed into the kitchen to pour a glass of wine.

Chapter 8

When Jazzi and Ansel pulled into Olivia and Thane's drive the next day, Leo was on his riding lawn mower, cutting his grass. He stopped to give a quick wave when he saw them. Jazzi had to admit, for a man in his early eighties, Leo certainly kept active.

They went inside, pulled on gloves, and got straight to work with Thane, tearing up carpet. The widow who'd lived here before them must have had a small dog with a bladder problem. There were too many stains to count. The padding smelled foul. George found a spot to supervise as far away from the action as possible.

Jerod didn't walk in the house for another half hour, and when he did, Jazzi was glad to see him. The thick pile carpet was heavy, easy to pull up, not so easy to carry out.

"Sorry I'm late, but I drove Franny to a house to pick up a bunch of antiques. She saw them advertised in the paper—everything for a hundred bucks. The owners just wanted to get rid of them."

That piqued Ansel's interest. "I saw that ad, thought the pieces must be mostly junk."

Jerod pulled on his work gloves. "No, we got some really nice stuff."

"Like what?" Ansel wrinkled his nose when he reached a particularly smelly patch of padding.

"A whole dining room set—buffet, table, and chairs." Jerod picked up his cutter and sliced off a huge section of carpet, then tugged on it. "Three double beds, a chest of drawers—nothing fancy, but solid."

Ansel whistled. "Franny hit the jackpot."

"She's in refinishing heaven. When I left, she was looking through all of her stains with a gleam in her eye."

Jazzi laughed. Jerod couldn't have found a better wife than Franny. In her mind, the girl looked like a grown-up version of Anne of Green Gables—with carrot-colored hair almost always up in a ponytail, gray eyes, and a face full of freckles. Add in a big heart, a practical nature, stubborn willpower, and Jerod didn't stand a chance.

Jerod rolled up his section of carpet and carried it outside to throw in the dumpster. "I bet she started on the buffet the minute I left for work."

Ansel gripped a large section of carpet and looked at Thane. "Do you like antiques?" Thane grabbed his side, and they tugged, peeling one big piece from the far wall to the front door. "I like whatever Olivia likes. It doesn't matter to me."

Jazzi blinked. Ansel was easygoing, but not *that* easy. She went to pull up the padding under the carpet they'd just removed. "We got lucky. There's a sturdy subfloor."

They had a good enough start. Ansel and Thane decided to continue yanking together and ripping up big pieces. Jazzi would follow, removing the padding and tack strips, and Jerod went to strip the indoor/outdoor carpet out of the kitchen. By eleven, all of the carpet was gone, and they started cleaning up to get ready to install new floors.

Even with the faded, stained carpet out of the house, the kitchen looked so dated, Jazzi was surprised it didn't use a wood-burning stove. The two bathrooms were just as bad. One of them, with no shower, offered lots of Pepto-Bismol pink.

They'd swept up enough carpet scraps to fill a big black trash can, which Jazzi carried outside to toss in the dumpster. She was turning to go back into the house when Leo called, "I'd like you to meet my wife."

Nuts. Leo wasn't usually outdoors at this time of day. She turned to see Olivia's neighbor pushing a woman in a wheelchair across the street toward her. Cocoa's leash was tied to one of the wheelchair's handles.

The woman held out a hand, and Jazzi hurried down the driveway to shake it.

"Hello. I'm Louisa. Leo's talked so much about you, and it's such a pretty day, I asked him to take me for a small walk. I hoped I might meet you."

Louisa wasn't what Jazzi had pictured. In her mind, the woman was stooped and frail. In real life, she was plump, with white, permed hair and sparkling brown eyes.

"I love what you're doing to Della's house," she told Jazzi. "Della and I were close until she couldn't care for herself anymore and had to move. We used to play gin most afternoons. I miss her."

"It's hard to lose a friend. I hope she's found a group of card sharks at the nursing center. I bet she misses you, too. Have you gone to visit her?"

Louisa shook her head. "It's hard for Leo to load my wheelchair in our car. The thing's heavy and awkward. It's such a bother, I just stay home anymore. Seth's promised to take me soon, though."

Cocoa tugged on her leash to start walking, but Louisa reached out to pet the Lab. "Give me a minute, girl." She looked at Jazzi. "Leo said he told you about the boy who disappeared a while ago. I used to work at the courthouse as a paralegal for a judge. I sorted through lots of crime photos to get things organized for court dates. Know a lot of cops and lawyers. I asked them to look for Miles, but they've hit a dead end."

"I hope they find out something, one way or another. It's easier to heal if you have answers." Jazzi thought of all the years her mom and grandma had worried about Aunt Lynda.

Louisa nodded. "Leo says you're working on your sister's house. It's nice to have family in town. Our daughter lives in South Carolina, married with two grown kids and two grandkids. We only get to see her once in a while, but she calls once a week. We try to stay in touch."

Jazzi glanced at the house. Louisa liked to talk as much as Leo did. She wished someone would stick his head out a door and call for her, but no one did.

Louisa went on. "My sister's boy lives in town, and he's good to me. My sister and her husband retired to Arizona, but Seth stops in to see me once a week. I'm crazy about him, even though Leo won't give the boy a chance. Some friends drop in once a week to play bridge, and Miriam—an old friend of mine—stays to have supper with us." She smiled and reached up to pat Leo's hand. "And no one could have a more wonderful husband than my Leo. I don't know what I'd do without him."

Leo smiled, and Cocoa tugged on the leash again. "We'd better move on, but I'm glad you got to meet Louisa. You young folks have a good afternoon." He tipped his head to Jazzi and started off.

Jazzi let out a long breath and hurried back into the house. She frowned at Jerod and Ansel. "It would have been nice if one of you had come out to rescue me. Those two can talk a long time. The only thing that saved me was Cocoa. She wanted her walk."

Jerod shook his head. "We thought about it and decided we'd just get caught, too. We decided to sacrifice you instead."

"Thanks for nothing." She gave Ansel an evil glare. He grinned and went to the fridge to get her a beer. Really? He thought that would be enough to get him out of trouble? But she took the beer.

"What if Jerod and I get the hardwood floor started while you cool off?"

She tipped back the beer and took a long swallow, then smiled. "That's a fair trade-off."

He bent to kiss the top of her head. "We'll lay the first few rows, and then we can all work on it together."

While they concentrated on that, Jazzi went to the refrigerator and made sandwiches for lunch. Olivia had bought deli meat and cheeses and left out a loaf of bread. The guys carried the wooden table that served as an island back into place and came to join her when she lined their lunches up on paper towels.

Thane grimaced. "Sorry. I forgot to buy paper plates. Olivia was going to make the sandwiches, but she left early this morning to give someone a perm."

"Doesn't matter to us." Jerod reached for the chips.

After lunch, all four of them got busy on the floor. When Jazzi touched the first piece, she frowned. "This doesn't feel like wood."

Ansel pointed to the box that held the pieces. "It's porcelain that looks like wood. I told Thane that you put it in your bathroom, and it's a good product. He liked the idea."

Jazzi nodded. It would be great in a kitchen. "I love mine. It's durable, will last forever."

The talking stopped, and they all focused on the work. By four, they were done.

"You guys are lifesavers," Thane told them. "We can start on the bathrooms tomorrow, and then all the big, heavy jobs are done."

Jerod snorted and glanced at the kitchen. "Really?"

Thane ran a hand through his longish, auburn hair. "I forgot about that, but you're right. Anyway, we can quit for now and dig in on the bathrooms tomorrow. We should have the kitchen done by the end of the week."

"Yes, master." Laughing, Jerod grabbed his gear to leave.

Ansel teased, "I see how this goes. He's last in, first out."

"Only because you're slow." Jerod nodded to Ansel's tool belt. "Grab your stuff, and let's go home."

Jerod was already gone when Jazzi and Ansel loaded their stuff into the van. Ansel lifted George onto the back seat and had slipped behind the steering wheel when another white work van pulled into the driveway, blocking them in. The driver jumped out and rushed toward Jazzi, waving a baggie in the air.

"Does the old guy who left this in my yard live here?" he yelled.

Chapter 9

The man stopped in front of Jazzi, waving a bag of poop in her face. She could guess what had happened. "Someone told me the chocolate Lab lives here."

Jazzi pushed his hand away, motioning to George inside their van. She wasn't about to rat out Leo. "Nope, we own a pug."

Mr. Blow Hard was her height—five eight. He leaned toward her. "You don't own a Lab?"

He was starting to annoy her. "That's what I just said."

He was so thin, she wondered if he had a problem with his metabolism or just didn't eat. His dark hair was going gray, and his pointy features conjured a mental image of a ferret. Ferrets were cute, though. He wasn't. "The old guy usually cleans up after the stupid dog, but he just left it in my yard today."

"What? Do I look like an old man to you?" Jazzi didn't appreciate bullies. She put her hands on her hips, glaring at him. "No old man lives here, and you're rude. So go away."

He stepped closer to her, trying to intimidate her. That irritated her more. "Look, lady, do you know where the old man lives? If you do..." He raised the bag again.

She'd be darned if she'd tell this idiot where Leo lived. She took a step to close the space between them and pulled her cell phone from her pocket. "I don't like people who threaten me. Get in your van and leave now, or I'm calling 911."

The man stared at her. He looked furious, but confused. "Why won't you tell me where he lives?"

"Because you're out of control. Go home and cool off."

He stood there, uncertain. Then he raised the bag again. "What about this?"

Ansel swung out of the van and stalked to Jazzi. He wedged himself between her and the man. Clamping his hand on the man's forearm, he shoved the bag down. "If you wave poop in front of her face one more time, you'll regret it."

The guy stared up at him and took a step backward. "Sorry, man, but some old timer let his dog take a crap in my yard and just kept going. He's the same old geezer who parked in front of my house when I was arguing with my wife."

"Does my girl look like an old geezer to you?" Ansel looked threatening. He'd never once struck her as intimidating. She didn't know he had it in him. She was wrong. His arm curled around her waist, a clear message that if the guy bothered her more, he'd wish he hadn't.

The man stumbled over his words. "No, but I asked her about the dog. Someone in the next neighborhood, well, he might have gotten it wrong. Anyway, he said he'd seen the Lab in front of a red house, so I figure she knows who owns it, and I thought maybe..."

"I don't care what you thought." Ansel squared his shoulders. "We don't have a chocolate Lab. And we have zero desire to help you, so go away."

"Do you know where he lives?"

Ansel glowered and took a step toward him, his hands balling into fists. "If I did, I wouldn't tell you. You have anger issues. I don't want to see you again."

The guy took another step back but kept arguing. "It's not me, man. I'm telling you, it's the old guy that's the problem."

Thane walked out of the house to join Ansel. The two of them towered over the man. Thane frowned down at him. "Who in blazes are you?"

"Ed, from two neighborhoods down. You live here?"

Jazzi rolled her eyes. Why didn't Ed just give up and go away? Did he have a death wish?

Thane plopped his hands on his hips. He didn't look happy. "Yeah, I live here. So what? You have a problem, mister?"

"I'm looking for a man who owns a brown Lab."

"Yeah, I've heard...over and over again. But *you're* the guy who seems like a nutso to me, a certifiable wacko. Wanna wave poop in front of my face and see what happens?"

The man swallowed. "I picked the wrong house. The wrong people. Look, I made a mistake, all right? I lost my temper. Sorry I bothered you."

Thane just studied him. "Seems to me you're only sorry 'cause we could kick your butt. If you ever bother my Olivia, I'll come looking for you. You don't have any right running around screaming at people. If I see you again, it had better be a lot more pleasant."

The guy nodded and scurried back to his van. It was white, like Ansel's, but had a company logo on the side. Gutter repair and siding.

As soon as the man was gone, Jazzi let out a long breath. "What a jerk! I'm going to Leo's place to warn him to stay away from that freak."

"I'll come with you." Ansel turned to Thane. "Keep an eye out for that one. He's weird."

Thane straightened his shoulders. "If he ever bothers Olivia, he won't have any teeth. He needs to see a counselor."

Ansel went to pet George. "You were worried, weren't you? We're fine. You stay, and we'll be right back."

The pug lowered his head onto his front paws and gave a deep sigh. Jazzi wondered if the dog ever whisked into protective mode and bared his teeth. But Ansel was his owner. Maybe George thought Ansel could take care of himself.

She and Ansel knocked on Leo's door and told him what had just happened. "I wouldn't walk in front of his house for a while," Jazzi said. "He didn't strike me as stable."

Leo nodded. "He thinks his wife is cheating on him. That's what they were arguing about. She didn't make him feel any better."

"Well, he's on the edge, barely holding it together," Ansel said. "I'd avoid him if I could."

Leo nodded. "Thanks for the warning. I always clean up after Cocoa, carry bags in my pockets, but Louisa was tiring fast, and I wanted to make sure I got her home."

On the walk back to his van, Ansel said, "I sure hope Leo listens to us. That guy was volatile, ready to blow."

Jazzi hoped Leo and the man with the guttering van never met. The man was looking for someone to release his venom on. Leo looked like a perfect candidate.

Chapter 10

Besides not liking to cook, Jazzi's sister, Olivia, wasn't fond of gardening either. Jazzi helped the guys gut the two bathrooms, but when it came to installing new drywall, moisture barriers, and floors, the rooms were small enough that Jerod said, "We can handle this. Why don't you clean up the landscaping a little? Pruning shears will make a big difference."

Fine with her. The temperatures had dropped to the high seventies, so it was a perfect day to work in the yard.

She'd played with the idea of tearing into the kitchen, but Olivia and Thane had to empty the cupboards and refrigerator first. So she concentrated on the flower beds. The yard had beautiful landscaping, but it was all overgrown. Azaleas, boxwood, forsythia, and hydrangeas grew in lush curves in front of the house. Jazzi was on her knees, weeding, when Cocoa trotted up to her, took hold of the hem of her T-shirt, and tugged for her to follow her.

Jazzi reached to pat the dog's head but hesitated. Matted blood caked the area close to her left ear. Was she hurt? Jazzi gently pressed her fingers under the dog's fur, and Cocoa whimpered. Dirt darkened her entire left side, and a boot print showed near her left leg. It looked like someone had kicked her.

Had Ed found Leo and Cocoa? Did he kick the dog and then hit her head so hard that he drew blood?

Jazzi sat back on her heels and looked up and down the street for Leo. Where the old man went, so went his dog. But Leo was nowhere to be seen. Had Cocoa slipped out of the house without him? And why was her left side covered with dried dirt? She looped her hand around Cocoa's collar and led her to Leo's house. She knocked, but no one answered the door.

Worry slithered up her spine. What would Gutter Ed have done if he found Leo? She knocked again and thought she heard a low moan. Had he kicked Cocoa, then forced himself inside the house? She turned the doorknob, and the door opened. Crap. She pushed it wider and called, "Leo? Are you home?"

She heard a faint voice. She stepped inside the house and followed the noise. "Leo? Louisa?"

She found Louisa lying on the floor. She was conscious, dressed in pajamas and a robe, struggling to push herself up on her elbows. Jazzi rushed to her. "Are you all right?"

"Leo never came home last night. I tried to call for help, but my phone was too high. I can stand, but when I stretched to reach it, I fell. I've been on the floor all night."

Jazzi pulled out her cell and called Ansel. "Louisa fell. Leo's missing. I need help."

Then she reached under Louisa. "Is it safe to move you? Can I help you to your feet?"

"I didn't hurt anything. I just can't get up."

"Ansel and Jerod will be here in a minute. It will be safer if they help me get you in your wheelchair."

Tears trickled down Louisa's cheeks. "Leo and Cocoa went out for their evening walk and never came back. Before they left, Leo got me into my pajamas, then they waited until it was dusk, hoping no one would see them. Leo didn't want to meet the angry man who came to yell at you."

Jazzi nodded, now sure that Leo was in trouble. "I have a friend who's a detective. I'm calling him. Do you mind?"

Louisa pinched her lips together, clearly frightened. "Leo always comes home. He'd never leave me here, alone."

"I know." Relief rushed through her when all three men poured through the front door. She raised her eyebrows at Ansel. "No George?"

"We left him at Thane's house. He wasn't happy about it, but we don't have to worry about him there."

"Makes sense." Jazzi called Gaff while Ansel and Jerod each slid an arm under one of Louisa's shoulders and lifted her into her wheelchair. She looked pale and nauseous.

"Can I get you something to eat? Drink?" Ansel asked. Her Viking made her proud.

Jerod went into the kitchen and returned with a bottle of Ensure. Her cousin wasn't half bad either.

"Something's happened to my Leo, or he'd be here. Cocoa didn't come home last night either."

After Jazzi hung up the phone with Gaff, she explained how Cocoa had come to her. The dog had seen her outside, working in the yard, and had come to her for help.

Thane went to fill the dog's food and water bowls. Cocoa scarfed down the food and drank most of the water. Then she looked at Thane and whimpered. He scratched her behind her ears. "You've had a rough night, haven't you?"

Jazzi turned to Louisa. "Is there someone I can call for you? Someone who might help you now?"

"Seth will be working at his bar, but Miriam will come." She gave her Miriam's number, and Jazzi called her friend and explained what had happened.

"I'll be there in less than an hour," Miriam said. "Tell Louisa I'm coming."

Jazzi passed on the message and took a seat on the aged, plaid sofa near Louisa. She finally looked around the house. Leo wasn't exaggerating when he said it was solid, but dated, just like the house Thane and Olivia had bought. Maybe somewhere along the way, even if they had enough money, people got tired of caring for their homes.

"Do you need anything?" Jazzi asked Louisa.

Tears fell in earnest now. "Only my Leo. Do you think he's dead?"

Oh, crap. That's exactly what Jazzi thought, but she hoped against hope that she was wrong. Cocoa went to lay his head in Louisa's lap, trying to comfort her. The dog whimpered while Louisa cried, and Jazzi felt so helpless, she wanted to scream.

Chapter 11

Detective Gaff was as good as his word and pulled into Louisa's drive ten minutes later. Cocoa hid behind Jazzi's legs when she opened the door for him to enter. The dog must be able to sense cop vibes, the intensity and authority. The man himself demanded attention with his salt-and-pepper hair, stocky build, and button-down shirt, but all three of her coworkers were big and strong, and Cocoa liked them. Could a dog sense that a cop could put people in jail?

Gaff sat across from Louisa and took out his notepad and pen. He motioned for Jazzi to sit across from him. "Start from the beginning."

Ansel, Jerod, and Thane took seats on the perimeter of the room.

Jazzi explained that she, Ansel, and Jerod were helping Thane and Olivia renovate their house. Leo and Louisa lived across the street from them. She filled in the rest, her explanation succinct, but thorough.

Gaff asked, "Could Leo have hurt himself on his walk? Is there anyone who didn't like him or Cocoa?"

Jazzi explained about the man who'd confronted them yesterday. She filled in the background of Leo annoying him when he argued with his wife.

Gaff looked at Ansel. "This Ed wouldn't leave, even when you told him to?"

Ansel shook his head. "He was revved up, and it didn't seem like he'd had too much to drink or was high on anything. He was just plain mad."

Gaff turned his attention to Thane. "You know the neighborhoods. Do you know where this guy lives?"

"We just moved in. I don't know the area very well, but I'd recognize his van if it's in his driveway. A working van, white like mine. He does gutters and siding."

Jazzi hadn't realized how many white working vans clogged the streets of River Bluffs. Lots and lots of them.

Gaff glanced at his watch. "He's probably not home now, but I'll have one of you ride with me later to look for it."

"I'd be happy to," Thane said. "I don't want that moron anywhere close to Olivia."

Cocoa walked to the door and whimpered so loudly that Jazzi went to her. The dog immediately tugged on the hem of Jazzi's T-shirt, nudging at the door.

"You want me to follow you, don't you?" Jazzi reached for Cocoa's leash and looked at the others. "Someone needs to stay with Louisa until Miriam gets here, but I feel sorry for this poor dog." She patted Cocoa's head. "Okay, girl, let's go for a walk."

"Nope, not alone." Ansel clicked the dog's leash to Cocoa's collar. "I'm going with you."

The dog tugged at the hem of Jazzi's shirt again.

Gaff frowned. "I'm coming too."

"So am I." Jerod rose and glanced at Thane.

Thane went to sit across from Louisa. "I'll stay with her until her friend gets here."

The four of them set off with the Labrador. Thankfully, it was a beautiful day. Blue skies. Temperatures in the high seventies.

The dog kept tugging at her leash. She wanted to get somewhere in a hurry.

"We're coming already," Jazzi said. "Calm down."

Cocoa led them to the bottom of the circle of the small housing development. They passed several ranch houses—each a different color and style—until they came to the narrow patch of asphalt that led to another neighborhood. The dog trotted into that subdivision—made up of mostly Cape Cods—and circled half of it. A German shepherd threw itself against a chain-link fence and barked until they moved on. Two terriers barked at them three doors down. Cocoa never slowed down. She kept up a brisk pace until another asphalt road opened into a third neighborhood. Older houses lined its streets, many of them small. Cocoa veered to the left. The golf course was far in the distance, and she kept going until a dry, dusty path rambled away toward the wetlands. She took that.

Brambles and weeds overgrew the narrow trail, but they followed the dog's lead. The path dipped, and the ground grew damp and spongy. A garter snake slithered into the tall grasses. A cluster of trees huddled ahead of them, and Cocoa strained against her leash to sniff there. She circled a spot and started to dig.

Geese honked in the distance. A mallard duck flew overhead. Jazzi had read that a pair of young eagles had made a nest in the line of trees across the street.

Damp dirt flew toward her. Jazzi stepped to the side, out of the way. The dog whined and dug faster.

Traffic hummed on the nearby four-lane street. A heron flew overhead and landed nearby, in the water of the wetlands.

Jazzi frowned. It looked like Cocoa had dug here before. The ground had been disturbed and tamped back down. She turned in a circle to survey the area. Had Leo come here with his dog and tripped and fallen? No one would see him if he was prone in the tall weeds and grasses. The dog yipped, and Jazzi turned to stare. She gasped.

Gaff went to see what Cocoa had found. A dark T-shirt with a red slogan sprawled across the front was partially visible under a foot of dirt. He tugged Cocoa away from the shallow grave. "Good, girl. Good job. We'll take it from here."

The dog sat on her haunches, panting. She looked proud of herself.

Jazzi knelt to pet the dog, and Gaff opened his cell phone to call for a scene of crime team. While they waited, Ansel and Jerod came to stare at the dog's find.

"Leo doesn't wear T-shirts," Ansel said. "That's not him."

"Then who is it?" Jerod asked.

"How would I know?" Ansel glanced at Gaff. "Could it be the missing kid?"

"That's my guess." Gaff shook his head. "My bet was on the dog leading us to Leo, not this."

Jazzi stood, the knees of her jeans damp from kneeling on the ground. She shielded her eyes from the sun and turned in a circle, searching for signs of a fallen person. It would be easy to trip over a fallen limb in dim light. She didn't know why Leo had come here near sundown.

Jerod started scanning the area, too, like Jazzi had done. If Leo had fallen, he was nowhere in the vicinity.

Cocoa moved a few feet away and started digging again. A cold coil of worry twisted in Jazzi's stomach. No, it couldn't be another body. The dog was probably just hyper. If it made her happy to dig, why not let her? *Please, don't let it be Leo.* Except once again, the dog yipped, and Jazzi stared at what looked like a flowered shirt with pockets. She recognized the style—scrubs—under a thin layer of dirt. Long, dark hair waved past slim shoulders.

"You guys are gonna wanna see this." It felt surreal. Cocoa had found everything *but* Leo.

"Oh, crap." Ansel came and looked down. "There's another one," he told Gaff.

Jerod came to see. They all stared at the cheery-patterned fabric.

"A girl?" Jerod asked.

"Looks like a nurse to me." Gaff glanced at the dog. "She doesn't want to dig another hole, does she?"

Lord, Jazzi hoped not. She frowned and tugged Cocoa a little way back. "Is Leo here?"

The dog lowered her head to the ground to sniff again and started toward a sport complex's asphalt drive a short distance in the opposite direction. Jazzi bit her bottom lip. "Ansel! Gaff and Jerod!" She pointed to weeds that had already been flattened, as if someone had dragged something heavy over them.

Leo? Was his body thrown in the wild shrubs on the side of the drive? When Cocoa reached the asphalt, though, she lay down and whimpered. She turned to look at Jazzi with a low, sad whine.

A dead end. What had happened to Leo? Had he crawled here to flag down someone for help? Jazzi noticed a piece of torn cotton fabric snagged on a shrub's branch. Blue and yellow stripes. Just like the thin sweater Leo wore the last time she'd seen him. Then she saw the rust-colored smears on the pavement.

"Crap."

Gaff glanced at Ansel, who nodded. "Leo was wearing a blue-and-yellow sweater the day he disappeared."

"Right after Ed, the gutter guy, tried to find him?"

Jerod wasn't buying it. "Who'd kill someone for leaving dog crap in his yard?"

Jazzi had to agree with him. "Ed had a screw loose. Nobody gets that mad over stupid stuff. Plus, there are two dead bodies now. From what I've heard, Miles didn't have a dog, just a bicycle. And he disappeared just like Leo did."

Gaff started to walk back to the shallow graves. "Let's hope Forensics can tell us something. More's going on here than we thought."

How could this happen to her twice? They were working on another house, and they'd stumbled onto more dead bodies. The only good news was that none of it involved Jazzi's family.

Cocoa hurried to hug her side. The dog quivered, she was so anxious. Jazzi reached down to pet her.

"Don't pet any fur with blood," Gaff said. "That could be evidence."

Ugh. Jazzi patted the top of the dog's head, avoiding the spot by her left ear where the killer had probably struck her. Poor Cocoa. Had she tried to defend Leo? Protect him? Jazzi thought about Louisa. She couldn't take the Lab for two walks a day, not even one. What would happen to her? She looked at Ansel, and as if he was reading her thoughts, he nodded.

"She's a good dog. We won't let her go to the pound."

Jazzi didn't really want another dog, but if worse came to worse, they'd take Cocoa in. The dog deserved a good home.

Chapter 12

They were quiet as they turned to walk back to the shallow graves. Cocoa didn't pull on her leash. She walked with her head down, as if she were in mourning.

When they reached the cluster of trees where they'd found the bodies, the crime team was there, taking pictures and gathering evidence. They'd removed the dirt, exposing two young people. Miles—at least Jazzi assumed it must be Miles—wore tight jeans and a T-shirt. He had on one red sneaker. His wavy, brown hair was caked with dirt. A pair of black-rimmed glasses sat lopsided on his nose.

"Did he have a wallet?" Gaff asked one of the techs.

The guy held up a baggy with a wallet inside. "Miles Lancaster, lived close to here."

"And her?" Gaff asked.

"Nothing. No purse, no ID."

Gaff looked disappointed. "That would have been too easy. Thanks, Ben."

With a nod, Ben went back to work. Gaff held up a hand, motioning for the three of them to stay a bit longer. He'd want to talk to them.

Jazzi couldn't help it. She studied the corpses. Part of her didn't want to, but the rest of her wanted to know what they looked like, how they'd died. The dead girl had long, dark hair and a heart-shaped face. She must have been really pretty before bugs and decay had started to work on her. She wore scrubs and sensible, white work shoes. A nurse or hospital tech? Both sides of Jefferson Street, which wasn't that far away, were lined with medical buildings until you reached the hospital, a little farther south.

Both bodies had started to decompose in their shallow graves. One body wasn't worse than the other.

Jazzi grimaced. She'd assumed Miles had been killed because of his voyeur tendency. He'd probably seen the wrong thing at the wrong time. Had he seen the killer attack the girl?

And what about Leo? He liked to rove the many pocket neighborhoods, "keeping an eye" on things. He'd left near sunset on his walk with Cocoa, anxious not to be seen. Had he set off in a different direction last night, trying to avoid Gutter Guy, and stumbled on the graves? Cocoa might have smelled them and led him to them, just as she'd led Jazzi to them today. Was Leo killed so he couldn't expose them?

Jazzi glanced at the dirt coating the dog's left side and silently voted for that scenario. She could picture Cocoa leading Leo to the cluster of trees, digging and exposing Miles's T-shirt, and then trying to protect Leo when someone came up behind him and bashed him on the head. Then had the killer bashed Cocoa, too, before dragging Leo off to load in the trunk of a car to take his body away? She thought about that. Could Leo's murder have worked that way? It seemed possible to her.

"Your wheels are turning," Ansel said, coming to wrap his arm around her waist. "I can watch them. You have that look. What have you come up with?"

Gaff walked over to join them. "What do you think?"

They tossed ideas back and forth as the four of them returned to the asphalt drive that circled the last neighborhood they'd visited. She bumped closer to Ansel, matching her stride with his. Jerod, walking behind them, turned to Gaff. "Jazzi's take on this makes sense to me."

"It's a good start. Maybe Miles saw the killer murder the pretty nurse. The killer realized he'd seen them and went after Miles."

Ansel dropped his arm from her and stepped onto the narrow asphalt strip that led to the next neighborhood's street. "You said Miles had his wallet. What about a cell phone? Did he carry one? And the nurse hasn't reported for work for a while now, right? Someone realizes she's missing. If you find out who she is, you can start setting the dominoes in place, right?"

Gaff loosened another button on his shirt and ran his finger under the collar. It wasn't hot today, but the exertion was enough to make anyone sweat. The field was clotted with weeds, and it felt surreal to hear cars whizzing down the highway while they followed a narrow path through a no-man's land. "Neither Miles nor the nurse had cell phones on them. We're going to have to check missing persons and hope someone fits our nurse's description."

Jerod gave his head a quick shake. "I wouldn't want to be called in to identify either one of those bodies. They don't look very good. That image would stay with you a long time."

"I thought they'd look worse," Ansel said. "They've been missing for a few weeks, haven't they? At least Miles has. That's when his parents called about him, wasn't it?"

"Bodies break down fast if left in the open air," Gaff said. "Burying them, even in a shallow grave, slows down decomposition. Bugs still feed on you, though."

Cocoa leaned her head against Jazzi's leg, and she stroked her soft fur. The poor dog looked depressed. "I wonder why the killer didn't bury Leo with the others."

Jerod gave Cocoa a sympathetic look. "Maybe he thought Cocoa would stay away from the graves if Leo wasn't buried there."

That made sense. Jazzi scratched behind the dog's ears. Cocoa raised her head and howled a long, sad note. Ansel, a sucker for dogs, leaned closer to pet her, too. "I hope George is all right. I've left him a long time in a strange house."

Jerod snorted. "He knows Thane's house by now. He's probably sleeping. I bet we wake him up when we get back."

"But he has to be worried by now," Ansel argued. "He doesn't like it when I'm gone this long."

Jazzi had never seen the pug too bent out of shape. He liked to snooze on the dog bed Ansel had bought to keep at Thane's while they worked.

When they reached Thane's, Cocoa tugged on the leash, anxious to be home. By the time they reached Louisa's house, Jazzi felt grateful she was with Gaff. He'd tell Louisa the sad news, not her. They entered the house in single file, and Cocoa went straight to her dog bed and flopped down on it. She laid her head on her paws and closed her eyes.

Thane, who'd stayed with Louisa, glanced at their faces, and Jazzi watched him brace himself. "How bad is it?"

Gaff glanced at Louisa. "Are you ready for this?"

She bit her bottom lip and nodded. He told them what they'd found. Louisa gripped the arms of her wheelchair and took deep breaths, struggling for composure. They all waited, giving her time.

Finally, she said, "You think someone *killed* Leo?"

Gaff nodded. "It looks that way. We have no body, but someone dragged him away."

She shook her head in denial. "Why would anyone hurt Leo? He was a kind, gentle man."

Just then a car pulled into the driveway, and an older woman rushed to the house. She knocked and hurried inside, going straight to Louisa. She had a cap of soft brown hair and stooped shoulders. Her slacks and top looked expensive. "I'm Miriam," she told them, "Louisa's friend. You called me to stay with her."

Louisa reached for her hand. "They think my Leo was murdered. Can you imagine?"

Miriam blinked and pressed her lips together. "Why in the world would anyone harm Leo? How dreadful. I'm so sorry, Louisa." She glanced at Gaff, the only one of them in a dress shirt and slacks. She must have decided he was in charge. "What makes you think someone killed Louisa's husband?"

Gaff motioned to the dog. "Cocoa found two dead bodies. We think she dug up their graves, and Leo was going to report them when someone stopped him."

"And why did you decide that?" Miriam asked.

"We followed a trail of smashed weeds and grass. There were rust-colored stains—dried blood. We think his body was dragged to a car and taken away."

Miriam stopped to consider that. "Couldn't the two bodies in the graves have been dragged there for burial instead?"

Gaff shook his head. "The weeds were crushed down in the other direction, away from the graves, toward the driveway."

"Oh dear, oh dear." Miriam's hand went over her heart, and Jazzi tensed. The woman's wrinkles implied she was as old as her friend. She wouldn't have a heart attack when she heard terrible news, would she? But then she bent to hug Louisa. "Losing my Charlie was the worst thing that ever happened to me. He was my helpmate for over sixty years. How many years were you with Leo?"

"Sixty-seven. I was twenty-two when I walked down the aisle."

"Oh my. It's going to be hard. I can stay with you as long as you need me."

Sixty-seven years? Jazzi glanced at Ansel. That was a long time! "Till death do you part" hadn't translated into twice the years she'd been alive when she thought about marriage.

Ansel quirked an eyebrow at her. "How long have your parents been married?"

"I'm twenty-seven...jeez! Thirty years?"

"Thirty *good* years," he told her.

Gaff looked at her, amused, then turned his attention back to Louisa. He took out his notepad. "Could I ask you a few questions before I leave?"

Nervously, she tugged her housecoat closer together. "I haven't had a chance to get dressed yet. I must look a fright."

"You fell," he said to reassure her. "Your husband wasn't here to help you. I'm just grateful you didn't get hurt."

"I don't know where Leo went last night. I can't help you very much."

Miriam pulled a chair next to hers and reached for Louisa's hand. "This isn't a quiz. I'm sure the lieutenant just wants to get some background information that might help him understand Leo and his routine more."

Gaff nodded. "Just some general information, nothing serious."

Louisa relaxed against the back of her wheelchair. Her voice still sounded a bit anxious, but she said, "All right."

Jazzi started toward the door. She could zip out of here while Gaff did his thing. They still had a lot of work to do on Thane and Olivia's house, and lunchtime had come and gone. They could grab something to eat and get back to renovating bathrooms. But just as she turned the knob to leave, the black Cadillac SUV she'd seen before pulled into the drive. Louisa's nephew jumped out and almost ran to the door.

Jazzi opened it and stepped out of his way. He looked to be in his late forties, only an inch or two taller than she was. His head was shaved, but somehow, it only made him sexier. He wasn't really good-looking, but he was attractive.

"Aunt Lou! Are you okay?" Ignoring the others, he knelt beside her wheelchair.

Tears filled Louisa's eyes when she saw him. "You were at work. I didn't want to bother you."

"At a time like this?" Seth leaned forward to hug her. "Miriam called me. I'm glad she did. Are you all right?"

"They think my Leo is dead, murdered."

He raised his eyebrows, surprised. "Leo? He could be a nuisance..." He stammered to a stop. "You can't stay here on your own. It's not safe for you to stand without someone around."

"Miriam's going to stay with me a while."

He looked relieved. "Good."

"I can't walk the dog, though." Miriam glanced at Cocoa, lying exhausted in her bed. "I get winded easily."

"I can come before I open the bar in the morning, but I can't always get away on my break before supper rush. Is that enough?"

Good. Jazzi had worried about the Lab.

Louisa turned to look at her. "Could you walk Cocoa before you leave your sister's house each day?"

It was a small favor to ask. "I'd be happy to, but we're only working here till the end of the week. I can do it that long."

Louisa sat up a little higher in her chair. She looked a little less shaken. "Thank you. Maybe I can pay someone after that."

Gaff clicked his pen, ready to ask Louisa questions. Jazzi started to the door to zip out again, but another car pulled into the drive. Another SUV, smaller than the Cadillac. A woman dressed in scrubs got out, frowning at the other vehicles in the drive, and started to the house. Again, Jazzi opened the door and stepped back to let her in. Good lord, how many people checked on Louisa most days?

The woman, who looked to be in her forties, glanced around in surprise. She frowned at Jazzi. "Did I come at a bad time?"

She was pretty in a quiet sort of way, slim with fair skin and long, dishwater-blond hair pulled into a knot. Mascara and lipstick were her only makeup. That's all Jazzi wore, too. It was pointless to wear more. It melted away while she worked. "Louisa just got bad news. We think someone murdered Leo and dragged his body away."

The woman's light brown eyes went wide. "I'm Amy, Louisa's visiting nurse. Maybe I should come back at a different time?"

"No. Stay. I need you." Louisa held out both hands to greet her.

Amy went to take them and squeeze them gently. "I'm so sorry to hear your news."

Louisa was growing less frazzled with each new visitor. She had a strong support group. "Amy, this is my longtime friend, Miriam, and my nephew, Seth. I'm so grateful you're all here."

Jazzi decided to make her break while she could. She gave a nod to Gaff, then slipped out the door. Ansel, Jerod, and Thane followed her.

Back at Thane's house, they all gathered in the kitchen. George came to greet them, so maybe he had noticed they were gone longer than usual. Thane made sandwiches and passed them out. Jerod handed out beers. They looked at each other and shook their heads.

"Can you believe it?" Jerod asked. "I mean, I like Gaff and all, but I didn't really want to see him for another case."

"I didn't want to see another dead body." Ansel took a long swig of his beer. "After seeing four of them, I'm getting cremated. Ashes look better than corpses."

Jazzi nodded agreement. "I didn't think about *how* a person became dust to dust, but it's ugly."

Thane swallowed his last bite of deli turkey and reached for another sandwich. "What difference does it make? You'll be dead. If they kick your body to the curb, it doesn't matter."

Jazzi wrinkled her nose, trying not to think about bugs crawling across her corpse and her bodily tissues collapsing. "I'd rather go up in flames and get it over with."

"Whatever suits you." Thane glanced through the hallway arch. "Do you think we can still get the bathrooms done today?"

Jerod nodded. "We'll divide and conquer. Ansel and Jazzi can take the guest bathroom, and you and I will work on the master. We can stay a little later if we need to."

That's all it took to motivate them. They finished their lunch and separated into teams. Ansel and Jazzi installed the floor first. Easy, since the ceramic pieces fit together. The room's drywall was good. It didn't need any work, so all they had to do were the backboard and the moisture barrier around the tub and shower. Then they taped and mudded the drywall.

When Jazzi finished her section, she glanced at Ansel, bending to finish the bottom of his piece. Not a bad pose. She'd never wanted a horseback ride more. But she resisted the temptation. His expression didn't invite play. He was in work mode, concentrating.

He covered the last of the tape and straightened up. "Ready to tile the shower area?"

Olivia had chosen small tiles connected to a sheet backing, so the work went fast. When they both bent to press the tiles on the end walls, their butts bumped. They turned to grin at each other.

"Promises, promises," Jazzi teased.

Ansel wiggled his eyebrows. "I always deliver. Rest assured."

When they finished the tiles, they couldn't do anything else until everything dried.

"Let's go check on Jerod," he said.

Yup, work mode.

They tracked down Jerod and Thane. The master bathroom was bigger, and the walls still needed to be mudded. Jazzi glanced at her watch. Almost six, but staying a little over was worth it. Her sister was still at the salon, and as much as she loved seeing Olivia, they'd get more work done when she wasn't here. When they came tomorrow, they could finish the bathrooms in a short time and then start work on the kitchen.

She was reaching for a trowel when the doorbell rang and Gaff called, "Hey, Jazzi, can I borrow you for a minute?"

She sighed and glanced at Jerod and Ansel.

"Go," Ansel said. He took the trowel from her hand and scooped up some mud. "I'll pitch in here."

Wiping her hands on her jeans, Jazzi went to greet Gaff.

"I was wondering if you'd go with me to talk to Miles's parents. I waited until after five to see if you could spot Ed's work van on the way there and back. He should be home by now."

"Miles's parents?" She grimaced. That would be worse than being part of telling Louisa about Leo.

"You have more of a feel for him than I do," Gaff said. "And you'll recognize the logo on Ed's van. You saw it."

She called to the guys in the back of the house. "I'm going with Gaff."

"Have fun!" Jerod yelled.

Her cousin could be a pain in the behind. But she liked his sarcasm better than anything maudlin. She tugged some stray strands of hair behind her ears and set off after Gaff.

Chapter 13

Jazzi spotted Ed's van in the third subdivision Gaff drove into. She pointed. "That's it."

The white van was parked in a gravel drive, outside a detached, oversized, two-car garage. Closer to the road, a single-story bungalow with a small front porch faced the street. Someone had recently painted it a pumpkin color with cream-colored trim. Jazzi liked it. Ed's neighborhood was filled with small, modest houses, all of them well-kept. A chihuahua on a leash in the backyard barked the minute they parked and stepped out of the car.

A woman wearing short cut-off jeans and a tight top walked out of the house to meet them. She looked to be in her late twenties, with shoulder-length black hair, lots of makeup, and a swagger. She crossed her arms over her chest. "What do you want?"

Gaff flashed his badge. "We'd like to talk to your husband."

The woman's lips twisted into a sneer. "What did the dummy do now?"

"We hope nothing. We just want to ask him a few questions."

She looked disappointed. She tilted her head toward the back of the house. "He's out there, painting his precious garage to match the house. I'll walk with you."

When they got there, the garage door was up, showing a muscle car inside. Jazzi knew enough to know that old cars took a lot of maintenance. "He must be a handy mechanic."

"I suppose. He's going to build me a three-season porch next. He's too cheap to hire someone to do it. I like sitting outside in the evening but hate mosquitoes."

Ed walked toward them as she finished her sentence and scowled at her. He looked tired. He bent to pet the chihuahua. "It's all right, Killer. We have company."

His wife gave him a dirty look. "I shoulda known you'd come to check on your mutt."

"He was barking. You could have picked him up to make him feel better."

"Don't think so. He's shedding." She glanced down at her black top.

Ed looked annoyed but shook it off. He looked at Gaff. "You wanted to see me?"

"You're the man who tried to track down Leo about leaving dog poop in your yard?"

Ed's shoulders drooped. "Look. I was having a bad day. Eve and I had a big argument, and then I stepped in the stuff. I lost it."

"You got angry with Leo when you and your wife were fighting before, didn't you?"

Ed glanced at Eve and frowned. "Things have been a little rocky lately."

Another sneer from Eve. "He thinks I'm cheating on him."

"Are you?" Ed narrowed his eyes, waiting for her answer.

"What difference does it make? You can't keep up."

Jazzi tried not to gasp. She swallowed her shock. She tried not to look at Ed and make it worse.

"You have a temper," Gaff said. "We found two bodies not that far from here, near the wetlands. Do you know anything about that?"

Ed's face drained of color. He stared. "Was one of them Leo? Do you think I killed them?"

Eve laughed. "He doesn't have the balls to kill anyone."

Ed's hands formed fists, and he closed his eyes, struggling for composure. "Will you just shut up? You're not helping anything."

Eve's lips curled, amused. "Sorry, I figure you have to be innocent. You're all noise, no action."

Jazzi bit her bottom lip, determined to stay quiet. But no wonder Ed and his wife argued.

Ed raised his eyes to the heavens, took a deep breath, and turned to Gaff. "I don't know what happened to Leo. He was annoying as heck, but I never wished him dead."

"What about the kid who lived in your neighborhood? Miles. Did you wish him dead?"

"No, I worried about him." He hesitated. "You said two bodies. Did you find Miles?"

"I'm driving to talk to his parents."

"Do you know how...? Miles was a nice kid, you know. He just didn't understand. He had a bit of a voyeur problem. I told his parents, but they didn't know what to do about it. They couldn't lock the kid inside twenty-four-seven."

"We've heard that before," Gaff said. "He liked to lurk in the shadows and watch."

Jazzi glanced at all of the windows in the bungalow. She'd guess you could see in every room after dark if the lights were on.

Ed jerked his head toward Eve. "He'd park his bike behind our big bush at night and watch Eve parade around in her thin, little nightie. I was going to run him off, but Eve sort of liked it, said the kid had to get some kicks somewhere."

Ed thought a minute. "You didn't say. Was Leo the other body?"

"No, we found a young woman's body in the grave next to Miles's." Gaff waited for Ed's reaction.

Ed stared. "Huh-uh. Miles would never hurt anyone. He didn't pull some murder-suicide thing and fall into an empty grave after he buried the girl."

"We never considered that."

Ed looked uncomfortable. "Don't tell his parents I told you about him watching, will you? They've been through enough."

"There's no reason for me to mention that," Gaff said. "Knowing he's dead might actually bring them some comfort. It's better than wondering."

Ed turned to Eve. "We should send them a casserole or something."

When she snorted, he turned to Gaff and Jazzi. "Am I a suspect?"

"For now," Gaff told him. "We're just starting to investigate. You don't happen to know a young nurse who went missing, do you?"

"A nurse?" Ed shut his eyes again and shook his head. "Did she live around here?"

"Don't know. We haven't ID'd her yet."

Ed looked worried, glancing at Eve. "No one's killing young women around here, are they?"

Gaff tried to reassure him. "It doesn't look that way. So far, our victims seem to be a young man, a young woman, and Leo."

"That's a weird combination," Eve said.

"Yeah, it has us puzzled. Is there anything either of you can think of that might help?"

Ed rubbed his forehead. "I don't know about the nurse, but Leo liked to snoop as much as the kid did. Maybe that's what got him and Miles in trouble."

Gaff closed his notepad and put it back in his shirt pocket. "Thanks for your time, and I'd appreciate it if you didn't leave town."

Eve laughed. "Like Mr. Cheapskate would pay for a ticket. No worries there."

"How could I afford one?" Ed snapped. "You spend money faster than I can make it."

How in the world could Ed put up with Eve? He struck her as a decent person, but Eve could audition for *Taming of the Shrew*.

They left them to their bickering.

Gaff raised his eyebrows at her. "Interesting, huh?"

"I'd cut my losses and divorce her."

"Some men want them young," Gaff said as he got into the car. "They're willing to put up with a lot to get it."

"Then they deserve what they get."

Gaff laughed and pulled onto the street. "You ready to see Miles's parents?"

"Not really." She'd never signed on to be the bearer of bad news.

"Me either. Thanks for coming with me."

She'd feel too guilty if she didn't, but she was dreading this next visit.

Chapter 14

Miles's parents lived in a modest ranch-style house with a basement. Jazzi had a thing for basements, if they were in good shape. You could hide from a tornado in a basement. You could store all kinds of stuff in them, and if you were lucky, your pipes would stay warm enough to never freeze in winter.

This house had tan vinyl siding and dark brown shutters. She and Gaff walked to the front door and knocked. When a woman opened it, Gaff showed her his badge.

"Mrs. Lancaster?" he asked. When she nodded, he said, "We have news for you."

She opened the door wider and invited them in. Her husband was watching TV in his recliner and turned off his program to hurry to hear what Gaff had to say.

Gaff took a seat on the sofa across from him, and Jazzi sat next to him. The wife settled on an armchair. Gaff took a deep breath. "I'm sorry to tell you that we found your son's body buried in a shallow grave."

The wife clasped her hands together. "Can you tell how he died? Was it fast?"

"The medical examiner hasn't confirmed it yet, but it looks like he died from a blow to the back of his head. Fast."

The wife looked at Jazzi. "Were you the one who found him?"

She nodded.

"Where was he?"

"Close by, near some trees by the wetlands."

The father looked relieved. "So maybe someone hit him with something hard, killed him, then buried him there. There was no..." He grimaced. "No one abused him sexually?"

"I doubt it," Jazzi said. "He was fully dressed."

The mother tried to explain. "There was a time when we wouldn't have thought much about that, but after the accident, Miles was so simple, so naïve. He could be talked into all sorts of things."

What a horrible burden, to have to worry about that. "What happened to your son?"

The mother glanced at a photo of a young Miles on their fireplace mantel. He was beaming, holding up a trophy, and extremely good-looking. "You'd never know it now, but he was an honor student, a basketball star, and very popular. He went to college, got a good job, and it looked like he'd get promoted. Then he went to Florida with his friends. He got so drunk, he fell off a balcony. His body landed in a bush, but his head hit the sidewalk. He was never the same."

"I'm sorry." Jazzi sat stunned. How many young guys had too much to drink and got stupid and survived it? When Jerod was young, he loved bars and didn't always stop drinking when he should. And he'd been lucky. It was sad when youthful sprees haunted kids for the rest of their lives.

The father folded his hands in his lap. "Our church has been there with us, every step of the way. Without their support, I don't know if we'd have survived this."

Gaff took out his notepad and asked, "We've heard that Miles loved to ride his bike. Did he ever mention any place or anyone that might have gotten him in trouble?"

Miles's dad sat up straighter. "He talked an awful lot about some girl in an apartment complex who was always nice to him. Every time she saw him, she said hi, asked him about his day. Miles had a crush on her."

The mom nodded. "We had to explain that she liked him, and she was a wonderful person, but he couldn't pester her all the time. He promised not to, but he still talked about her a lot."

"Did he ever mention a name?" Gaff asked.

The dad locked gazes with his wife. "It was Meghan this and Meghan that. He was so happy someone was actually nice to him! Most people avoided or ignored him. He was devoted to the girl. He'd never harm anyone. Ever. If anything, he'd try to defend her if someone was bothering her."

"That's what we think, too," Gaff said. "There was a woman's body buried close to his. We think Miles died trying to defend her."

The husband let out a long breath and reached for his wife's hand. "He died fast, trying to do the right thing."

They both looked like a heavy burden had been lifted from their shoulders. Jazzi thought about finding her Aunt Lynda's body, and even though it was questionable that she was trying to do the right thing, it had still been a relief to know what happened to her.

Gaff stood and smiled. "When I hear anything more, I'll let you know."

Everyone got to their feet, and Jazzi followed Gaff out to his car. He drove her to Olivia's and dropped her off. "Thanks for going with me. It helped."

"No problem. The parents can heal now." Her mom was still healing after everything she'd learned about Lynda.

He gave a wave and pulled away. Olivia opened the front door of the house and looked Jazzi up and down. "You look like you've been dragged through the mud. You're staying with us for supper tonight."

Jerod stepped out of the house behind her. "Not me. Franny's parents took the kids to a movie tonight. It's just me and my woman for a few hours. Franny's getting big as a barn, but I have a thing for pregnant women, and she can't resist lasagna from Casa's." He wiggled his eyebrows. "She won't be able to keep her hands off me."

"You wish." Olivia laughed when he wiggled his hips on his way to his truck. "You picked a keeper. Franny's fun to see at family get-togethers."

"What did you expect when I had so many to choose from?" Jerod slid behind the steering wheel.

Jazzi laughed at him. Her cousin was full of himself. "Get all the romance you can before the baby keeps you up all night."

Jerod hesitated before starting the engine. "I'm voting for the birth to happen *after* Valentine's Day. Then I might get lucky. Franny's voting for before. She's ready to kick the kid out. No more free room and board. No cushy womb. He'll have to deal with the real world."

"Like it matters. You and Franny will be happy either way. You won't be able to keep your hands off the baby." Jazzi watched him pull away and then grinned at her sister. "Those two sure love their kids."

Olivia wrinkled her nose. "They can have them. Messy on both ends. But I'm hungry. Let's go inside and order pizza."

Chapter 15

They ordered three pizzas—one for Ansel, one for Thane, and one for Jazzi and Olivia to split. They were sitting around the wooden table that served as a kitchen island, sipping beers, when the delivery man pulled in the drive. When he rang the bell, Olivia grabbed for her purse. "Come in!"

A college-age kid stepped through the kitchen door and brought the pizzas to the island. He was a cutie—tall, with dark, curly hair, golden-brown eyes, deep dimples—and he knew he was Charm Perfected. His practiced grin gave him away. He glanced at his surroundings. "Lookin' good. You've been working hard again."

Thane smiled. "Thanks, it's getting there. You getting tired of delivering pizzas here?"

"You kidding? You guys are good tippers. You can order every night." His dark gaze skimmed their faces, then settled on Jazzi. "I wondered why my regulars ordered three pizzas. You a friend?"

"I'm helping my sister fix her house."

He looked her up and down. "I believe in sisterhood. Always happy to rescue stranded ladies who aren't in the mood to cook. I hope this makes your night better."

Ansel exchanged glances with Thane. "Does that mean free breadsticks? We've been working hard, too."

"No freebies for you, not unless Blondie orders them." He stared at Jazzi. "I'd bend the rules for you. Enjoy your meal."

When his little, red SUV pulled away, Olivia laughed. "I think he fancied you, sis."

Jazzi rolled her eyes. "I think he's a college student who fancies lots of things. He probably thinks if he flirts, he gets a better tip."

"Not when he flirts with the sister who's *not* digging in her purse."
Olivia pouted. "He ignored me."

"Yeah, like you don't turn enough heads. Besides, he knows you're with
Thane." Jazzi reached for the box that contained the thin-crust Supreme.

"Who did he think I was?" Ansel asked. "Hired help?"

Jazzi studied his dirty T-shirt and worn jeans. "You could have been
one of Thane's work buddies—an unknown."

"Maybe I should put a ring on your finger."

Was he serious? "To let a college kid know I'm off-limits? That's silly."

He would have argued, but Thane pushed his pizza in front of him.
Talking came to an abrupt halt while they all demolished the food. When
they finished, Jazzi helped throw away paper plates and cardboard boxes.
She yawned. "I'm dragging. Thanks for supper, but we need to go home.
See you in the morning, Thane. Love ya, sis."

"If you want to sleep in tomorrow, go ahead," Olivia called after her.
"You had a long day. Thane and I can figure out how to finish the kitchen."

Thane's jaw dropped, horrified. Ansel looked offended.

Jazzi laughed. Her sister with a hammer in her hand? That was a scary
thought. "You're great with hair, but hopeless with a tool. I *am* going to
skip our Thursday night out tomorrow. I'm staying home to become one
with the couch."

"Fair enough, and thanks, sis! You, too, Ansel."

George waited for Ansel to lift him onto the back seat, and then they
drove home. When they got there, the lamp in the bow window welcomed
them. They'd set it on a timer. The front entry lights were on, too. Jazzi
let out a sigh of contentment. Their stone cottage always lifted her spirits.

When they put the van in the garage and stepped inside the back door
to the kitchen, Ansel pulled her close and kissed her.

"What's wrong with an engagement ring?"

She pressed closer to his hard chest. Mmm, he felt good. "I have lots
more things I'd rather spend money on than a diamond."

He looked puzzled. "I thought every woman wanted a diamond—the
bigger, the better."

"Not me. I'd snag it on nails and bang it on trim. Besides, things are
too hectic right now. We can worry about rings later."

He ran his finger along her cheek. "If you don't want a ring, I have a
guaranteed way to make you feel better."

"Let me guess." She smiled, tilting her head back to look at him. "You
think sex heals everything."

"Doesn't it?"

So far, spending time in bed with a tall, golden Norwegian bent on bringing her pleasure had worked well. "What about George? He already feels ignored today."

"I've already thought of that. Stay here." He hurried to the kitchen and filled George's bowl with his favorite food. The dog's toenails tapped on the wooden floors, followed by the sounds of happy scarfing.

Ansel went to the stairs and told George, "I'll be back for you later."

The dog ignored them. He knew what that meant.

On their way up the stairs, Ansel grabbed her fanny. "You're tired. You don't have to do anything. I'll try extra hard tonight."

Her body was already gearing up for action. "You don't have to. It's always good, whether you take your time or hurry."

He picked her up at the top of the stairs and carried her to their room. "It has to be better than good this time, so no young college kid tries to compete."

Her heart sped up. "Like he could."

Two hours later, after they'd taken their showers and padded downstairs in their pajamas, Jazzi was positive College Boy could learn a thing or two from Ansel. They dropped on stools at the kitchen island, and Ansel sipped a bedtime beer. Beer wasn't good enough to celebrate a great romp in bed. She enjoyed a glass of wine. George sprawled on the floor beside Ansel's bare feet, and they were all enjoying the moment.

Ansel's cell phone buzzed. He glanced at the ID, frowned, and ignored it. "Who was it?"

He shrugged, his broad shoulders rising and falling. He wore only pajama bottoms, and Jazzi enjoyed the view. She took another sip of wine. "My mom."

She stared. "Aren't you going to answer it?"

"I know what she's going to say."

"But she's your mom."

"Mmm-hmm, and how many times has she called me?" He tipped his beer and took a long draw.

Jazzi bit her bottom lip, trying to remember. When Ansel had been with Emily, had his mother called him? "*Has* she called you?"

"No." He pushed his phone aside, and they finished their drinks. Then he picked up George, and they went upstairs to bed—to sleep.

Chapter 16

On Thursday, they finished the bathrooms, then started laying the new floor in the open-concept room. The porcelain tiles looked like wood but were easier to care for. Olivia had chosen a warm brown that resembled maple floors. Besides the living room, dining room, and kitchen, Thane had decided to do the hallway that led to the bedrooms.

They had a lot to get finished today if they wanted to install new cabinets and appliances tomorrow. Jerod and Jazzi started work on the tiles in the living/dining area right away while Thane and Ansel ripped out the old kitchen and tossed everything out the back door. They'd carry the old cupboards and appliances to the dumpster later.

They'd taped heavy plastic over the archway to the back rooms. Dust flew everywhere they worked. Jerod worked as hard as ever but had dark circles under his eyes. Jazzi looked at him with sympathy. "Did you get any sleep last night?"

"Franny tossed and turned. The baby kept kicking."

"An active one, huh?"

"Franny thinks he's doing cartwheels inside her."

"I'm never having kids."

Jerod laughed. "Keep telling yourself that. They're twenty-four-seven, but you wouldn't trade them for anything in the world."

Jazzi wasn't so sure. "George is a big enough commitment for me."

"Yeah, I could see how he'd wear you out. He sleeps most of the time. The thing about kids is that they have more energy than you do."

"That's what worries me."

He went to get another box of tiles while she finished the row they were working on. Olivia and Thane had painted the walls a soft cream last weekend, and the wood look was a perfect match for them. At lunch, there was no table to eat on. They balanced their sandwiches on their laps. Echoes bounced in the empty space. When they finished eating, all four of them worked on tiles, and things went fast. Every room was finished before five. Then they worked on trim.

Ansel straightened after pounding the last of the baseboard in place. He looked at Jazzi. "Why don't you go walk Cocoa while we clean up? The dog probably only got a short walk this morning. And she'll be missing Leo. Give her a little extra attention."

Jazzi stood, rolled her shoulders, and stretched her back. They'd been bent over all day long, but when she glanced at their work, she had to admit, it looked wonderful. Thane let out a low whistle.

"This looks even better than I pictured it. It's great."

Jerod grunted when he straightened his back. "Jeez, I'm stiff. I'm going to take a long, hot shower tonight." Then he studied their handiwork. "Just wait till we get the new cabinets and counters in here. This room's going to be reborn."

Plenty of scraps of wood and dust covered the floor. Thane reached for a broom and shooed Jazzi away with his other hand. "We'll clean. You do dog duty. Cocoa likes you."

"Are you sure?" Jazzi glanced out the kitchen door at the pile of cupboards and appliances. "There's a lot to do."

"Go," Ansel told her.

A walk might feel good. Jazzi left and headed to Louisa's house. Miriam's car was still in the driveway.

When Miriam saw her, she opened the front door wide. "Thank goodness! Cocoa's getting restless. She keeps going to the door and whining."

"It will take her a while to adjust to how things are now." Jazzi reached for the dog's leash, and Cocoa bumped against her, anxious to get outside.

Louisa glanced at the grandfather clock in the corner. "Seth came and took her around the neighborhood this morning before he went to work."

"That was nice of him." Jazzi clipped the leash in place. "Cocoa's not used to walking that early. She was used to Leo's schedule."

"I know, poor thing." Louisa laid her hands in her lap. "It's hard for all of us."

Jazzi couldn't think of anything to say, so gave a quick nod. "I might take her farther than usual, try to work off some of her nervous energy."

They slipped outside, and Jazzi started toward the small span of asphalt that connected their subdivision to the next. Cocoa's step picked up. She realized they were going farther than just a big circle. A squirrel ran across the street in front of them, and Cocoa barked.

"No chasing squirrels," Jazzi said, "or we'll turn around and head back."

Leo must have said the same thing, because Cocoa watched until the squirrel scampered up a tree, but she didn't bark or tug on her leash. It was a gorgeous day, in the mid-seventies, so they kept going until they reached the very last subdivision.

A field, full of weeds and small bushes, stretched toward the businesses that lined Jefferson Street. For the first time, Jazzi noticed a small apartment complex on a short street behind the sandwich shop and dry cleaners. Cocoa bent her head and sniffed until she found a narrow path through the weeds. It led to a row of evergreens that lined the apartment's parking lot.

The dog started down the path. Jazzi thought about tugging her back, but it would take the men a while to clean up. Curious, Jazzi followed behind her. The trail was too narrow to walk side by side. And then Jazzi realized that it was a bicycle trail.

The hairs on her arms stood on end. Did Miles use this?

When they reached the yew bushes, a large patch of weeds had been flattened between two of them. Jazzi studied the town houses and realized that Miles could hide here and see into the last town house at the very end of the development. There were no curtains at the windows. In the dark, with lights on, he could watch whoever lived there.

Cocoa moved farther down the bushes and was poking her nose in the weeds while Jazzi scanned their surroundings. When Jazzi looked at the dog again, she had a red gym shoe in her mouth.

Jazzi inhaled a sharp breath. Miles was missing a gym shoe in his grave. She reached for her cell phone to call Gaff when her phone buzzed. He was calling her.

"Hello?"

Gaff said, "We checked missing persons, and a young nurse never came to work and never called in sick. The floor supervisor said it wasn't like her not to be dependable and punctual. Our victim is probably Meghan Fuller."

She interrupted. "Did she live in an apartment complex off Jefferson Street, close to South Bend Drive?"

Gaff paused. "What have you got for me?"

She told him about the bike trail, the matted-down weeds, and Miles's gym shoe. "I can't get the shoe away from the dog."

"No problem. I'm on my way. I'm bringing the techs."

Jazzi called Ansel to tell him she was going to be gone longer than she expected. She told him the news. And then she waited for Gaff.

The detective and his team pulled into the apartment complex and parked at the very back, within easy walking distance of her. As Gaff approached, he unwrapped a small hamburger and held it out for Cocoa. The dog dropped the shoe, and a tech picked it up and bagged it.

Jazzi shook her head. "That's sort of sneaky."

Gaff grinned. "It worked, and I didn't have to play tug-of-war for the sneaker."

She stayed until the techs got serious, then said, "I've got to get Cocoa back, and the guys are ready to call it a day."

Gaff nodded. "I might give you a call tomorrow. When we finish here, we're going to look at Meghan's apartment. It's the one on the end, the one Miles watched at night."

She'd suspected as much. With a wave, she started back to Louisa's.

Chapter 17

On their walk to Louisa's, Jazzi and Cocoa passed Ed's house. His work van wasn't in the drive, but the pizza guy's older-model red SUV was parked close to the door. Jazzi wondered if Ed worked late some nights, finishing up a gutter or siding project. Eve didn't strike her as a cook, so she probably ordered out when she ate supper alone.

She'd walked two houses farther down the street when Jazzi heard footsteps running behind her. She turned and saw the pizza guy hurrying to see her.

He smiled, dimples showing. He really was good-looking with his wavy, dark hair and golden-brown eyes. He was in great shape. "Hey, good to see you again," he called. "Is your sister ordering pizza tonight?"

Cocoa sat down next to her. The dog must be used to Leo stopping to chat as he made his rounds. "Don't know. Ansel and I aren't staying for supper. I told Louisa I'd take Cocoa for a walk before we left, though, since Leo's gone."

"Yeah, Eve told me about that, said you'd stopped with a detective to grill Ed."

"Gaff didn't grill him." She lifted her chin, aggravated, ready to defend her friend. Eve would put it like that. "Gaff did ask questions, though, since Ed had been so mad at Leo."

"She said you found the missing kid, too."

"We think Leo and Cocoa stumbled on the bodies buried near the wetlands, and it looks like someone dragged Leo's body off so Cocoa wouldn't dig there again." She waited to see how he'd react. People might as well know that someone around here was dangerous. Did the killer know that the bodies had been discovered by the cops? That the deaths were being investigated now?

The kid shrugged. "The world isn't safe anymore, I guess. Who'd think murder would come to this little neck of the woods? It might not be safe for you to be out walking alone. Doesn't your boyfriend worry about you? I would."

Jazzi rolled her eyes. "I think I'm pretty safe on the streets around suppertime. Doors are open, and a few people are in their yards."

"What's with you and the blond hulk? I don't see a ring on your finger. Are you two married?"

This was the perfect time to let him know she was off-limits. "Not yet, but we're living together. We're serious."

He grinned. "But you're not hitched. You haven't made the commitment yet. Not even engaged. You might want to try something new before you make the big plunge."

She'd reinforce the message. "Not my style. I'm the one-man-at-a-time type girl, and right now, the only man in my life is going to be Ansel."

"That's a waste. If you two don't work out, you've made a bad investment."

Cocoa tugged on her leash, ready to walk some more. Jazzi nodded at the dog. "Gotta go. She's ready to be home."

"If you change your mind, if your Ansel doesn't work out, I'm Peyton, and I like older women. You're super attractive. I could show you a good time."

He was nothing if not persistent. She studied him. "How old are you?"

"Twenty-one."

Young enough to feel invincible. "I'm twenty-seven, and I'm *having* a good time. So I'll pass. I'm sure you can find plenty of other women who'll fall all over you." She turned to walk away.

"Hey! If you ever want to meet up, you know which pizza place to call. Just ask for Peyton."

"Will do, but don't hold your breath."

He laughed. "I like it when women play hard to get."

Hard to get? She turned, hands on hips. "I'm not playing. I'm not interested."

"I can be patient. Just let me know when you're ready."

Was he for real? She huffed a sigh and stomped away. He was freaking annoying. Cocoa growled low in her throat. The dog didn't like him either.

Chapter 18

Jazzi dropped Cocoa back at Louisa's house before crossing the street to see Olivia and Thane. Olivia wasn't home yet, but the men had finished their cleanup and were sitting at the island, nursing beers, waiting for her.

Jerod glanced at her face, and his eyebrow went up. "You were in a good mood when you left."

She told them about finding Miles's gym shoe.

"Sorry, cuz. But I bet Gaff loves you by now. You keep finding new clues for him."

She grimaced. "I think the poor girl who died lived in that town house at the end of the complex. All the things that have happened were close to each other."

"Makes sense," Ansel said. "Miles didn't go very far."

"But doesn't that mean the killer has to live around here, too?" she asked.

Thane's eyebrows furrowed in worry. "I'm not letting Olivia leave our yard until Gaff puts this nutjob behind bars."

She told them about meeting Peyton near Ed's house. "I'm not saying he's the killer, but Olivia had better watch herself around him. He thinks every woman should cave to his charms."

Ansel shook his head, amused. "I'm surprised he lived when he kept pestering you. You Zanders girls don't suffer fools gladly."

Jerod finished his beer and went to toss the empty bottle in the recycle bin. "Ain't that the truth? You should have grown up with them. It wasn't safe to get on their bad sides. They'd team up and make you miserable."

Jazzi snorted. "As though you were ever innocent and didn't deserve it."

He laughed. "I did like to ruffle their feathers every once in a while."

"Or more." Jazzi waved away the beer Thane offered her and looked at Ansel. "Ready to go? I'd like to put today behind me."

He and Jerod both stood. Outside, Jerod went to his pickup and drove south to his Franny. She and Ansel put George in his van and headed north for home.

Gaff called while they were on their way. "Our team went over Meghan's apartment, and there were signs of a struggle. We found blood. Probably hers. I'd bet she died there and Miles either watched the whole thing or ran in to rescue her. The manager was out of town while we worked there. Want to come with me tomorrow to talk to him?"

"What time are you going?" She surprised herself. She wanted to hear what the manager had to say about Meghan. She was beginning to care about these people and what had happened to them.

"I can pick you up at ten at your sister's place."

"That'll work. Thanks for telling me what you found."

"No problem. We'd still be posting Miles and Meghan as missing persons if you hadn't gotten friendly with that dog."

It was sort of sobering how easily people could disappear, and what a fluke it was that she'd stumbled on their bodies. "See you tomorrow," she said.

"Ten o'clock." Gaff hung up.

Ansel glanced sideways at her. "She died in her apartment, didn't she?"

"It looks like it. Miles was probably watching when the killer went in it. Gaff wants me to go with him to see the manager tomorrow."

"Good, maybe you'll learn something new."

"That would be nice." Maybe the manager had seen Meghan's visitor and could describe him. Maybe Meghan had been friends with someone across the hall or in one of the other buildings, and she'd talked to them about a new boyfriend.

Ansel pulled into their driveway and parked by the kitchen door. He let Jazzi out, then drove on to put the van in the garage. Jazzi had thawed shrimp to make for supper, with New Orleans barbecue sauce. They'd decided to be lazy and opened a bag of readymade Caesar salad. She put a foil bag of garlic bread on the counter top and started heating the oven.

She loved to cook shrimp. The recipe tonight was quick and easy. Twenty minutes after Ansel and George ambled into the house, supper was ready. Jazzi had saved a half dozen plain shrimp for the pug. George didn't like garlic or spices.

Cleanup was a breeze, so in a short time, they were ready to head upstairs to shower and change into their pajamas. George followed them to the steps, but Ansel shook his head and said, "Later."

The pug gave him a dirty look but lay at the base of the stairs.

Jazzi raised her eyebrows. "Now?"

"Might as well get down and dirty before we shower." He stepped behind her and wrapped her in his arms. "Besides, I feel pressured to keep you satisfied so the pizza guy doesn't start to look tempting."

"No worries there." Usually she'd get hot and bothered just thinking about going to bed with Ansel. Tonight, not so much. It had been a long day...a long week. If she sat down on the bed, she'd probably fall asleep.

He turned her to face him and gripped her fanny with both hands, pulling her close. Then he bent his head and ran his lips up and down her throat.

Oh, crap, he was playing dirty. Every nerve in her body zinged into alert. His hand moved up her back, sending tingles up and down her spine, then cradled the back of her head. His lips tasted hers, then the kiss deepened. She was no longer sleepy, almost intoxicated. A coil of need tightened in her belly. Her body went on high alert. Every cell craved his touch.

When they came up for air, they hurried up the steps to their bedroom, and a good hour later, Jazzi felt so satisfied, she didn't want to move. She let him take the first shower, because her legs felt like noodles.

When Ansel went down to get George, she stood under the hot water a long time to wash away a bit of her desire. It lingered in her pores. She'd never get enough of Ansel. When she felt more normal, she dried off and pulled on her oversized white T-shirt and pajama shorts. Then they climbed into bed together. She pressed against his back, and they fell asleep.

Chapter 19

It was freakishly hot outside when they woke Friday morning. The first day of September—not fall yet. But really? Who wanted the high eighties to start the month?

They were going to work on Thane and Olivia's kitchen today, hopefully finishing it up. New cabinets were going in, new counters and backsplash. The old worktable was being replaced with an island, topped by an oversized slab of granite with an overhang. Four stools could slide under it. If all went well, they'd get everything done, and this would be their last day there.

On the drive across town, Jazzi glanced at store windows. Fall clothes draped every mannequin. She cringed. "I don't even want to see heavy fabrics and sweaters right now."

Ansel smiled, keeping his eyes on the traffic. It was always heavier on Fridays. "You look so good in sweaters, though, I'm a fan. You have a black one with a V-neck that's my favorite."

She knew the one he meant, which was more form-fitting than most. "I didn't think you paid attention to what I wore."

"I was with Emily then, but I loved that sweater. And you always wore it with tight jeans. You have plenty of curves, and every one of them is dangerous."

She laughed. He always made her feel desirable. The man loved sexy underwear, and she had zero in her drawers. She'd have to buy something sexy to make him happy.

They made the turn onto Sycamore Drive. The strip mall with Seth's bar sat on the north corner, and the few small businesses with the apartments behind them sat on the south. They passed the open field that separated the businesses from the housing developments. Halfway down the street to Olivia's turnoff, an old brick church sat on the left side near a corner. Cars were always parked in its back lot. Its members must be active. Jazzi wondered if Miles's parents went there. When they pulled next to Thane's, she noticed Seth walking Cocoa back to Louisa's. He gave them a wave and stopped to pet the dog. Cocoa's tail waved her happiness.

Jazzi had to give Seth credit. When Louisa needed him, he'd stepped up to the plate. "I think Seth likes Cocoa."

"She's great." Ansel glanced in the rearview mirror at George. "Not as special as our guy, but pretty nice."

When Ansel helped George out of the van, the wonder pooch in question went straight to his dog bed in Thane's living room to supervise the work they did.

The cabinets were delivered a few minutes later, and Jazzi started unpacking them while the guys arranged them in the right order. They worked together to drill and screw the cabinets in place. Gaff came at ten, and Jazzi had to leave before they were finished.

"I'm always interrupting your work," Gaff told her on the drive to Meghan's apartment complex.

"If it helps catch a killer, it's worth it." Driving from this direction, Jazzi studied the backs of the businesses that bordered Jefferson Street. She hadn't realized how many there were. Back-to-back strip malls stretched as far as she could see. "There are lots of people who come and go around here. I was thinking the killer might live in the area, but it could be someone who's a regular at one of the restaurants or stores."

A ditch ran behind Seth's strip mall. Trees lined it, and someone had hung bird feeders from their branches. She remembered that there was an outdoor seed store farther down Jefferson. Her dad bought suet there.

Gaff interrupted her thoughts when he turned into the apartment's parking lot and found a spot by the office. "There are lots of possibilities. Let's hope the manager can tell us something."

The office was nice, but unpretentious—a desk with two chairs across from it, filing cabinets, and a cheap picture on the wall. The manager, however, almost burst with personality and energy. He held out a hand to greet them.

The man looked to be in his forties, shorter than Jazzi, with dark coloring. He wore dress slacks and a button-down shirt. "A pleasure to meet you. You came about Meghan."

Gaff nodded. "It looks like she was killed in her apartment. We know she was a nurse. We've notified her parents—they live out of town—and we're interviewing the people she worked with, but we were hoping you could tell us more about her. We've gone door to door, but she didn't seem to have any friends here. Do you know if she had a boyfriend, visitors, anyone we could interview?"

He motioned for them to take seats and went to sit behind his desk. "She was the friendly sort, always had something nice to say when she came to pay her rent, but she worked two jobs. Didn't have time to make many friends."

"Two jobs?" Gaff opened his notepad.

"She worked two nights at the wings restaurant down the road from here. She was saving for a house. Wanted a big down payment. It was mostly work and sleep for her, but everyone liked her. She was just plain nice."

"Did you see anyone come or go from her apartment?"

"Sorry." He shook his head. "She was the last unit, and any visitor would have parked behind her town house. I wouldn't see them. I leave here every night at six, so I wouldn't see any evening visitors."

"Anything at all you can tell us?"

He shook his head. "Sorry. She was a few days late on her rent, but she was so dependable, I just left a note in her mail slot. I thought maybe she'd gone home to visit her parents and stayed longer than she expected."

Gaff rose. "I appreciate your seeing us. Thank you for your time."

"No problem, I liked Meghan. I hope you find whoever hurt her."

"We're trying." Gaff nodded to Jazzi, and she followed him out of the room. When they reached his car, he asked, "Have time to stop by the wings restaurant?"

"Sure. Why not?" Someone had killed a young guy with mental issues and a nurse who sounded like a truly nice person. And Leo, who struck her as naïve. She wanted whoever killed them in prison for the rest of his life.

It only took them five minutes to reach the restaurant. It wasn't open yet, but people were inside, working. Gaff pounded on the door and pressed his badge against the glass. A worker opened it for him.

"Is your manager here?"

The kid pointed toward the kitchen. "He's in there. We're expecting a big crowd tonight. He's overseeing prep."

"Would you tell him I'd like to ask him a few questions?"

The kid headed to get him. Jazzi studied the place. Comfortable, but not fancy. It was known for its ribs and chicken wings. Booths surrounded the outside walls; tables filled the center. When the manager came toward them, he wore a frown. "How can I help you?"

"We want to ask you a few questions about one of your employees, Meghan Fuller."

His expression turned sour. "What about her? She was always dependable, never missed a night, never came late, and then she just didn't show up. Didn't even call. When I tried to call her, she didn't answer. Just quit. Left us in the lurch."

"Not her fault. She was murdered."

The man blinked. "She's dead?"

"Yup, killed in her apartment and buried in a shallow grave."

He rubbed a hand across his forehead. "I just thought she was a no-show. I get a lot of that with kids today. They don't even give notice."

"We're trying to find her killer. Do you happen to know anyone close to her, someone she might have confided in about a new boyfriend, anything new in her life?"

"She didn't talk much to anyone here. Just did her shift and left." He thought a minute. "You might try the bar three doors down. She went there after work to chill out. I think she had a crush on the bartender there."

Seth? Louisa's nephew? Jazzi frowned. He was too old for Meghan.

"Did Meghan ever talk to you?" Gaff asked.

The manager shook his head. "She mostly kept to herself."

Gaff handed him his card. "Thanks for your time. If you think of anything else, let me know."

Jazzi wondered how many times detectives did the meet and greet, question and thanks. Probably more than she could stand. They left the restaurant and started down the sidewalk to Seth's bar. A furniture store, pet shop, and department store were on the other end of the mall. An ice cream shop and upscale restaurant anchored its center. Seth's bar sat on the far end, closed, too, but people were inside, getting ready for the lunch crowd. Once again, Gaff knocked and showed his badge.

Seth noticed them and hurried to open the door. Words rushed out. "Is everything all right with my aunt?"

Jazzi felt bad. She'd never thought about what Seth would think when he saw them there. "Everything seemed fine at her house. I just came with Gaff about the murders."

His shoulders relaxed, and he turned to the detective. "You've learned something about Leo?"

Jazzi noticed he didn't call him *Uncle* Leo. She wondered if Leo had *ever* been fond of him. When Seth was ten, he wouldn't have been running a bar. Did Leo disapprove of him even then? She decided to ask. "Were you close to him?"

Seth motioned them to a booth. "Never. Leo didn't like my mom. Thought she was too rough around the edges. She worked as a dispatcher at a trucking firm, knew all the guys. A little on the salty side. My dad worked in a factory. We weren't classy enough for Leo."

Jazzi could see Leo being a little on the particular side. "He told me he didn't like bartenders."

Seth laughed. "Maybe, but that's only part of it. I'm not sure he would have liked me even if I became a college professor. He'd already made up his mind about our side of the family."

Gaff took out his notebook. "We've come because your uncle's death ties in with two other murders. We think the nurse, Meghan Fuller, was the first victim, and the others were killed because they saw something they shouldn't have."

"Meghan? Did she have soft dark hair? Pretty and soft-spoken?"

"That would be her," Gaff said.

"She came in here a lot after work, after her shifts at both the hospital and the wings place. She always sat at the bar and ordered nachos and two beers. Had a thing for my bartender, Greg."

Relief seeped through Jazzi. Meghan hadn't been flirting with Seth. She'd had a crush on his bartender.

"Is Greg here now?" Gaff asked.

Seth shook his head. "Won't show up until the evening shift. Fridays are always busy."

"Were Meghan and Greg an item?"

"She wanted to be, but Greg's like a flame for women. They line the bar, flirting with him. After his ex, though, he's not ready to commit to anyone. Keeps a safe distance from all of them."

Jazzi had taken some time to lick her wounds when she broke up with Chad. It had surprised her how much she'd misread him. Maybe Greg felt the same way. She'd distrusted herself for months. They'd been happy, happy, happy until they moved in with each other. Then he'd wanted to change everything about her. Didn't like it that she worked with Jerod. Wanted her to stay home and have his babies and take care of their apartment. She wasn't ready for that yet, but he'd wanted it *now*. She finally moved out.

A young, attractive waitress went from table to table, filling ketchup bottles and salt and pepper shakers. Her shorts stopped at mid-thigh and her V-necked T-shirt showed a decent amount of cleavage. A blond waitress with a snug T-shirt that showed off large, firm breasts was wrapping silverware. "How can female customers compete with your work staff?"

"Bailey and Lexie? They both have steady boyfriends. They dress for success—big tips."

Maybe Peyton was on to something. Being cute and flirting probably filled your pocketbook.

Gaff asked, "Was Meghan interested in any of the customers who came here? Did anyone come on to her?"

"Not that I noticed. She wasn't good at flirting and shut down most guys, but she really liked Greg."

"It wasn't mutual?" Gaff poised his pen above his notepad.

"Greg liked her, but not like that. When Greg hits the bar, he turns on. He becomes Mr. Showman. He's great for business."

"Anything else you can think of that might help us find her killer?" Gaff asked.

Seth shook his head. "Sorry, she was a steady customer, but I didn't talk to her much." Then he hesitated. "You know, she did talk about an EMT who got a little too infatuated with her. Came up to her outside the hospital a few weeks ago when she waited for the shuttle. Shook her up a little."

"Do you remember a name?"

He shrugged. "Maybe you can ask one of the nurses she worked with."

Jazzi waited for Gaff's magic words, and he didn't disappoint. "Thanks for your time. If you think of anything else, give me a call." He handed Seth his card.

On the drive back to Thane's house, Gaff said, "I'll drop you off, then go to the hospital and ask around about the EMT who had the hots for Meghan. I've talked to a few of the nurses before. I'll let you know what I find out."

"Thanks. Seth made me curious about the guy." Gaff pulled into the driveway, and Jazzi got out of the car. As he pulled away, the sound of kids' voices drifted from the school's playground. They were low-key today, sluggish. It was too freakin' hot.

Jazzi hurried into the house to help finish up the kitchen. The cabinets were all installed and the counter tops had been delivered and put in place. Wow. Her sister had a thing for white. White cupboards and white granite counters with gray streaks. Not Jazzi's thing, but it looked gorgeous.

While the guys worked on getting the stainless-steel appliances in place, she started installing aqua glass tiles for the backsplash. The pop of color made a big difference. They stopped for quick sandwiches for lunch, and by four-thirty, their work in the kitchen was done. This weekend, Olivia and Thane could put up finishing touches, fill cupboards, and buy stools for the kitchen island.

Thane grinned. "Are you going to miss me next week? We'll all be back to our regular jobs."

True. Thane would go back to fixing and installing furnaces and air-conditioners. Jerod, Ansel, and Jazzi would start work on their new fixer-upper off Anthony Boulevard. All of its bones were great, but no one had lived in it for eight years. The owner had flown to California to stay with her aging mother, met a nice man there, and decided to stay. She didn't want to return to sell it, so she put it up for auction. They'd gotten it at a great price.

Jerod laughed at Thane. "Hate to tell you, buddy, but I'm happy enough just seeing you on Sundays at Jazzi's house. We can catch up then. I don't need to see you every day."

Thane grew serious. "I sure appreciate all the work you guys have done. It would have taken us forever doing it ourselves. All Olivia and I have to do now are small things."

"You're family," Jerod said. "And Zanders take that seriously. Don't ever cheat on Olivia or we'll track you down, draw and quarter you."

Ansel and Thane exchanged glances. "We'll keep that in mind."

"Do that."

"And if you ever cheat on Franny?" Thane asked.

Jerod just stared at him. "Why would I do that? Franny's my everything."

Ansel sent her a sizzling look. "That's how I feel about Jazzi."

Really? His everything? He felt that way now, but they'd only lived together a short time. Chad was happy when they'd first moved in together, too.

Jerod gave a quick nod. "When you hook up in our family, it's till death do you part. If you try to wiggle out ahead of time, you'll only *wish* you were dead."

Jazzi turned to him with a frown. "What about Chad?"

"That was different. We were all happy to see him go."

"Everyone was always nice to him."

Jerod stared at her as if she had two heads. "You moved in with him. What were we supposed to do? We weren't fans, but we respect you."

"What if Jazzi leaves me?" Ansel asked.

"Then it will be your fault. You did something wrong, and we'll all stick up for Jazzi. You'd better move far, far away."

Ansel liked that answer, she could tell. Why, she had no idea. It sounded unfair to her, but Ansel valued families who stuck together. They said quick good-byes, and Jerod beat it for home.

Ansel glanced at George. "I'm starving. Can we leave George here while we grab supper somewhere close?"

Thane looked at the pug, still napping in his dog bed in the living room. "He's a lot of bother, but I can manage. He can help me clean."

Ansel went to pat the dog's head. "We're leaving for a minute, but wait here. We'll be back soon, and I'll bring you something."

It was the oddest thing, but the dog seemed to understand. He licked Ansel's hand, then stretched out again, content.

When they reached his work van, Jazzi asked, "Where to?"

"You made Seth's bar sound good. Want to give it a try?"

"It had fried calamari on the menu."

"That's a yes then." And it was only five minutes away.

When they walked in, the place was packed. There were two seats at the bar, and they snagged them. They'd just settled when the door opened and a group of girls rushed to stand behind a friend who sat at the bar's other end. They all preened and posed, trying to impress the man taking their friend's order. Ah! The bartender Seth had told them about who cranked up hormones. Jazzi craned to catch a glimpse of him.

Chapter 20

At first, Jazzi was disappointed. The guy behind the bar couldn't hold a candle to Ansel. Of course, if Ansel were a bartender and smiled and smirked, that bar might be standing room only. Girls tripped over themselves when he didn't even notice them. They were happy just to look.

She watched Greg in action, though, and he had swagger and style. He might not want a woman in his life, but he sure enjoyed flirting. The girls crowded even closer, but he held up a finger and winked at them. "Ladies, behave! Two customers came in ahead of you, but I'll be right back."

He came to take her and Ansel's orders. Calamari for an appetizer, and a burger and fries for each of them. Beer for Ansel, wine for her. Greg held her gaze a little too long. "You're new here, aren't you?"

"We don't live close, only visiting. Nice bar."

He grinned. "Hope you have to come back soon."

Ansel glared, and Greg returned to his fawning crowd. He wasn't handsome, but his personality made him appealing. And he was good at bartending. Every customer had a drink. Even with the overflow of girls, no one was neglected.

When their drinks came, Ansel took a sip, then looked at her. "I rushed you tonight. You still need to walk Cocoa, don't you?"

"Yeah. I'll get her when we go back for George. But Louisa said she'd find someone else to walk her from now on. She knows we've finished work at Olivia's."

"Good, I'd hate to drive back every night." A bowl of popcorn sat close to them, and Ansel grabbed a handful.

"What do you think of Olivia and Thane's house? I think it turned out great." It wasn't Jazzi's style, but that didn't mean she couldn't appreciate it.

"It's going to be a showstopper, but I love our place."

Our place. She liked the sound of that every time he said it.

Seth hurried from the kitchen to them with the calamari. "Order's up! Hope you like it. If you don't, don't tell my aunt."

Jazzi laughed. "It'll be our secret."

"I'd better get back behind the bar again and help Greg. A guy bumped a waitress and made her drop an armload of plates. I had to help out for a minute, but everything's smooth now." He dipped behind the bar, and Greg gave him a grateful nod.

Families finished their suppers and left. New customers rolled in. Seth whisked away their empty appetizer plate and delivered their burgers. People lined up at the front counter for takeouts. The place was bustling. Seth and Greg made a perfect team. People got welcomed, served, and checked on.

Jazzi and Ansel ate, waved a good-bye to Seth, then drove back toward Louisa's house.

"I like that bar," Ansel said. "Wouldn't mind going there again."

"We could stop some night when we visit Mom and Dad. Their house isn't that much out of the way."

He grinned. "Your parents might start seeing more of us."

"Lucky them." Jazzi probably only stopped to see them once a month.

"Hey, they like me, welcomed me into the family with open arms."

She chuckled. "They like me, too, but seeing me every Sunday might be enough for them."

They pulled into Louisa's drive and knocked on her door. When Cocoa saw Jazzi, her tail started wagging.

"She's ready for her walk." Louisa handed Jazzi the dog's leash.

Ansel started across the street. "I'll go get George and bring him with us."

Jazzi couldn't hide her surprise. "Does George walk that far? We're going to the end of the subdivisions and back."

Ansel hesitated. "Maybe I'll wait. I'll walk with you, *then* get George. And don't let me forget to buy him a takeout burger on our drive home. I promised him one."

The pug was nothing but spoiled. She and Ansel walked side by side, taking the Lab through one neighborhood after another. Jazzi hoped whoever took her place with Cocoa knew how far the dog was used to going. When they reached the field that separated the houses from the businesses, Cocoa started a high-pitched whine and strained against her leash.

"No, you can't cross the street!" Did Leo let her walk farther on Fridays? Surely, they didn't go through the parking lots. Jazzi tried to pull the dog closer, but Cocoa leaned into the leash, almost ripping it out of Jazzi's hands. "What's wrong with you?"

"Do you think she's hungry?" Ansel motioned to the back of Seth's bar. "Maybe Leo let her cheat once in a while. Louisa only gives her dry dog food. Maybe she has a thing for burgers."

"I don't know, but I'm taking her over there and walking her on that side of the street. If she breaks free from her leash, who knows how far she'll run? I don't want her to dart in front of a car on the highway. There's not a lot of traffic on Sycamore Drive."

Ansel grabbed the dog's collar, and they waited for a few cars to pass, then crossed over. The parking lots for the businesses didn't connect to Sycamore Drive, but there was a wide grassy strip they could walk on. The dog went ballistic when they got close to the buildings, whining and barking, lunging toward Seth's bar. And then Jazzi saw it. She clamped her left hand over her mouth. "Oh crap!"

Ansel followed her gaze and let out a surprised grunt.

A hand stuck out of the dumpster behind the bar. Why hadn't someone noticed it before now?

Ansel took Cocoa's leash. "You'd better call Gaff. Cocoa knows who that hand belongs to."

"Leo?"

"Unless there's more dead bodies lying around here."

Jazzi pulled out her cell and dialed. Ansel knelt next to Cocoa and held her close, stroking her and talking to her in a soothing voice. "It's okay, girl. You can't go near him until Gaff gets here, but then we'll let you say good-bye to him."

The dog leaned into him, whimpering, then slumped onto the ground and laid her head on her paws.

Chapter 21

Jazzi called Thane and told him that they might be late picking up George. She explained about the hand in the dumpster.

Olivia got on the phone. "Are the heavens punishing you? Are you cursed to go around town, finding dead bodies?"

"Not funny." Jazzi had asked herself the same question.

"Do you have to stay for Gaff?" Olivia asked.

"Yeah, he just thought he got to go home and be off duty."

"And he still likes you?"

"So far." Jazzi let out a long breath. "We have Cocoa. Gaff'll probably want to go with us when we take her home. He'll want to talk to Louisa."

Her sister's voice softened. "Sucks to be you. Want a glass of wine when you get here?"

"Have you had a chance to eat? We don't want to interrupt your supper."

"I picked up takeout on my way home. We had enough to share with George. Tell Ansel his dog likes lo mein."

Jazzi laughed. "George likes almost everything, even green beans."

"Well, he's happy for the moment. We're just going to be putting things in our cupboards. I can finally get the stuff out of our spare bedroom. See you whenever you get here."

"Thanks, Olivia."

Gaff and his team pulled in as soon as she hung up. They stretched yellow tape around the area, went straight to the dumpster, and got to work. Flies and bees circled the garbage bags, but they ignored them.

"You should let Seth know we're here," Gaff said. "I'll want to talk to him."

Jazzi gave him a look. She wasn't officially part of his team, but dark circles cratered his eyes, and his white shirt was more rumpled than usual, so she let it go. She ducked into the restaurant, caught Seth's attention, and told him the news.

The color drained from his face. "In my dumpster?"

She nodded.

He called, "Cover for me!" to a male waiter and walked out the door with her. When he joined Gaff and Ansel and saw Leo on top of his trash, he looked like he might be sick.

"Hang in there," Gaff said. "I need some information from you."

Seth straightened his shoulders. "What do you need to know?"

"You've been at the restaurant all day. Has anyone used the dumpster?"

"I have. I tossed big bags in it after the lunch crowd. Leo's lying on them."

Gaff looked surprised. "So someone brought his body here and dumped it while you were at work?"

Seth crossed his arms over his chest. He wrinkled his nose at the smell. When the dumpster was closed, it was bad enough. With the lid open, it reeked. "Had to. Fridays are always busy. I took Cocoa for a walk, then came here. I don't leave until after closing and cleanup, usually close to three in the morning."

"And you don't leave to make a bank deposit or take a break any time during the day?"

Seth grew thoughtful. "I usually do. I make a bank run around three in the afternoon, but today was one of those days; lots of little things kept going wrong. I stayed to deal with crap, and our head waitress deposited the money for me."

Gaff paused to think a moment. "Is there anyone out to get you? It feels like someone was trying to pin Leo's murder on you."

"On me? He's my uncle."

"And I'd bet his body went in the dumpster when you're usually on break, when you wouldn't have an alibi."

Seth shook his head. "I'm not buying that. I don't have any enemies I know of. *I'd* bet someone wanted a convenient way to get rid of Leo's body. The collection truck empties the dumpster early Saturday morning."

Jazzi tried to block an image of a garbage truck emptying Leo's body into its crusher. "But where was Leo's body in the meantime? He's been dead a while."

"Good question." Gaff looked at Ben, one of the techs, who was close enough to hear their conversation. "Got any answers for us?" he called.

Ben came to join them. "There's no decomposition. No bugs or dirt. I'd say he was in a freezer."

Jazzi's mind painted a mental picture of Leo cradled among frozen peas and chuck roasts. She pushed it away.

Seth stared. "Someone froze him, then came and tossed him in the trash? What sense does that make?"

"A lot," Ben said. "I'd guess the killer dragged the body to his trunk but wasn't sure where to get rid of it, so he tossed it in an empty chest freezer. He didn't want to keep it there, though, and he'd buried two other bodies close to here and wanted to dump Leo in the same area. If he could point us in the wrong direction at the same time, so much the better."

Jazzi raised an eyebrow at Ben. The tech was pretty impressive.

Gaff looked at Seth. "You have a big freezer room, don't you?"

Seth straightened to his full height, clearly offended. "Yeah, but it's full of chicken wings, burgers, and supplies. People walk in and out of it all the time. If Leo was in there, someone would notice."

"Mind if we take a look?"

Seth motioned toward the bar's door. "Come on. Be my guest."

Gaff nudged Jazzi to follow him. She glanced at Ansel, and he nodded for her to go. He'd stay with the dog.

Just as Seth had told them, there was a lot of food in the cooler, nothing else. On the way out, Jazzi glanced at the kitchen full of bustling cooks. Windows opened onto a small space outdoors, surrounded on three sides by a high, wooden fence.

"Employees go out there to smoke," Seth told them.

Jazzi's attention focused on a pair of binoculars hanging from a hook near the kitchen door. "Binoculars?"

Seth grinned. "You wouldn't believe it from a bunch of guys like mine, but they like watching the bird feeders at the end of the lot. We get a big variety since there's a creek back there."

"How far can you see? If you aim them at the back of those apartments across the street, could you see Miles checking out Meghan's apartment? Could you watch Leo take Cocoa for her walks?"

Seth looked stunned. "I don't know."

"Let's find out," Gaff said.

They went out the kitchen's back door. Gaff took the binoculars and looked across Sycamore Drive. He let out a low whistle. "You could watch Leo turn onto the brambly patch that led to the wetland from here."

Jazzi rubbed her arms. Someone who worked here could have seen Leo follow Cocoa toward the buried bodies. Come to think of it, though, so could someone from the wings place a few doors down. And Meghan had worked there. Did they have binoculars, too?

Gaff flipped back through the pages of his notepad. He aimed his words at Seth. "You might as well know that the coroner looked at the other two victims. Miles had a lot of scratches and bruises, probably defense wounds. It looks like he rushed into Meghan's apartment to try to save her and ended up dead, too. The back of his head was bashed in. So was Leo's. Meghan was strangled."

Seth rubbed his forehead, turning pale. Finally, he said, "Why would anyone watch Miles from here? It doesn't make sense."

"I don't think they did," Gaff told him. "But I do think someone noticed Leo heading to the wetland, and he panicked and went to make sure Leo didn't report any shallow graves."

"Couldn't someone from the wings restaurant have seen him, too?" Jazzi asked.

Gaff shook his head. "Look at the line of trees. They would block the view. The bar's on the end of the strip mall. This is the one and only place that would work."

"Unless someone from one of the housing developments killed him," Seth said. "I can't see any of my employees as a murderer. It could have been someone from her apartment complex, too. Or someone she worked with."

Jazzi liked that Seth had a high opinion of his staff, that he stuck up for them.

When they walked to where Ansel was waiting for them, Jazzi stepped closer to him. He could always tell when she was upset and wound his arm around her waist. She told him about the binoculars, and he thought for a minute. "That does look bad, but what about the EMT who had a thing for Meghan? Couldn't he park his ambulance around here and keep an eye on things? I've seen EMTs on break, pulled into an out-of-the-way place."

Gaff nodded. "I talked to him, and he admitted he wanted to hook up with Meghan, but when she wasn't into him, he said he hooked up with someone else who works on the fourth floor."

Jazzi snorted. That didn't mean he gave up on Meghan. "Are you going to look into him more?"

"Want to come?" Gaff clicked his pen shut. "I thought I'd talk to the nurse he's seeing."

When she nodded, he tucked his notepad into his shirt pocket. "I'll call you when I can interview her, but it might take a while. I'm working another case, too. For now, we can take it from here. And thanks for helping me...again."

Seth started back into the restaurant. Ansel and Jazzi walked Cocoa back to Louisa's.

"I'll be there soon," Gaff told them.

A new car was in the driveway when they got there. A woman in her early fifties opened the door for them.

"I'm Penny." She motioned them inside. "I'm Louisa and Leo's daughter. I'm staying with Mom for a couple of weeks."

Thank heavens! Relief flowed through Jazzi. Besides Miriam, Louisa would have family staying with her, and Penny looked fit enough to walk Cocoa in the evenings. She could cross those two things off her worry list.

When Ansel removed Cocoa's leash, she hovered close to Jazzi's legs. Jazzi bent to stroke her fur and comfort her. The poor dog looked traumatized.

Gaff dropped in fifteen minutes later. "Did you tell them?"

Jazzi shook her head. "That's your job."

Penny put her hand on her mom's right shoulder. Miriam stood on her left side. Gaff told them the news.

Louisa pinched her lips into a tight line. She took a moment to compose herself, but her hands kept busy, her fingers wringing each other. "You found him in a dumpster?"

Gaff was as positive as a detective can be when delivering bad news. Louisa didn't handle it well, and Miriam went to get her a "happy" pill the doctor had prescribed. When Miriam and Penny finally got Louisa calmed down and in bed, Gaff, Ansel, and Jazzi left.

Gaff headed back to the station. Ansel and Jazzi crossed the street to Olivia and Thane's. Olivia opened the door and handed Jazzi a glass of wine. "Tell us about it."

They settled around the new island. "This was a tough one," Jazzi said. "No one wants to hear that their husband's body was found on top of trash bags in a dumpster."

"Or was frozen for a while." Olivia gathered their dirty glasses and carried them to the sink.

Thane hooked an arm around Jazzi's shoulders. "Sleep in tomorrow. You've had one heck of a week."

"After I mow the grass, I'll help you clean the house," Ansel offered.

How could she have better friends and family? And who could be a better boyfriend than Ansel? A knot of emotion clogged her throat. She swallowed it down and shook her head. "You guys are the best."

Ansel stood to hug her. "It's late. Let's get George and head home. Dead bodies make me tired."

He had a point. She hoped she didn't see another one for a long time.

Chapter 22

They slept in on Saturday. They always worked hard, but they'd put in more hours than usual the last two weeks, and a little extra sleep felt good. Jazzi woke with Ansel curled against her, his arm draped over her shoulder. She lay still, enjoying the moment, but Ansel had a built-in radar that sensed when she was awake. He stirred and pulled her even closer.

He nuzzled his face into her messy hair. "Mmm, good morning."

She turned to face him, tipping her head for a kiss. "We have a whole day to ourselves."

His hand reached to tug her close. "We should celebrate, go out for supper tonight."

She believed in acknowledging all of the good things life offered—birthdays, holidays, and a hot man lying next to her in bed. "Someplace special?"

"Why not?"

They lay there, enjoying the moment, until Jazzi pushed away. They had a long list of chores to do today. Still..."We could let everything go and spend the day in bed."

He sat up and swung his legs over the side of the bed. "No rest for the wicked."

"I haven't been *that* bad."

He chuckled, then padded into the bathroom. When he returned, he was wearing an old pair of drawstring shorts. They hung low on his hips. He went to the chest of drawers and pulled on a sleeveless T-shirt. "The yard needs to be mowed."

The yard. His personal obsession. Lightning might strike them if the grass got too long.

He went down to start the coffeepot while she got dressed in short-shorts and a loose T-shirt. She cleaned on Saturdays and worked in the flower beds. Her family would come for the Sunday meal tomorrow, but she was keeping it simple, marinating skirt steaks in a beer mix so Ansel could grill them, along with onions and peppers. She'd bought tortillas to make fajitas. She'd have red beans and rice in the slow cooker and toss a big salad to finish the meal. Admitting she was lazy, she'd bought three brownie mixes to make for dessert.

When she met Ansel in the kitchen, he pushed a cup of coffee across the island to her.

"Want a quick breakfast?" Four slices of pumpernickel popped out of the toaster, and he went to butter them. She added cherry preserves to hers, peanut butter to his.

George begged, and Ansel gave him the corners of each slice of bread. When they'd finished eating and Ansel started outside, George stepped half in, half out the door. It wasn't as hot as yesterday, but it wasn't cool either. George watched Jazzi reach for her dust mop and headed to his dog bed.

Ansel laughed. "George would go anywhere to get away from Emily. He's getting spoiled living with you."

"He's going to have a tough choice when I'm finished cleaning. I'm going outside to work on the flower beds."

Ansel glanced at the pug, stretched in his dog bed. "He might survive. A little movement is good for him."

They both got busy. Ansel started mowing, and Jazzi dived into her cleaning. This house was a lot bigger than her apartment had been, and it took her longer. At noon, she stopped to make lunch. They ate sandwiches every day on the job, so she took a little time to make a pot of minestrone. Ansel loved soup. She'd even bought a round of crusty bread. He'd be happy when hunger called him to the kitchen.

When he stepped inside the house, he sniffed the air appreciatively. "Do I smell soup?"

She'd finished the floors and dusting. He'd completed mowing around the pond. "I thought I'd spoil you today."

He heaved a satisfied sigh and went to get bowls and spoons. "You always spoil me. I have to pinch myself sometimes. Emily never cooked."

They'd finished eating when Ansel's phone buzzed. He scowled. "My sister."

"You're a sucker for Adda. Go ahead and talk to her. Take all the time you want. I need to scrub sinks and tubs."

He looked pained, but answered his phone. "Yeah?"

Jazzi got busy on cleanup. She poured the rest of the soup into a storage container and put the bread they hadn't used in a Ziploc bag to freeze. She was wiping down the counter when Ansel finally spoke.

"No, and there's no reason for you to help with the milking either. I'm surprised you lasted a week. No wonder you're tired. You can't do your job in town *and* help Mom and Dad. The farm's a full-time commitment."

He listened to something on her end before adding, "I can't help you. If I leave here, I don't have an income. If you take days off, you have no vacation time. They got themselves into this mess. They can figure out how to fix it."

Adda said something else, but Ansel only shook his head.

"I can't come. I did what they wanted. I left. I have a job and a life. I can't just drop it now. And for what? When Bain's leg is healed, they'll kick me out again. I'm not interested."

When he hung up, Jazzi came to sit across from him. "You know my income can pay all our bills."

He scowled at her. "Would you go back after they told you to leave?"

She didn't know what she'd do. "I'm a wimp with my family. You know that. I don't know if I'd cave or not."

"I'm not going to." He stood. "I want to finish mowing around the house. Thanks for the soup. You're the best." He kissed her forehead. "See you later."

It was a little abrupt, but she understood. When his family called, it upset him. She went back to work, too. She finished cleaning and made three pans of brownies. Then she and George wandered outside to work on the flower beds.

They'd finished for the day and showered when her phone rang. It was Olivia. It sounded like a party was going on in the background. "Hey, sis! Mom and Dad stopped in to see the house. They invited Jerod and Franny and their kids. Mom's ordering wings and fries. Thane's making a beer and wine run. Want to come celebrate our unofficial open house?"

Ansel was standing close enough to hear. When she glanced at him, he nodded, so she said, "Sure, we'll be there soon." They could go out to eat some other time.

"Great! Tell Ansel that Mom will order a lot more wings." Chuckling, her sister hung up.

Jazzi raised her eyebrows at her Viking. "You okay?"

He didn't look like he was in a party mood. "Yeah, I've settled down. I'm over it."

Work could be a blessing. It took your mind off your worries. Jazzi looked down at herself. "Guess I changed into my pajamas a little too early."

"You look cute to me." He smiled and glanced at his bare torso and sweat pants. "We might be a little too casual, though."

She laughed and started upstairs. "If Olivia's neighbor girls saw you like that, you'd be attacked. And I wouldn't blame them."

He pinched her fanny as she climbed the steps ahead of him. "You're just as bad. The pizza guy would have a coronary. Maybe we should put some clothes on."

Fifteen minutes later, with Ansel carrying George, they went to her pickup. The drive across town went fast enough with only a little traffic. They stepped into laughter and kids running around Olivia's kitchen island when they joined the party. Jerod's little girl, Lizzie, one and a half years old, wrapped her arms around Jazzi's leg, and Gunther, four, attached himself to Ansel.

Jazzi scrubbed her knuckles over Lizzie's head and bent to hug her. Ansel grabbed Gunther's leg and hauled him, upside down, into the air. The little boy screamed in delight. Then he and his sister went back to their mad dash.

"Hey, kid!" Mom came to kiss Jazzi on the cheek. "Dig in. Everything's still hot."

Her dad came to talk to Ansel. "You guys did a great job here. It could be on HGTV."

The conversation turned to remodeling, the nearby school and golf course, and the murders in the neighborhood. Mom raised her eyebrows at Olivia. "When you have kids, will you send them to the local school?"

Olivia laughed at her. "If I ever have any. Maybe. We were thinking about a cat instead."

"A cat?" Jazzi had a thing for cats.

The conversation took off from there. It was a great, fun night. By the time Jazzi and Ansel left, it was later than usual. George fell asleep the minute Ansel put him on the back seat. The temperature had dropped, and they could roll down their windows and enjoy the night air.

They were halfway across town when Jazzi glanced in the side mirror and saw a car that looked a lot like Peyton's, the pizza guy's—an older-model, red SUV. Wasn't it odd that as soon as you saw a car, you saw lots of others that looked like it?

She didn't think much about it until Ansel turned onto their road, and the car followed. She half worried that when they turned into their drive, the car would park behind them. But it didn't. When Ansel drove to their garage and pulled inside, the car kept going. She laughed at herself. She was getting paranoid.

When they walked into the house, Ansel grabbed George, and they headed upstairs. It was past their usual bedtime. And they were tired.

Chapter 23

Jazzi didn't have to rush to get things ready for the Sunday meal. Ansel helped her get the red beans and rice started in the slow cooker; then they put the skirt steaks in the marinade. Finally, they plopped opposite each other in the living room to read the Sunday paper. At noon, they started chopping greens for the salad and setting the table.

Jerod and Franny walked into the kitchen first, as usual. And as usual, Franny brought her vegetable tray. It went well with the Mexican corn salad that Jazzi and Ansel made at the last minute. When people arrived, they tossed money on the counter to pitch in for the food. Jerod and Ansel went outside to start the steaks on the grill, and Franny settled on one of the stools at the kitchen island. The kids zipped out the back door to run in the backyard.

"Starting to feel being preg-o?" Jazzi asked.

Franny rubbed her belly. "I always feel better when I start to show, get super horny. Jerod swears I'm wearing him out."

Jazzi laughed as she carried food to the island to be served buffet style. "Is that possible?"

Franny's lips curved in a smile. "No."

Mom and Dad walked in, along with Jerod's parents, Eli and Eleanore. Gran and Samantha came next, followed by Olivia and Thane.

"Smells good in here," Eli said.

Ansel and Jerod brought in the slices of steak and warm tortillas, and everyone found their usual spot at the long farm table. People got up to fill their plates at the island and, once they'd settled again, started to interrupt and talk over one another as they caught up on the week's events.

Jazzi was happy to see that Gran was clear and lucid today. Her eyes sparkled, and she kept up with the conversation. Having Samantha move in with her helped her feel secure, and that helped her live more in the present and less in the past.

Jerod was going for thirds—yes, thirds—when the doorbell rang.

Ansel went to answer it. He returned, looking like a thundercloud, with a young woman and a man slightly older following him. The woman was pretty, tall, and willowy with Ansel's coloring. The man looked like he was in his late thirties with brown hair and blue eyes, an inch shorter than his wife and a little heavier. Everyone stopped and stared. Ansel said, "This is my sister, Adda, and her husband, Henry."

Adda looked uncomfortable, so Jazzi jumped to her feet to greet her.

"Hi, I'm Jazzi. You came at the right time. It's a long drive from Wisconsin. There's plenty of food, and you can meet everyone in my family and try to keep us straight."

Adda's smile wobbled. "I'm sorry to interrupt. I wanted to talk to Ansel. I didn't realize you were having a family get-together."

Ansel snapped, "You didn't see the cars in the drive?"

Jazzi stared. "They'd already driven all this way. We do this every Sunday. Grab two plates and join us."

Jerod went to get two more chairs, and people scooted closer to make room for them. Ansel returned to his chair, ignoring them. Adda looked so miserable that Jazzi and Olivia tried harder to make her and Henry feel welcome. Adda tried hard, too, and soon the three of them were laughing.

Jazzi liked Ansel's sister. They hit it off, and it was clear that Adda's husband was crazy about her.

When plates were empty, Jazzi and Jerod cleared the table and people went to get brownies. Ansel stayed where he was, refusing to move, so Jazzi brought one to him, along with another beer. People lingered longer than usual, introducing themselves to the visitors.

"We love your brother," Mom told them. "He's perfect for our Jazzi."

"He'll make a great husband. He always stuck up for me," Adda said. "He's my favorite brother."

Jazzi glanced at Ansel, but his scowl only deepened.

Jerod pulled Jazzi aside. "I feel sorry for Ansel. No one likes to be caught in a squeeze play. Why don't we take Monday off? I have a feeling you guys are going to have a crummy night. Then we can start work on the house on Tuesday."

Jazzi agreed. She wasn't sure what was going to happen when her family left. She wouldn't be surprised if Ansel kicked his sister and her husband out. But whatever happened, he was going to be in a horrible mood.

Adda kept glancing at him, but Ansel stayed on his side of the room, ignoring her. Jazzi made an urn of coffee. It and all three pans of brownies emptied before people started to wander to the door.

On her way out, Gran grabbed Jazzi's hand and squeezed it. "You need to be more careful, Sarah. You don't realize how attractive you are, and men mistake smiles for more than they mean."

Nuts. Gran was in the past again. She must have felt the stress in the room. Jazzi glanced at Samantha, the widow who'd moved in to help care for her. For weeks now, Gran had been sharp and with it.

Samantha smiled. "We've had murders and stress again recently, but she'll be fine once we get home. She'll probably be her old self again next week."

Jazzi relaxed. The meal had been fun, but the tension between Ansel and his sister couldn't be ignored. No wonder poor Gran was scrambling back to better times.

When everyone was gone, Ansel went to help Jazzi with cleanup. Adda and Henry sat in the small sitting area by the front window. Finally, when there was no other way to stall, Ansel and Jazzi walked to join them.

Ansel glared at his sister. "You shouldn't have come."

She had Ansel's mouth, full and generous. "I'm not asking you to like them. I don't. But I'll regret not helping them. So will you. We're better than they are. Always have been. If you can give us two weeks, Dad will be on his feet again. You can fix the roof. They can't. And then you can leave again and never look back."

His hands curled and uncurled. "I miss you. You know I do, but we were always second-string players to them. They drilled that into us every day."

She nodded. "Wisconsin isn't that far away. You and I can start getting together more. But give us two weeks, Ansel. That's all I'm asking."

Ansel turned to Jazzi. "I don't want to leave you. It took me forever to get you to hook up with me."

She put her hand on his thigh and squeezed it. "I'm not that fickle. I'm not going to chase after some other guy the minute you pull out of the driveway."

"I see guys lining up already."

She found it incredible that he kept worrying about losing her. *He* was the hottie.

She rolled her eyes. "Go. Help your family. I'll be here when you come home. In the meantime, let's get your sister and her husband comfortable in the guest room. They can spend the night, and then you can all head to Wisconsin in the morning."

He nodded but didn't look happy.

Jazzi stared at him. "You have to trust me a little more than this."

"I haven't sealed the deal. We're only living together. There's no ring on your finger."

"Quit being a dork. I'm monogamous, always have been. I don't cheat, and I won't go behind your back."

"No, you'll just break up with me when I walk through the door. And it will be my fault. I will have left you too soon."

She pushed to her feet. "Get over it. I'll be here, waiting for you. Now let's get your sister and Henry settled."

Chapter 24

Ansel, Adda, and Henry left early Monday morning. Ansel took George with him in his work van. The pug jumped up to press his nose against the back window. He stared at Jazzi, confused. She always came with them to work. Jazzi stood in the door and waved them off. The minute they were gone, the house felt too big, too lonely. She glanced at the security system, grateful she'd installed it.

She didn't want to sit around all day in an empty house so decided to use her key to look at the house on Anthony. She locked up behind herself and drove to check it out. Jerod's truck was in the driveway. She walked in the open door and called, "Hey, cuz, I thought we were taking Monday off."

Jerod came from the kitchen and frowned at her. "What are you doing here? I thought you'd be getting to know your sister-in-law better."

"She's not my sister-in-law. Ansel and I aren't married. They left for Wisconsin already. I didn't want to sit around in an empty house."

He nodded. "Franny's doing stuff with her family today. Kids, too. It's been so long since we've been here, I thought I'd write down ideas for fixing the place."

They walked through it together. Wooden floors, but they all needed to be refinished. A small living room and smaller dining room, connected to a large, odd-shaped kitchen that was dated. Walls had to come down. Only one was load-bearing. Solid foundation, but the deck on the back of the house was close to collapsing.

"Nothing major," Jerod said.

"Kitchen and bathrooms, like usual." She studied the walls and ceilings. "No cracks. All we need to do is paint."

"Let's sit down and plan it out." They discussed what they wanted to do with each room, measured, and graphed what they decided on. It took a couple hours, but when they finished, it was lunchtime. They drove downtown and ate at Coney Island. After that, they drove to order cupboards, appliances, and paint. They were finished by two-thirty.

"Looks like we're set for tomorrow," Jerod said. "Franny will be home by now. Do you want to stop by our place? Have some company? It must feel weird without Ansel."

Weird was putting it mildly. It felt wrong, but Jazzi turned him down. "I'm going to go shopping for things I usually put off."

He stared at her. "You? Shopping?"

"It happens sometimes."

"Yeah, when all of your clothes have holes in them. Buy a couple of knockout outfits, will you? I've seen you in the same stuff for years now."

She tried to think of a decent retort but couldn't. He was right. "Wish me luck," she told him.

He laughed at her. "May the garment gods shower you with blessings."

Now he was pushing it. They walked out of the house together, and he headed home to his Franny, and she headed to Victoria's Secret. Ansel had been so unhappy about leaving, she planned to have one doozy of a welcome for him when he came back. Then she walked the mall and stocked up on new long-sleeved T-shirts, V-necked sweaters, jeans, and dress slacks. She even bought a long skirt and knee-high boots. He wouldn't know what hit him.

She bought fast food on her way home and ate it in front of the TV. She'd done that after she left Chad, spent most of her evenings alone, grateful he wasn't there to pressure her. It was different this time. She missed Ansel. She loved spending time with him, hanging out. She finished her crispy chicken sandwich while watching the news. It was as depressing as usual. *Wheel of Fortune* was starting when her cell buzzed. It was Gaff.

"I wanted to let you know that the results on Meghan are back, and she was pregnant when she died."

She inhaled a surprised breath. This felt too much like déjà vu, like her Aunt Lynda.

Gaff went on. "This was her first child. She wasn't far along. Not exactly like your aunt."

"It still feels freaky."

"We have the fetus's DNA. We might be able to identify the father if his DNA is on file."

Jazzi thought about that. "Has anyone mentioned someone she was involved with?"

"Not yet. It's still early."

He hung up, and Jazzi felt restless. She surfed the movie channels. An old Meg Ryan and Tom Hanks movie had just started, and she settled in to watch.

At bedtime, she climbed the steps to their room, but the sleigh bed looked too big without Ansel. She had wandered into the hallway when her cell phone rang.

"Hey," she said, "how's it going?"

His voice sent shivers through her. "It's been a long day. The drive here felt like it took forever, but I think that's because I didn't want to come. It was awkward meeting my family. I wanted to punch all of them. But then we started working, and I settled in. Radley and I spent all day cleaning out the barn and hosing down the milking stations. I'm beat."

"How early do you have to wake up to milk?"

"Too soon. It takes a while. We have a big herd."

She told him about Gaff's call.

"Meghan was pregnant? Does he think that's why someone killed her?"

"Why would someone kill her because of that?"

"All sorts of reasons. The guy was married and didn't want his wife to know he had an affair. Maybe Meghan lied to him and said she was on the pill when she wasn't so she could pressure him into marrying her." He yawned.

She saw his point, but Ansel was exhausted. "I get it, but you sound like you'd better get some sleep. We can talk tomorrow."

"I miss you."

"I miss you, too, but you'll only be gone two weeks. We'll live."

"Maybe. 'Night, Jazzi."

"'Night, Ansel." She hung up, missing him more. She ended up in the spare room. The amethyst walls made her think of him, how happy he was when he chose the paint color. She thought she'd never be able to sleep, but she snuggled under the covers and drifted off. The security system would alert her if anything went wrong, but she felt safer with Ansel beside her. She dreamt about him most of the night. He kept slowly fading from sight while she battled enemies to reach him.

Two weeks was only fourteen days. Less than half of a month. She'd survive, but she feared the days he was gone were going to make her more miserable than she expected.

Chapter 25

Jazzi gave up and got up early. She'd tossed and turned most of the night, every time she'd reached out to feel empty space. She'd never felt this needy. No, not needy, but she'd never *wanted* someone so much.

She glanced at the empty dog bed when she went to their room to grab clothes. She even missed George. What was wrong with her? Ansel would be gone two weeks. That's all. She needed to get a grip and deal with it. She stalked into the bathroom and got ready for the day.

She beat Jerod to the house on Anthony and was emptying cupboards and boxing up linens when he got there. The owner had taken any personal items with her when she went to live with her mom, but she'd left everything else, expecting to return. A truck would arrive soon to collect the furniture and anything else worth saving. It was all in good shape, but nothing they wanted. Too modern. They were donating them to Mustard Seed. Some family could use them after fire claimed their belongings or some other disaster struck.

Jerod scowled when he saw her. "How long have you been here?"

"An hour."

He gave her a pitying look. "No fun at home without your big blond?"

"I miss him, but I'll get over it. I'll be okay."

"Sure you will. You should come out and have supper with Franny and me some night. I'll fire up the grill."

"Maybe I'll buy some steaks to bring. That would be fun."

He clicked things off on his fingers. "I can bake potatoes, heat anything that comes in a can, and open a bag of salad. Just so you know."

She laughed. "Works for me."

He looked at the boxes piled in the center of the kitchen. "Cleanout day?"

"Yup, then we can start gutting rooms we're going to redo."

He rotated his shoulders to loosen them. "Let's do this."

They had every drawer and cupboard emptied by the time the truck showed up to take things away. Then they stopped for lunch. Jazzi had brought her cooler full of drinks and sandwiches.

Jerod took a bite of the tuna salad on toast and sighed. "I missed your food while we worked at Olivia's. She bought those awful deli meat packages at the store, the variety pack that comes in neat little squares. No lettuce. No pickles. Nothing. Just mayo and sorry meat. Her sandwiches were just plain sad."

Jazzi couldn't argue. "My sister isn't into cooking."

"Cooking? She's just plain cheap. And we were working for her for free."

"She's great at takeout."

"She only springs for that for supper, and even then, only for special occasions. I love Olivia, but if I ever have to depend on her for meals, I'd rather eat at the soup kitchen."

"I know food's important to you. If I'm still around, I'll feed you."

"I'm holding you to that."

She told him about Gaff's call. Jerod's lips pinched in anger. "Then her death's a double homicide. Whoever killed her killed her and the baby."

"Ansel thinks she might have been killed *because* she was pregnant."

"That's just sorry, but he might be right."

He looked upset enough that Jazzi said, "Gaff said they might get DNA from the fetus, so maybe that will help him find the killer."

"I hope so." He visibly shook off his mood. "Let's work."

They finished their lunch and then got started on the three bathrooms in the house. By the time they left for the day, two of them were gutted.

Jerod turned to her before climbing in his pickup. "Want to follow me to my place? I can scrounge up something for supper."

She'd seen her cousin scrounge before. His kids weren't picky, and Franny was just happy when he cooked and she didn't have to. He'd made her ramen noodles with pork and beans one time. She wasn't that desperate. "Thanks, but I'm going to the store on my way home. I'm out of milk and coffee. I'll grab steaks and a bag of salad for tomorrow."

He gave her a thumbs-up. "Good, I can pick up the house a little tonight. I'll be ready for you tomorrow night."

They went their separate ways, and Jazzi stopped out north to grab the few things she needed before going home. She was trying to decide between T-bones and rib eyes when someone stepped up behind her and said, "This looks serious."

She turned to see Peyton, the pizza guy, smiling at her. She smiled back. "I'm a rib eye fan, love the extra fat, but Jerod likes T-bones. I'm going to buy a few of each."

"A woman who's willing to compromise. A good thing."

She laughed at him. "Don't you think most women try to please the people they care about?"

"That's not a for-sure. I've met plenty of females who think men should bow down and serve them because they're hot and sexy."

Jazzi decided she must be hanging out with the wrong men. "That never worked for me."

"Only because you didn't expect it to. You wouldn't like it if someone treated you like a princess."

"I'd barf." She frowned at him. "What are you doing on the north side of town anyway? Don't you live on the south side?"

"Yeah, but my parents live close to Ivy Tech. I'm studying for a nursing degree, and I stop at their house every Tuesday for supper. Mom asked me to grab a few things for her."

"Nice. Your family must be close."

"My parents are the best." He glanced at the steaks in her cart. "You must have someone coming for supper, too."

"No, Ansel's out of town. I'm taking these to my cousin's tomorrow." The minute the words slipped out of her mouth, she regretted it. Why announce that she was alone in a house that sat on lots of property? Neighbors were too far away to be of any help.

He pounced on her slipup. "You're alone tonight? What if I take you out for supper?"

"I thought you were eating with your parents."

"I do that every week. I'd change things up for you." He grinned.

"Thanks, but I already have plans." A little lie never hurt anyone. He wouldn't know one way or another.

He followed her to the checkout lanes, and they walked outside together. He started to his car, and she walked toward her pickup. She stopped and frowned. "Your SUV has black stripes on the sides."

He squirmed.

"A red SUV with stripes followed us home a few nights ago."

He looked uncomfortable. "That was me. I was driving to my parents' house and recognized your work van. I was curious where you lived, but when you pulled in your drive, I figured it would freak you out if I stopped to say hi."

"It would have been odd," Jazzi admitted. It sort of gave her the creeps. "Once we go home, we're ready to collapse and relax."

He nodded. "That's what I suspected. Anyway, you have a neat house."

"Thanks, we remodeled it ourselves."

He shuffled his feet, then smiled. "Hey, anytime your boyfriend takes off, give me a call. I'll buy you a supper."

"Thanks." It would never happen, but why make a big deal out of that? She got in her truck, and he drove away.

On her way to the house, she kept reminding herself that she had a security system. And Detective Gaff's number was in her cell. And Peyton was just young and impetuous. No cause to worry.

Chapter 26

Jazzi's cell phone rang five minutes after she walked in the house. It was her sister, Olivia.

"Hey, why don't you come here for supper instead of eating alone somewhere? I promise I won't order pizza. Thane's in the mood for Shigs in Pit. Are you craving barbecue?"

Her sister was offering free food again? She must be feeling frisky since her house was done. It wouldn't last, so Jazzi decided to take her up on it while she could.

"I'm craving company. I'll be there." And then, if Peyton happened to drive by the house, she wouldn't be there, like she'd said. She tossed her groceries in the fridge and turned around to drive across town. She didn't want to sit alone in an empty house tonight.

When she passed Louisa's house, she noticed that the visiting nurse was there. So was Seth's SUV. When she looked up the street, he was rounding the corner, walking Cocoa, and waved at her. She turned into Olivia's drive, and Seth came to say hi.

"You're not working tonight?" she asked.

"It was slow. I left for a couple hours to check on my aunt. I feel more comfortable stopping to see her now that Leo's gone. That sounds terrible, but we never got along that well."

"He was a little particular."

Seth grinned. "My aunt called me at work. She never does that, but she wanted to tell me that the visiting nurse was at her house."

Jazzi couldn't make the connection. "Does that make her nervous? She has Miriam and her daughter here, doesn't she?"

"I didn't get it at first either, but once I commented how attractive Amy was, and now Lou's trying to play matchmaker. I dashed over here when she called, thinking something was wrong, and she was pretty obvious about trying to push us together." He chuckled.

Cocoa tugged on her leash and came to nuzzle her head against Jazzi's leg. Jazzi bent to pet her. "Should I expect to see you in the engagement column of the newspaper anytime soon?"

"I doubt a nurse would be interested in a bartender, so don't hold your breath."

The man had to be in his late forties. Jazzi couldn't help being nosy. "Have you ever been married?"

"No, I work too many hours, always have. Who'd want me?"

She suspected there were plenty of women who could live with his hours but kept her opinion to herself. "You meet lots of women at the bar."

"Most of them are young. I don't hire anyone over thirty. Young, pretty women bring in customers. And they're great scenery. A man can look, right?"

"I think it's instinctive." But maybe he was one of those men who was only attracted to younger women. She thought about Ed and Eve. Ed had a young wife, but he sure didn't seem happy.

Seth nodded toward his aunt's house. "Well, I'd better get over there, or Lou's going to want my head."

She blurted, "Did you know Meghan was pregnant when she died?"

He looked surprised. "She never came in the bar with anybody. She was always alone."

He sounded as though the news threw him. "I was hoping you might have some idea who the father could be."

"No clue. Pregnant." He paused. "She was such a nice girl. This makes her death even worse. This is going to bother me."

"Sorry. I thought you should know."

"Thanks." He didn't sound thankful. "I'd better get to my aunt's."

"Nice seeing you." And it was. She liked Seth. He was good to his aunt, and she respected that. And he'd acted genuinely upset about Meghan. But her sister was probably wondering what she was doing, so she headed into Olivia's house.

Her sister laughed. "My neighbors talk more to you than they do to me."

"It would be easy for you to change that."

Olivia shook her head. "No, I'm fine with things the way they are." She went to the kitchen island and poured Jazzi a glass of wine. "Thane should be back soon. I hope you're hungry."

Jazzi realized she was. She ate more when she was with people. Alone, she grabbed something to fill her belly, that's all. She and Olivia started yakking, and they were still gossiping when Thane got back with the food. He spread out smoked brisket, pulled pork, coleslaw, and spoon bread. Jazzi loved the stuff.

She had a really good time visiting with Olivia and Thane. When she finally left, her stomach was full and her mood lifted. She drove through the subdivisions on her way home and spotted Peyton's pizza car parked close to Eve's house again. Ed's van was nowhere in sight. Peyton must have eaten a fast supper with his parents and then hightailed it over here. It made Jazzi wonder. Did Eve enjoy pizza, or did she enjoy the delivery man? And where was Ed?

None of her concern. She listened to music on the drive home, and when she walked through her front door and turned on the security system, she was ready to watch some TV and relax.

She was getting up to get ready for bed when her cell rang. She looked at the ID and smiled. Ansel.

"Hey, babe." His voice soothed every frayed nerve in her body. She wished she could pull him through the phone and hug him close. She couldn't let him know how much she missed him, though. He'd want to come home.

"Hi, handsome. How's it going?"

"All I do is work. The place has been pretty neglected. The grass needed to be mowed. Mom's flower beds were a mess. Bain and Radley don't care about those, and Dad hasn't gotten to them. My brothers might work the dairy farm, but they don't bother with anything else. They have their own house on the property, and it's in good shape, but there's no landscaping, nothing but the basics. Mom was so happy when I weeded her flower beds, she almost cried. But it's her own fault. I'm the one who always took care of the yard for her."

She heard the frustration in his voice. "It's nice of you to care for them now."

"It hurt me to see them so bad." His tone changed. "I miss you. How are you? What have you been doing?"

She didn't want to feel sorry for herself, to tell him that it was lonely here without him. She didn't want him to worry about her. He had enough things to think about. She put a lilt in her voice. "Jerod and I started on the house on Anthony. It's going to be easy—all surface repairs. I had supper at Olivia and Thane's tonight. They ordered in from Shigs in Pit. Seth was walking Cocoa when I got there, and I caught up with him."

"So you're doing all right?" He sounded worried.

She forced a laugh. "Me? I'm doing fine. I've been worried about you, though. Sounds like I don't need to. You've got things under control."

There was a pause. "I really miss you."

"I miss you, too." She didn't want to make too much of it, though. He sounded sort of down. "Have you run into any old friends?"

"Jezebel came to say hi already. She heard I was home and stopped in."

A knot twisted in Jazzi's stomach. "Who's Jezebel?"

"She went to school with my sister."

"Is she married?"

"Not now. She married some rich guy and got a big settlement. Doesn't even have to work. Mom said she's been sniffing around after my brother Radley."

Jazzi felt the tension ease out of her. "Does your brother look like you?"

She could hear his smile. "Honey, you got the best of the litter."

He was so modest, she laughed. "Feeling a little full of yourself, are you? Good. Jezebel will have to settle for second best."

He yawned. "I'd better get some sleep. Tomorrow's going to be worse than today. We're going to look at the roofs and buy materials to fix them."

"Hang in there," she told him. "I love you."

"Love you, too. And Jazzi?"

"Yes?"

"Don't fall for someone else while I'm gone."

"I'm not that fickle."

"I left at a bad time. I don't want to lose you."

She wasn't crazy about Jezebel dropping in to welcome him, so she understood. "If we can't survive two weeks apart, we're doomed anyway."

"I guess, but timing makes a big difference sometimes."

"I'll try to be good," she told him.

"You do that." When he hung up, she shook her head. He was worried about nothing. He didn't realize what a prize he was. But she'd be here in two weeks when he came home, and he could put that worry behind him.

Chapter 27

Jazzi packed sandwiches for lunch on Wednesday and then, in another cooler, packed the steaks and bags of salad she'd bought for supper. She'd put them in the refrigerator at the house on Anthony before she took them to Jerod's house. When she saw her cousin, though, she grimaced.

"You look like crap."

"Thanks." He had dark circles under his eyes. "Both kids have the flu. I emptied buckets all night."

"School started. It happens every year. Kids get together to share their germs."

"I can still grill steaks for you." He would, too. He didn't want her to be lonely.

"Thanks anyway, but I'll send the food home for you and Franny, and I'll go out to eat. I really don't want to get sick if I can avoid it."

"Don't blame you. If the brats weren't mine, I wouldn't go near them either."

She felt sorry for him. "Do you want to go home? Take a nap?"

"I want to stick it out today. I'll probably be tossing my cookies in a couple of days. I brought the machine to do the floors. If we get them refinished, you can paint while I'm worshiping the porcelain throne."

"I can do the floors if you want to do something else."

"I'll gut the kitchen. Every floor needs to be done, upstairs and down."

"I'll start upstairs to stay out of your way."

Jerod was a big man, tall and burly. By the time they stopped for lunch, the kitchen cupboards were gone. So were the old stove and dishwasher. Those sat in the open garage, but he'd brought their heavy-duty dolly back inside. "Want to start taking out walls?"

"Might as well. It's easier with two people working together."

They ate quickly, then got to work. The walls took longer, and they didn't get them finished by the end of the day. Jerod looked wiped out.

Jazzi held up a hand and said, "Quitting time. If you're not here tomorrow, I can work on floors and paint rooms upstairs. So go home."

He grinned. "Yes, Mommy."

"And take the steaks and salad. That'll be an easy supper for you and Franny."

He didn't argue. "You care. Thanks, cuz."

She shooed him off and drove home. She hadn't thawed anything for supper, since she thought she'd be eating at Jerod's, so she took a quick shower, changed into better jeans and a clean T-shirt, and drove to Seth's bar. Wednesday was fifty-cent wings and half-price beer. Greg and someone she didn't recognize were working behind the bar. She took a seat, and Greg came to take her order.

"Zinfandel and ten wings," she told him.

"I'm on it." He handed in her tab, then turned and quirked an eyebrow. "Where's the big guy? Did you kick him to the curb?"

The girls crowding Greg's side of the bar focused on her, glaring.

She glanced at them. They had no worries from her. "Not likely. He had to go to Wisconsin to help his parents."

"But he's out of the picture for a minute?"

"He's out of town, but we're committed." She nodded to the new guy. "Where's Seth?"

"He never works Wednesdays, goes to Big Brothers Big Sisters to pick up the kid he took on." He smirked. "How exciting is that?"

Jazzi couldn't hide her surprise. Seth didn't look the type to plug into a kid. "Actually, I'm impressed."

A customer raised his hand for a refill, and Greg went to get him another beer. Then, to her surprise, he returned and leaned on the bar, invading her personal space. "It blew Meghan away, too, when she heard about Seth. He really milked it with her. Are you into kids?"

"As long as they belong to someone else. I thought Meghan had the hots for you."

He shrugged. "Lots of girls come in here to enjoy some safe flirting. But Seth had a thing for Miss M. He was always picking up her tab, over and over again. Everything was on the house for her."

"But she still flirted with you?"

"Yeah, it was a little awkward. Seth wasn't too happy about it, but it wasn't my fault. I didn't treat her any different than anyone else."

"You weren't interested?"

"She wasn't my type. You, on the other hand..."

She shook her head. "Would interest you for about ten minutes. I'm not into that."

"If you get lonely while the big guy's away, I can be discreet."

"I'll remember that." She hesitated a moment. "Did you hear that Meghan was pregnant when she died?" She couldn't bring herself to mention murder.

Greg stared. "I didn't think she'd go to bed with someone until she was married. She seemed the Old Testament type to me."

"She must have met someone who changed her religion."

He thought hard on that, then shook his head. "I never saw her in here with a guy. Maybe someone from the hospital?"

"Maybe." She remembered Gaff telling her about an EMT. She'd have to call him to find out more about him. Her food came, and the girls craving Greg's attention started clamoring for refills. More customers came in. He got busy. She ate, set money on the bar, then left.

She stopped to rent a movie on the way home. By the time the last scene ended, she was more tired than she expected. Ansel called before she went up to bed.

"How was your day?" she asked before he could talk.

"Both the house and barn roof need to be replaced. They're in too bad of shape to patch. No one's done anything around here."

"Not even your dad?"

"Dad's knee's been getting worse every year. He could do less and less. My brothers have kept the dairy running like it should, but that's all."

"Sucks to be you."

He laughed. "What about you? What have you been up to?"

"I was going to go to Jerod's house for supper tonight, but his kids have the flu. So I went to Seth's bar for wings."

"And Greg hit on you."

How did he know? She wasn't going to confirm that. "The place was packed. Great wings."

"There's a wings place just down from there in the strip mall."

"It's a family place. I don't want to sit in a booth alone. It's different at a bar."

"A curvy blonde, alone on a bar stool, is like a magnet for men."

"Not for supper." She was tired of talking about it. "Did Jezebel stop in today?"

He hesitated. "It's apple season. She brought us a pie."

"That she baked?"

"She's not into cooking."

Was he really that naïve? "Has she ever brought a pie to Radley?"

"It wasn't apple season before."

"She's hitting on you."

He sighed. "It won't do her any good. I told her that. I told her I had you, waiting at home."

"And she looked at your ring finger."

Another sigh. "I bet Greg looked at your ring finger, too."

"It doesn't matter what they do. Plenty of people who wear rings cheat."

"That's just plain sad."

"It's life. People can either trust each other, or they can't."

"I trust you."

It sure didn't sound like it, but she let that pass. "I trust you, too." But she didn't trust Jezebel.

"I hate this." He sounded upset.

"Just get your family in good shape and come home."

"Home." His voice lingered on the word. "George doesn't like it here either."

"Tell your brothers to sneak him treats."

"That's the thing. They have. He won't eat them."

She didn't believe it. George had never met a food he didn't like. "You've got to be kidding. George eats everything. What are they giving him—broccoli?"

"We're in farm country. Bits of steak. Chicken."

Jazzi was concerned. "Is George feeling all right? Is he sick?"

"He misses you...and home."

"Holy crap. I thought George would eat in spite of anything."

Ansel sounded downright gloomy. "Well, I'd better go upstairs to bed. They put me in my old room. No happy memories there."

"Do you want me to jump in my pickup tomorrow and drive to Wisconsin? I could roof next to you."

"That's tempting, but we already lost work time and money when we helped Olivia and Thane. I'm costing us money by staying here. I'm sleeping in a twin bed—no room for you—and believe me when I tell you that my parents wouldn't make you feel welcome."

"Even if I came to help?"

"They want me to stay and be a good farm boy again. They'd think of you as a strong enticement to leave. They'd let you know they didn't want you here, and that would make me mad, and then..."

"I get it. If I came, it would make everything worse."

"But you get a gold star for the offer. It made my day. Love you."

"Love you, too." But this was sure one bump in the road they didn't need.

After they hung up, Jazzi went upstairs to the spare bedroom, but it was hours before she went to sleep.

Chapter 28

Jazzi and Jerod made good progress at the house on Anthony. Jazzi had to pinch herself. Things were going almost too smoothly there—no messed-up wiring when they tore down walls, no leaks or mold. It was almost as though the heavens were blessing them since they didn't have Ansel there to help them.

She missed him but pushed that thought away. She was going to have fun tonight. Thursday was her and Olivia's girls' night out. They'd decided to try the Mexican restaurant close to Olivia's house. Jazzi lusted after chimichangas.

She worked on sanding floors downstairs while Jerod painted bedrooms upstairs, and they finished earlier than usual. Jerod still looked tired, so they decided to call it a day. Jazzi drove home with enough time to leisurely get ready for her evening out. She showered and dressed in her new jeans and a snug top that showed off her figure. She took more time with her hair and makeup, too.

She still had plenty of time before Olivia got home from the salon, so she decided she'd stop at Louisa's house and check on her. She was walking to her pickup when her cell buzzed.

"Gaff here. Just wanted to let you know we got back the results on the DNA. I didn't expect them so soon. It usually takes a while, but when the techs heard it was a mother and baby, well...the lab didn't find any matches in the system."

"It's never that easy, is it?"

"It was a long shot. Just means the dad's not on file. I don't have time to talk, but I wanted to let you know."

"Wait! You talked about an EMT who had a crush on Meghan. You asked me to go with you to talk to his new girlfriend."

"Yeah, a nurse on another floor. She took a few days off but works again next week. I thought I'd try to grab you on Monday."

"Works for me."

"See you then." And he hung up.

Abrupt, but nice. After meeting Gaff, Jazzi was glad she'd never become a detective. Too much stress. She drove to Olivia's neighborhood. Louisa's drive was full, so she pulled into her sister's and walked across the street to knock on Louisa's door. She recognized the home nurse's vehicle and Seth's SUV.

Miriam opened the door for her, and Jazzi was disappointed when no Cocoa came to greet her. When she glanced at the empty dog bed in the corner, Miriam smiled. "Seth will be back soon. He stopped in to take Cocoa for a walk...and other things." She winked.

Jazzi smiled, too, and glanced at the home nurse, Amy.

Louisa chuckled. "Seth's gotten attached to Cocoa. He even takes her in his SUV on Wednesdays when he runs errands. The boy he does things with for Big Brothers Big Sisters loves Cocoa. He's getting attached to my Amy here, too."

Amy blushed but didn't deny that.

Louisa rushed on. "I have more good news. Miriam's selling her big, old house in the country to move in with me."

Jazzi looked at Louisa's friend in surprise.

Miriam waved away her concern. "My bedroom at home is on the second floor, and stairs are becoming a problem for me. The house and yard are too big, too much for me to keep up with. A one-level house will be a lot better, and I'll have company instead of living alone. We both have our houses paid off, so we don't have to worry about money arrangements. It's a win-win."

Jazzi was happy for them. She thought about Gran and Samantha. "A widow moved in with my grandma a while ago, and they both like it."

"See?" Louisa grinned at Miriam. "She understands. Seth likes the idea, too. Both of us will have someone to rely on."

The door opened, and Seth came in with Cocoa. When the Lab saw Jazzi, she went over to be petted. Jazzi bent to hug the dog and scratch behind her ears. She was probably a little too happy to see her. Who knew she could miss George so much?

Seth went to stand beside Amy. He looked pretty happy being close to her. She was in her early forties, and very attractive. If Seth had a hang-up about young women, he'd gotten over it. "Hey, nice to see you. Are you stopping at your sister's tonight?"

"We go out almost every Thursday night. Sister bonding. Since I was in the neighborhood, I thought I'd stop to see how everyone was doing."

He nodded. "What can I say? Leo's death knocked us off kilter, but we're handling it pretty well."

Louisa misted for a minute but blinked away unshed tears away. "I'm the luckiest woman in the world. I have so much love and support."

A car flashed by the front window, and Jazzi motioned toward Olivia's house. "My sister's home, but I'm glad you're all coping so well. Take care." As she left, she crossed Louisa off her worry list. Grief still clung to her, and it would for another year or two, but she had a great support team. Even Cocoa would be well taken care of. It wouldn't surprise Jazzi if Seth claimed her as his dog soon.

She was walking down Olivia's driveway when Peyton pulled in behind her.

"No fair!" he called. "I'm not working tonight. You two didn't order pizza, did you?"

He wasn't working. So why was he here? Jazzi frowned. "What are you doing here? If you have the night off, why aren't you out and about with buddies?"

He blushed and stumbled for words. "I came to check my work schedule, and it's just habit to drive through the neighborhood."

Yeah, right. Jazzi had driven past Ed's house, and Ed's van was parked near the garage. How many women did Peyton deliver to when their husbands were gone?

"Why are you here?" he asked.

"My sister and I go out on Thursday nights. Girls' night out."

"Take me with you." He glanced at Olivia as she walked out of the house. "You two women are out of my league. Let me hang out with you and learn a few things."

Olivia shrugged. "Sure, why not? Do you like Mexican?"

"I like whatever you like."

Jazzi rolled her eyes. What was her sister thinking? It was *girls'* night out, not girls and one guy. But what was done was done, so the three of them crammed into her pickup—which luckily had a back seat—and she drove to the restaurant.

They ended up in a booth, and Peyton wasn't the dingbat Jazzi thought he was. She knew he had to be smart. He was studying to be a nurse, for heaven's sake, but he didn't come off as very mature.

"I love working with patients." When Olivia looked surprised, he added, "I know some people titter about male nurses, but it's a good, interesting job. I've done all my book work, so now I'm training on the floor. I just worked in med-surg for a week. Talk about tubes!"

"Which hospital are you training at?" Jazzi asked.

"Lutheran, not that far from here."

The hospital where Meghan worked. She hadn't put that together when he'd first talked about nursing. "Did you meet a girl named Meghan?"

"Yeah, she lived in an apartment close to Sycamore Drive. She told me if I got hired, her complex is a good place to live." He grimaced. "I was sorry to hear she was killed. Talk about naïve. She wasn't very worldly, grew up in a small town, an only child, really sheltered. She told me the first time she saw a penis, she almost fainted."

An only child. Jazzi felt for her parents. "Did you talk to her very much? Learn anything about her?"

Peyton looked smug. "Women talk to me, you know? She said her parents were really old-fashioned. She moved to River Bluffs to have more freedom."

Too much freedom? She didn't sound like a wild child. Getting pregnant shouldn't get you killed.

The waiter came to take their orders. Peyton ordered Dos Equis, Olivia went with a margarita, and Jazzi chose sangria. When the waiter left, the talk changed to what was happening around town and fixing up houses. Peyton and Olivia both had their pulses on the latest gossip.

The waiter returned with their drinks and to take their food orders. River Bluffs was obviously a happening place, because Olivia and Peyton talked all through their meal. By the time they'd finished eating, Jazzi felt like she was in the know again.

When they paid their bills, Peyton grinned at Jazzi. "Remember, I'm almost ready to graduate from nursing. If you start feeling poorly, give me a call, and I'll come to check you out. If you get a fever, though, I hope I'm the one who makes your temperature rise."

Oh, brother. "How many times have you rehearsed that line?"

He laughed. "Too many. It's not working on you, though, I can tell."

"I'm taken."

"The Viking left town. If you get lonely, I'll bring you a free pizza and any sides you want with it."

She laughed. Peyton was persistent, she had to give him that. And lots of women seemed to appreciate his charms. They walked to her pickup, and she drove them back to Olivia's house, waved good-bye, and then headed home. On the drive across town, she decided Peyton was harmless. He was a player, but too conspicuous to worry about.

The TinCaps must be playing at Parkview Field, because there was more traffic than usual. People dressed in elegant outfits walked past the Botanical Gardens toward the Embassy theater, and Jazzi remembered the Philharmonic Orchestra played there tonight. The restaurants lining Clinton Street were busier than usual, too. It took her longer than she expected to pull into her drive.

She was in her pajamas in front of the TV when Ansel called at ten.

"How's it going?" she asked.

"Radley and I got half the roof done on the house. We can finish it tomorrow. And we got all the milking done in the morning and again at night. We milk, roof, then milk again."

"How are you and your parents getting along?"

He huffed a nonverbal comment. "Every night at supper, Dad explains how much Bain did around the farm before he broke his leg. Tonight, I finally told him I didn't give a crap. Bain and Radley can do whatever they want, I don't care. I'm only here for two weeks because Adda begged me to come, and then I'm gone, and I'm not coming back."

His dad obviously pushed Ansel too far. "What did he say to that?"

"He mumbled around for a while and then shut up."

Ouch! But Ansel's dad deserved it. So did Bain. So did all of them. "Are your dad and Bain doing any better?"

"Dad can do more with his new knee, and Bain's better on his crutches. By the time I leave, they'll be able to do the basics, and Radley will have to do extra, but they'll manage."

"And your mom?"

"She nods to whatever Dad says. If her flower beds turn to weeds, I don't care."

"I'm sorry. You deserve better."

"I have better. I found you. What did you do today?"

"I finished sanding the floors, and Jerod painted the upstairs. Then I went to Olivia's, and we went out. Peyton ended up coming with us, and he knew Meghan."

"The pizza guy?" His tone had an edge to it.

"Olivia invited him."

There was a long silence. Finally, he said, "Sounds like you're doing all right while I'm gone."

"I'm fine, but I miss you."

He sounded happier. "Keep missing me, and don't get any ideas until I get home. I'll be back in less than two weeks."

"I'll be here."

"I can't wait to be home, Jaz." And they hung up.

On her way upstairs, Jazzi shook her head. What was wrong with Ansel's family? Were they just plain stupid or so self-centered they couldn't see the big picture? She'd forgotten to ask Ansel if Jezebel brought new treats today. She dug her nails into her palms. If she had to guess, she'd bet she did.

Chapter 29

Jazzi walked into the house on Anthony, took one look at Jerod, and shook her head. "Are you sick?"

"Not yet, but Franny started throwing up this morning. She felt good last night. We went to get a huge, old armoire that she saw online for twenty bucks. The thing's covered with layers of paint, but she can't wait to restore it." He shook his head, frowning. "I'm not sure she should be breathing in paint-remover fumes, but she swears it's fine. She wears a mask."

"I don't think you could keep Franny away from her furniture for nine months."

"I know. And she restored stuff during her other pregnancies and was fine. The shed has plenty of ventilation, but the heat wears her out now that she's bigger. By the time she finishes sanding a table, she's whipped. I played with the kids last night to give her a break. I'm feeling it today. We might not make it to the Sunday meal."

"Okay with me. I don't want your germs." Jazzi loved him, but she hated tossing her cookies.

"Well, I'm here now. Let's finish painting this place, and then we can stain the floors and get to the fun stuff next week."

"You look like you should sleep for a few days."

He didn't argue. "I'm going to live on the sofa this weekend, but I want the basics done here."

Jazzi nodded, and they got busy. She ended up staining the upstairs floors while he painted downstairs. The man looked like he was going to collapse by the end of the day. She kept her distance from him. "If you can't make it on Monday, I can stain the downstairs floors by myself."

"Got it. You're telling me not to show up sick."

"Exactly."

"Don't think I could make myself move if I catch the kids' bug. Pray for me."

She laughed. "I'll light incense." Not really, but Jerod looked pitiful.

He went home to his family, which sometimes was more work than he did with her, and she hurried to get ready to meet Isabelle and Reuben for supper. She and her old neighbor tried to get together once a month. They wanted to keep in touch.

Isabelle, Reuben's future bride, always looked dramatic and sophisticated. Jazzi couldn't compete with her raven updos, sweeping black eyeliner, and designer clothes, but she did try to look better than usual when she met them. She took time with her hair and makeup and slipped into a summer dress she'd found on clearance and a pair of wedged shoes. They were meeting at the Gas House, their old standby. It was downtown, on the river, and if you didn't make reservations on a Friday night, you were out of luck.

She saw Reuben's car in the lot when she pulled in. The waiter led her to their table, and Isabelle looked radiant. Being with a man who loved and adored her worked wonders. She'd loved Cal for years before he died, and he'd liked her back. As usual, she was dressed in designer chic—one of the new blouses with cut-out sleeves to show her shoulders and a slim pencil skirt.

"You look wonderful," Jazzi told her.

"Thank you. You wore a dress tonight, too."

After they ordered their drinks, the first thing out of Isabelle's mouth was, "Ansel will be home before our wedding, won't he? We're both partial to your...special friend."

Jazzi grinned. "It's hard to find the right word, isn't it? He's more than a boyfriend, but *significant other* sounds a little too weird. He should be back in time. He's working his fanny off at his parents' farm."

Reuben glanced at the menu, and it amused Jazzi. He always ordered the salmon, no matter what else was on offer. Then he looked at her, confused. "I thought his family kicked him out, left him on his own, and that's why he started working with you and Jerod."

"It's a long story." The waiter came with their drinks and took their dinner orders. That out of the way, she explained about the problems on the farm.

Reuben sniffed. "Just because you're born into a group of people doesn't mean you have to like them. When I didn't marry and became an interior designer, my family decided I was gay. They cut all ties with me. As far as I'm concerned, good riddance!"

Isabelle's red lips curved. "I could assure them Reuben's not gay, but they showed their true colors. Who needs them?"

Reuben emphatically nodded, more opinionated than usual. "I'm surprised Ansel even bothered with his family."

"It won't happen again," Jazzi said. "He's let them know."

Reuben changed the subject. "How did your sister's house turn out? With your help, I'm guessing it's stunning."

She gave him a look. Reuben was the one who did stunning. "We got all of the big stuff done—gutted the kitchen and bathrooms, new floors, and a new roof. They can take it from there."

The waiter came with their food, but that didn't slow down their conversation. Reuben leaned forward, excited. "Olivia lives close to a woman who's the aunt of a friend of mine."

"Seth?"

"That's him. I swoon for that man's drinks! He used to hire out for parties and was known as the city's top mixologist."

Swoon? There might be a reason his family thought he was gay. "Really?"

"His martinis are marvelous! He taught me how to make my favorite one when he decided to retire and concentrate on his bar."

"Are you allowed to share the recipe?"

"Heavens no! I was sworn to secrecy." He glanced at Isabelle. "I've only shared with one other person."

Jazzi swallowed another bite of her blackened shrimp. "Why did Seth retire?"

Reuben finished his martini and motioned to the waiter for a second. "Such a sad story. Seth lived with Annabelle Burton, a well-known local chef, for years. Annabelle's appetizers were to die for. They catered parties as a team. But Annabelle's mother had retired to Florida and went into a decline. Annabelle drove down to help her and ended up staying there."

That's what happened to the woman who auctioned her house to them. Jazzi's mind went to Ansel. He returned to Wisconsin to help his parents. Jezebel, with money to burn, was stopping to see him every day. What if his brothers finally appreciated him? What if his parents offered him part of the dairy farm? That's what he'd wanted before they kicked him out. Would he be tempted to stay? She pushed those thoughts away.

Isabelle took up Seth's story. "Once Annabelle left, Seth sort of spun out of control. He had no desire to bartend at parties without her."

They'd shed a different light on Seth. He'd loved and lost, didn't sound like a player trying to score with younger women. Or maybe losing

Annabelle had made him that way. "I heard he only hit on women under twenty-five, that he liked them young."

Isabelle's perfectly shaped brows rose in surprise. "Seth?"

Reuben chuckled. "That's business. People like young, attractive waiters. But I ran into him at the 07 bar on Broadway and Bluffton Road. He told me his young employees made his teeth ache, always fussing about something, too many hormones."

Jazzi had driven past that bar, and it looked interesting. "Did you like it there?"

"The owner wants it to be a neighborhood hangout, and that's exactly how it feels. Not a huge menu, but good food, good drinks, and low-key." He lowered his voice. "They serve sausage rolls."

He knew her too well. She'd have to try it out. She moved to a new topic. "You heard about the murders in Olivia's area. One of them was a young nurse, really pretty, practical, and level-headed."

Isabelle shook her head. "If you're thinking Seth might be a suspect, you're wrong."

"Even if the girl got pregnant on purpose?"

"Then he'd still do the right thing and marry her," Reuben said. "Seth doesn't duck out on his responsibilities. I've heard that the bartender he works with wants to start doing parties, and Seth's agreed to work with him for a while to get him started. If that's true, Isabel and I will hire them to throw an open house."

"Greg and Seth?"

Isabelle pushed her half-empty plate away. "Is that his name? Greg? Rumor is he's a woman magnet."

Jazzi nodded and finished her meal, too. She'd eaten every shrimp. "That would be Greg. Girls line the bar to see him."

Reuben tipped his glass to sip the last drop of his martini. "I've missed Seth and his drinks at events. I'd love to see him at parties again."

They all passed on dessert and paid their bills when the waiter returned, then went their separate ways. Jazzi always enjoyed getting together with Reuben and Isabelle. On the drive home, she wondered if a young girl who was serious and practical would have appealed to Seth. From what she'd heard, Meghan acted older than her age. Something about her must have appealed to him or he wouldn't have kept giving her free drinks.

Chapter 30

Jazzi woke up grumpy. Ansel hadn't called last night. She was guessing he'd sat down on the edge of his bed and fallen over, and sleep had claimed him. Either that or Jezebel had talked him into going to dinner with her and he'd lost track of time. She tried to picture what a Jezebel would look like. Probably long and lean with perfect abs, perfect skin, and long dark hair. She'd never met her, but she already didn't like her.

She looked up at the ceiling and sighed. Chore day. She always cleaned and brought in groceries on Saturdays, but she had to mow today, too. It was close to ninety degrees outside, and she was going to look like a melted puddle before she got done. Ansel usually took care of the lawn, but since he was working for his parents, she had to do it all.

Quit whining. But what if Ansel didn't come back? What if he and his family all joined hands and skipped together through green pastures in Wisconsin? What if Jezebel hopped into his bed every night?

She was being silly. Time to get a grip. She pushed out of bed and tossed on old clothes.

She started with the yard. It hadn't grown much since they hadn't had enough rain lately. Most of it was still green, but spots were turning brown along the driveway. It took her a solid three hours to mow it, and Ansel wouldn't approve. She didn't bag the grass around the house. But he wasn't here, was he? When the yard was done, she gave the rooms a quick dust and scrub. Nothing to brag about. Then she ran to the store to buy lots of rotisserie chickens and cartons of eggs. She planned on making chicken salad and pavlovas for tomorrow, things that were easy to make ahead. Then she threw in some deli meats and added ham salad at the last minute. On impulse, she tossed braunschweiger into the cart, too—one of her secret pleasures. She didn't plan on cooking next week. Finally, she grabbed lots of cartons of fresh strawberries and whipped cream.

She was putting groceries away when Gaff called. *Uh-oh, there weren't any more dead bodies, were there? He hadn't changed his mind and decided to question the EMT's nurse girlfriend today?* She answered cautiously. "Yes?"

"It's hotter than Hades," he complained. "You offered to let me and my wife use your pond sometime. Is the offer still good?"

"The water's perfect. Come on over."

"Will we be interrupting your supper?"

"I have ham salad and braunschweiger. Take your pick."

"We'll bring chips. See you soon."

Jazzi was already in her modest bikini with an oversized T-shirt pulled over it when they parked in the drive. At the moment, she didn't look or smell good, but it was only Gaff. If his wife looked like Isabelle, she'd kick herself for not dressing up to meet them, but she was too hot and sweaty to care.

The car doors opened, and Gaff led his wife to meet her. "Jazzi, this is my Ann. Ann, Jazzi."

Jazzi liked the woman the minute she saw her. Warmth and vitality radiated off her. Totally gray-haired, with deep laugh lines, she looked to be five-three and a little overweight—a perfect person to hug.

"I've heard so much about you!" Ann held out her arms, and Jazzi stepped into them.

"I don't know how you do it, being married to a cop."

Ann laughed. "Neither do I, but the kids and I still like the guy."

Gaff and Ann were both dressed in their swim suits with cotton robes pulled over them. Jazzi grabbed the stack of towels she'd put on the patio table and led them over the rise Ansel had created with the backhoe to give the pond privacy.

Ann inhaled a quick breath. She took in the gazebo and the landscaping. "This is beautiful."

"Let's jump in." Jazzi reached up to yank off her T-shirt, and they stripped down, too.

Her words were braver than she was. She was a dip your toes in the water and inch in type of girl. Gaff and Ann lunged in and swam out a ways, like Ansel did. Ansel had dug the pond so that the bottom fell away gradually. Jazzi could walk until the water was up to her shoulders. Then she lowered herself back and floated. It was a perfect way to end a Saturday.

They swam and chatted until they were cooled off and relaxed, then walked through the backyard. Newly mown grass stuck to their feet, but they hosed it off on the back patio. Ansel would have told her that if she'd bagged the grass, that wouldn't have happened. Jazzi led them into the house, where they made sandwiches together. Gaff drank a beer, and Ann shared a bottle of wine with Jazzi.

"Do you want to take another dip?" Jazzi asked when they finished.

"No, this has been perfect," Gaff told her. "Thanks for sharing your pond with us."

"Any time." And she meant it. She'd enjoyed having them here. She had a soft spot for Gaff, and his wife was wonderful. She hadn't enjoyed them just because Ansel was out of town, either. Ansel would have liked having them over, too.

Gaff heaved a long sigh. "I haven't felt this relaxed for a long time. Think we'll head home and enjoy a quiet evening. Thanks again."

She was in an especially good mood when they left, so went upstairs and showered, then changed into her pajamas. She turned on music and went to the kitchen. She sang along to the CD as she skinned and chopped the rotisserie chickens to make a huge chicken salad with dill. She loved dill. Then she whipped the meringues for three big chocolate pavlovas for dessert. She took loaves of bread out of her freezer and put them on the kitchen island to thaw, adding cans of a variety of olives and a jar of marinated artichoke hearts. She wouldn't put the cheese out until the last minute.

With the meal prepped, she padded to the living room, plopped on the sofa, and turned on the TV. She must have been searching for movies the last time she had it on, because a woman was running down a hotel corridor with a crazed, knife-wielding maniac chasing after her. Horror. Ansel would be thrilled.

There was no way she was watching it alone. She flipped to the Food Channel instead to watch a whole different kind of chopping and dicing. More her speed. Once it was ten, she was having trouble keeping her eyes open, so climbed the stairs to the guest room and crawled under the blankets before Ansel called.

She answered on the third ring. "Is the roof done?"

He sounded tired. "For the house. The barn's next. That's going to take most of next week."

She felt sorry for him. "It was hot today. Gaff and his wife came over, and we cooled off in the pond."

"No pond here except for runoff. Believe me, you don't want to step foot in that. It would be easy enough to dig out a swimming hole. It won't happen."

"What did Jezebel bring you today?" The image of a willowy, perfect brunette mocked her.

"They're for me and my family, especially Radley."

"Right, she didn't bring Radley anything before."

His sigh traveled over the distance. "Specialty ice cream sandwiches. They were really good."

"She's a humanitarian. I'm impressed." Sarcasm dripped from her tone.

He laughed. "You're such a smart-mouth. What are you making for the Sunday meal?"

"Chicken salad and pavlovas."

"I love pavlovas." He hesitated. "My mom puts supper on the table every night, but nothing's changed. Every Monday's goulash."

"You like goulash."

"I like *your* goulash. Tuesday's fried chicken."

"You love chicken."

"Not every Tuesday. You get the idea."

"It's only for two weeks."

"This is going to be the longest two weeks of my life."

That made her feel better. She missed him, too. "When you finish the barn roof, can you come home?"

"You'd better believe it. I don't care if they have to crawl to milk the cows after that."

She laughed. "Tomorrow's Sunday. Do you get to sleep in?"

"Cows don't understand that concept. Since we'll be up anyway, we're starting work on the barn. Adda's invited us all to her place for supper. That'll be nice."

"What does your parents' place look like? And what's the town like where Adda lives?" She'd never seen either and couldn't picture them.

"Mom and Dad have a big, square, white two-story with an addition on one side. The roof's high, but simple. And thank heavens the long, red barn has a regular roof, not a rounded one. The milking shed has a metal roof and sides. It's in okay shape. Lots of pasture land."

"And the town?"

"A main street lined with brick buildings. The post office is on the corner across from the city/county building. Nothing to brag about."

"I bet it took you a while to adjust when you moved here."

"It was like hitting the big time—lots of places to eat and tons more traffic. My parents would hate it."

"I'm glad you came and liked it."

"So am I. I met you."

She was having trouble staying awake. It had to be harder for him. "Enjoy supper at your sister's tomorrow."

"I'll try. I just want this over."

So did she. "I love you, Ansel."

"Don't forget that. I'll be home soon."

Chapter 31

Sunday's meal was full of news. Jerod, Franny, and the kids were MIA. Jerod had finally succumbed to the kids' flu. Jazzi put together a quick vegetable tray. After everyone settled at the table, Mom and Dad announced that they were going to Michigan for a week to play.

"Thought we'd start in Grand Rapids, then follow Lake Michigan's shoreline until we're back in Indiana," Mom told them. "I worked a lot of hours to squeeze in clients for cuts and colors before we go."

Olivia nodded. "It's going to be quiet working by myself for a week. I'll miss you, Mom."

Jazzi could relate. It felt too quiet without Ansel in the house.

Oliva grinned. "Thane and I had a big card party at our place Saturday night and ordered pizzas. Peyton asked about you, sis. Asked if your boyfriend was home yet."

Gran frowned and looked around the table, upset. "Where *is* Ansel?"

Jazzi realized everyone else knew Ansel had left, but she hadn't told her grandmother. It was a balancing act these days. Sometimes Gran lived in the present, and sometimes she didn't. That's why the family was so happy Samantha had moved in with her. Every time Gran got stressed, she retreated to the past, so Jazzi tried not to upset her. Gran liked Ansel. A lot. Jazzi tried not to make Ansel's absence a big deal. "His family needed help in Wisconsin, so he drove there."

Gran shook her head. "You shouldn't have let him go. That awful girl has been after him for years, and now she has another chance."

Mom looked confused. "What awful girl?"

"The girl with the long dark hair," Gran said. "She's divorced now. Ansel doesn't need a girl like her."

Jazzi blinked. So Jezebel *did* have long, dark hair. If Gran said so, she believed her. Ever since Gran slipped a little from reality, she saw things that proved to be true. But only when she was upset, and Jazzi didn't want to agitate her. "He'll be home soon, Gran, and he calls me every night."

Gran gave her a pitying look. "You're so pretty, hon, but the Wisconsin girl knows men and how to play them. She's dangerous."

That's the feeling Jazzi had. Ansel didn't pay much attention to her, but everyone had a weak moment. Those were the moments that tested you. "He either loves me, or he doesn't. If he doesn't come home, we had problems anyway."

Olivia rolled her eyes. "Let Jezebel take her best shot. Give Ansel some credit."

Thane nodded agreement. "No one could steal me away from Olivia. This girl could dance naked in Ansel's bedroom, and he'd send her away."

Everyone turned to stare at him. Thane usually stayed out of any serious conversations.

He shrugged. "I like Ansel. Someone has to stick up for him."

"Thank you." Jazzi meant it. She'd let doubts creep in when she shouldn't have.

Olivia changed the subject. "I'm not worried about Jezebel. I want to ask you for a favor. I saw a baker's rack for sale on Craigslist that would be perfect in our kitchen, but we can't fit it in our van. Later today, would you help us pick it up?"

Jazzi was happy to talk about something besides Ansel. "Sure. After cleanup?" There were times when nothing beat having a pickup.

"If that works for you. I want to buy it before someone else does."

Jazzi shrugged. "Why not? When everyone leaves, I have free time." What was she going to do? Watch another movie?

"You can't rush our desserts, though," Mom warned. "I live for those."

"We're on it." Jazzi stood to clear away plates, and Thane pushed to his feet to help her. The chicken salad had been a good choice for today. There was only enough left for one sandwich. They put all the dirty dishes in the deep farmer's sink and carried the pavlovas and fixings to the table.

Jerod's dad looked at the pavlova. "What is that?"

"A big meringue. It's crisp on the outside, gooey inside."

He cut himself a large slice, then pointed his fork at Doogie—Jazzi's dad, his brother.

"Eleanore and I don't close the lake cottage until late October. You've only made it up once the entire summer. Things have been busy, but I'd like you guys to come up some weekend."

Jazzi half-listened to them, her thoughts drifting to Ansel. He'd be eating at his sister's house today. She wondered how the dynamics were at his family's table compared to hers.

When the last of the dessert was gone, people starting milling around to leave. Olivia and Thane stayed behind to help her with cleanup, and then they climbed in her truck to go buy the baker's rack Olivia wanted.

The price was great, but it was a half-hour drive north of town. When they left the city, farmers' fields stretched along the highway. Corn, soybeans, and wheat rotated mile after mile. Occasionally, chickens scratched in house gardens, running free. Jazzi loved how green Indiana was. Her parents had done a fair amount of traveling while she was growing up, and she'd fallen in love with many cities and states, but she was always glad to come home. For her, there was something vibrant about River Bluffs.

Three rivers came together here, and the city planners were finally talking about creating river walks. Downtown, once bordering on becoming a ghost town, was coming back to life. The ball diamond and event center brought in lots of people. The bike and walking trails stretched north and south.

Once you left the city and its suburbs, you were in farm country. She liked that, too. Olivia's seller lived in a small town with a domed, old-fashioned limestone courthouse in its center. The woman's house was well-kept. Jazzi waited in the truck while Olivia and Thane went to look at the baker's rack. Jazzi was pretty sure they were going to buy it, so she got out to spread the padding she'd brought in the truck bed. She didn't want the piece to get scratched. It was black wrought iron, but it still needed to be protected.

Thane and an older man—probably the seller's husband—carried the rack out of the house a few minutes after she finished. Money exchanged hands, and after securing the piece, Jazzi was ready to drive to Olivia's house. The drive back took longer since Olivia lived on the south side of the city. But once Jazzi parked near the kitchen door and she and Thane carried the piece inside, it looked as though it was meant to be in the spot Olivia had chosen for it.

Her sister smiled. "It's perfect."

It was. "It ties the kitchen and eating area together."

"Want to stay for a drink?" Olivia asked.

It had ended up being a long day. All fun, but Jazzi was ready to call it quits. "Thanks, but I'm ready to go home and do nothing."

Thane rode back with her to get Olivia's car. As she backed out of the drive, she glanced across the street and noticed that Louisa's daughter's car was gone. "Penny must have returned to Carolina."

Thane motioned to Miriam's car, parked near the back door. "Those two will enjoy living together."

For no particular reason, Jazzi decided to drive through all the small neighborhoods to reach Sycamore Drive. She hadn't done it for a while, and it was an interesting area. When she reached Ed's house, though, Ed had Peyton pinned against his red SUV, and Ed's hands were around Peyton's throat. Eve was tugging and kicking Ed, screaming at him.

Jazzi stomped on the brake.

Thane reached for the door handle. "What the heck?"

Jazzi parked and jumped out of the truck, running behind Thane. Thane plowed into Ed, knocking him sideways. Peyton took a huge gulp of air and hurried to stand on the other side of his SUV, away from Ed.

Ed lunged toward him, but Thane grabbed the back of his collar, hauling him backward. Eve ran to shower more blows on him, and Jazzi grabbed her arm and pulled her away.

Ed yelled at Jazzi. "Stay out of this! What do you think you're doing?"

"Trying to keep you from going to prison for murder."

His face contorted with frustration. "He's been sleeping with Eve!"

Jazzi looked at Ed's wife. "And she's been sleeping with him. But killing either one of them isn't going to change that."

Eve stabbed a finger at Ed. "You were going to be gone. Again. Fishing with your buddies. The only reason you came home is because Rory was sick and couldn't go, and he owned the boat."

"That's no reason..." Ed started toward Peyton again, and Thane jerked him back. Jazzi lost patience. "Quit being an idiot. You and Eve have problems. Either fix them or get a divorce." She looked at Peyton. "Get out of here while you can. And think about what you're doing. This could happen to you again."

He opened the passenger door on his SUV, scooted to the driver's seat, and raced away.

Ed whipped around to confront Eve. "Pack your bags and get out. We're done."

"Just like that, huh? I'm the bad guy. What about you? You've been staying away more and more."

"I wonder why." He started to his van. "All you do is gripe and ask for more stuff. Keep the car and everything I bought you. But we signed a prenuptial. I've already paid more for you than you're worth. I'm going out. When I come back, you'd better be gone." He got in his van and left.

Eve glared at Jazzi. "Happy now? I've lost Ed, and Peyton will have an even bigger crush on you."

Really? How stupid was this woman? "*You* lost Ed, and Peyton's just a kid. All you had was lust." She wasn't going to stand here and argue with Eve. She turned on her heel and walked to her pickup, along with Thane.

When she finally got home, Thane gave her a quick shoulder hug. "Bet you wish your life was boring for a week or two. Thanks for everything." Then he drove off in Olivia's car.

Jazzi poured herself a glass of wine and sagged onto her favorite spot on the sofa. She reached for the remote and clicked on a food show she'd recorded. *The Kitchen.* Nothing demanding. No angst. Just something to entertain her and give her ideas for new recipes. It helped clear her mind.

When it was over, she called Gaff and told him about Ed and Peyton. Gaff still considered both of them suspects, even though Ed had only shown up, angry, about Leo watching him argue with Eve and letting Cocoa take a dump in his yard. Not much to go on. But Gaff never discounted a man with a temper. And Peyton? Well, who knew all of the women he juggled? He'd worked with Meghan, maybe even slept with her.

Had he gotten her pregnant? Why would he admit to that? Especially now.

Gaff listened to her and said, "You know, I might just visit both of those men again. Somebody has to know something. I'd be happy to learn some new bits of information to look at. Thanks for the help."

She felt better. She didn't think Ed or Peyton had killed anyone, but Gaff was right. One odd little piece of news could lead an investigation in a new direction.

When she hung up, she turned on a Hallmark mystery and was half into it when Ansel called.

He plunged right into the gist of the conversation. "My parents and brothers talked and asked me to stay on the farm. They'll figure out a way to make it work."

Her stomach knotted until it hurt. She could barely get the words out. "Do you want to?"

"Heck, no, they just need me now. They're worried about what will happen if there's another emergency and I don't come back to help them. Once they get past that, it will be the same old, same old. Besides, I don't want to live here. I like River Bluffs. I want our house. I want you."

The knot eased. "Does it make you feel better that they asked you to stay?"

"Not much. It's more about them than me. I like Radley, but Bain's still Mr. Big Shot and Dad's still...Dad."

"What about your mom?"

"We were always close, but she'd throw me under the bus if she had to decide between me or the farm."

"Your family's ruthless."

"Yeah, and that's on a warm, fuzzy day when you haven't done anything wrong."

She laughed. "How much longer will you have to stay there?"

"I gave them a week to finish the roof on the barn."

"Were they unhappy when you turned them down?"

"Pretty ticked, but that's their problem."

She couldn't help it. "Was Jezebel at Adda's house?"

"She just happened to drop in, and Adda invited her to stay."

"Does Adda like her?"

"As an acquaintance, not for me, but Jezebel's been bringing food to the farm. Adda almost had to ask her to stay out of courtesy."

Jazzi thought about Ansel's brother. "How does Radley feel about Jezebel throwing herself at you? Hadn't she been interested in him before you went home?"

"I asked Radley if he was interested in her, and he said she scared the heck out of him. Told me he didn't want to be bossed around by a dominatrix. Dad thought Radley should hook up with her because she has money and could help them, but Radley said he couldn't picture her putting one penny into the farm."

"Your brother's not as naïve as I thought he was."

"He told me he grew up a lot when Mom and Dad tossed me out of the house. Said if they didn't need two hands to help with the farm, he'd probably be gone, too."

"That's just sad."

"Bain took after Dad. The farm's always going to come first. No, that's wrong. Dad and Bain are always going to come first." She heard someone yell in the background, and Ansel sighed. "Gotta go. A section of fence fell, and our cows are walking down the highway."

The picture that painted in her mind made her laugh. "Have fun."

He growled but had to leave.

She didn't turn her mystery back on. She sat and brooded for a few minutes. His family would try to think of ways to make Ansel stay longer. She hoped they failed. Was Jezebel like Eve?

If Ansel ever cheated on her—which she didn't expect; he wasn't the type—she'd want to kill Ansel, not his temptress. But Ed had gone straight for Peyton's throat. She thought about that a minute and then decided, in all fairness, that she'd want to kill both of them.

That put her in the perfect frame of mind to start her TV mystery again. It was a lot cozier than her thoughts. When it ended, she climbed the steps to bed.

Chapter 32

Gaff was picking her up early in the afternoon to visit the EMT's girlfriend at the hospital, so she drove to the house on Anthony earlier than usual to get some work done first. Jerod called on the way to say he was taking a sick day. Perfect. She didn't have to worry that he'd try to do too much while she was gone.

They'd gutted the upstairs bathrooms and bought the ceramic tile for the floors. Jerod had painted both rooms, so she got busy laying tile. She'd finished one of the rooms before Gaff came.

"She's expecting us," Gaff said on the drive across town. "She's going to talk to us on her break."

Jazzi cringed as a car peeled off a side street in front of them. A common occurrence these days. Everyone's time was more important than yours. Gaff had to jam on his brakes.

"The whole world's in a hurry," he grumbled.

Jazzi waited for the traffic to flow smoothly again before she asked, "Why do you want to talk to the girlfriend and not the EMT?"

"Oh, I want to talk to the EMT, but I want to get his girlfriend's take on him and Meghan first. Then, if he rearranges facts and stretches the truth, I might be able to tell."

"Smart." Jazzi would never have thought of that.

Gaff grunted. "I've been at this a while."

A half hour later, they sat in a small conference room with a petite, thin woman who had brown hair pulled into a ponytail that hung halfway down her back. She didn't wear a speck of makeup. Jazzi and Jerod had worked on a house once for a woman who wasn't allowed to cut her hair or wear makeup or jewelry. Did this nurse not want to bother with them, or did she belong to a religion that forbade them?

Gaff smiled, trying to relax her, and introduced himself and Jazzi. "Hello, Tonya. Thank you for meeting with us. We're investigating the death of Meghan Fuller. You worked with her, and your current boyfriend showed a lot of interest in her. Did they ever date?"

She shook her head. "Meghan turned him down."

"How did he react to that?"

She blinked. "He wasn't happy about it. Meghan thought she was better than everyone else."

Gaff looked up from his notes, surprised. "We've heard over and over again how nice she was. Did you ever meet her?"

"Only in passing. We worked on different floors."

"What was your impression of her?"

"That she was a competent nurse."

Tonya's hands lay on the conference table, clasped together. Jazzi got the impression the girl was going to tell them as little as possible.

Gaff asked, "Did your boyfriend wait for Meghan in the parking lot and accost her for turning him down?"

Before Tonya could answer, the door to the room banged open and a large man strode inside, slamming the door behind him. "Instead of picking on my girlfriend, why don't you ask me what really happened with Saint Meghan?"

Gaff studied him. "You must be Mack Leffers. You were the next person on my list to see."

Mack took the seat beside Tonya. He had longish, ash-blond hair and very dark eyes—almost black. He looked like a human version of a pit bull, ready for a fight. His lips curled back. "Do you always start with the easy targets and work your way up?"

Gaff didn't appear to react to Mack's aggressive attitude. Jazzi gave him credit. Mack intimidated her. Flipping through a few pages of his notes, Gaff said, "I interviewed lots of nurses who knew Meghan, but I didn't realize that Tonya might be the most important person I should question here. So I came back."

Mack's heavy brows tugged into a scowl. "And why might she be the most important?"

"Because she might be jealous of Meghan and resent her because Meghan was your first choice."

Tonya's hands clenched more tightly together. She focused her eyes on a middle spot of the table, not connecting gazes with anyone.

Gaff went on. "And I wanted to get a feel for what happened between you and Meghan, so that I could tell if you were lying to me or not."

Mack's hands balled into fists. "I'll be happy to tell you about Meghan. She was beautiful, and she knew it. She lived in her own little bubble and wouldn't let anyone in. All she talked about, on and on, was some bartender she had a crush on. Everyone knew he didn't give a crap about her. Never would. She was nice, just stupid. And a tease. She was all smiles and nos. I tried to explain that she should date other guys, give up on Mr. Perfect, but she wouldn't listen."

"Was this a friendly conversation?" Gaff asked.

"It started out friendly, got a little heated at the end. You couldn't budge Meghan once she made up her mind about something."

Gaff stared at Mack. "You have a temper, don't you? I looked you up. You were in a bar fight four months ago."

"Give me a break. The guy on the stool next to me got mad because I got my drink before he got his. I didn't take the first swing, but I sure as hell took the last."

Gaff raised an eyebrow to Jazzi. "What do you think?"

She locked gazes with Mack. "If Meghan had changed her mind and agreed to go out with you, would you have dumped Tonya?"

He inhaled a deep breath. "That wouldn't have happened."

That statement, in and of itself, was an answer. Jazzi turned to Tonya. "Did you hate Meghan because she could take Mack from you?"

Tonya unclenched her hands and pressed her palms against the table. "Yes. I hated her. But I'm always the last person a man looks at. I'm used to that."

Jazzi wondered why she didn't up her game then. She wondered what made Tonya tick. "How did you meet Mack?"

"He was upset. I could tell. I asked him if he was all right and listened to him."

Mack reached for her hand and squeezed it. "She's a great listener."

Gaff gave an understanding nod. "You became his shoulder to cry on."

Tonya blushed, embarrassed. "Something like that. I looked forward to seeing him whenever I could, whenever he brought a new admit to the hospital."

Jazzi heard the desperation in her voice. How much would she resent Meghan? Men tripped over themselves to vie for her attention, and all she cared about was Greg. Was Tonya desperate enough to kill Meghan to snag Mack? Was that possible?

Gaff turned to Mack again. "Do you usually have luck with women?"

Mack shrugged. "I do okay."

"But Meghan wouldn't give you the time of day."

"Meghan was delusional. She didn't live in the real world."

"Did you know where she lived?"

Mack frowned, clearly thrown off balance. "How could I? She never agreed to go out with me."

"What about you?" Gaff asked Tonya.

She stared at him. "We weren't friends. She never invited me to her place."

Gaff closed his notepad and stood. "Thanks to both of you for seeing us."

Mack and Tonya both looked a little surprised that the meeting was over. Mack took Tonya's hand, and they stood, too. "Is that it? Are we done?" Mack asked.

Gaff nodded. "If I have more questions, I'll let you know."

They all exited the room, and Jazzi walked out of the hospital with Gaff to his car. On the drive back to Anthony Boulevard, she said, "Both of those two were interesting."

"When I get back to my office, I want to find where both of them were on the night Meghan died."

"Do you have a time frame now?" She knew when Leo died. He took Cocoa for a walk and never came back. The same as Miles. He left his parents' house and disappeared. So he probably died that night, along with Meghan.

"We have a little more to work with. Each inch leads us to a new clue. Hopefully, we'll end up with the truth."

Murder was a lot more complicated than Jazzi realized. She couldn't imagine the killings that were impersonal—the drive-by shootings she read about in the paper, gang and drug deaths. People's lives didn't mean anything to those killers. But the personal murders at least had motives she could understand, even if she couldn't relate to them.

When Gaff dropped her off and she let herself into the house on Anthony, she decided to take a lunch break before she started work on the second bathroom floor. If Jerod were there, he'd distract her, but the house was too quiet, and she kept turning suspects and motives over in her mind. She turned on music and pushed those thoughts away. By the time she left, both bathroom floors were done, and she was ready to drive home and have a quiet night.

Chapter 33

Jazzi walked around the house, restless. She wasn't sure why, but Mack and Tonya bothered her more than most of the people Gaff put on his suspect list. Mack felt like he could blow at any moment. She felt sorry for Tonya. The girl pictured herself as a walking victim, like life had beaten her down somehow.

She tried watching TV but kept losing interest. She picked up her book but couldn't concentrate. Finally, she turned to a last resort. She set up a jigsaw puzzle she'd bought on the kitchen table and lost herself as she tried to put it together. When she glanced at the clock and it was ten, she was relieved. Time for bed.

Ansel called before she drifted off to sleep. "Sorry it's so late. We worked right through supper tonight. Got a lot done. Every part of my body is sore."

"You're pushing yourself too hard."

"I want to come home. I want this finished."

"I want you here." She told him about Mack and Tonya.

"It sounds like either one of them is a good candidate for Meghan's murder."

She nodded, then realized Ansel couldn't see her. "Gaff's going to check out their whereabouts when it happened."

She heard a thunk, and he cussed. "This room is too small. I just hit my elbow on the chest of drawers. I feel like I'm sleeping in a closet."

"Are you?"

He laughed. "Pretty much."

"Work hard, Norseman, and come home."

"I'm trying. I miss you, babe."

"Miss you, too." They hung up, and Jazzi turned off the bedside light. As she drifted to sleep, she wondered which was worse—living with people you weren't too fond of or being in a house by yourself, lonely. She couldn't wait until Ansel came back.

She was dreaming about shingling a roof that went on and on when her security system beeped a warning through the house. She sat up in bed and tried to see in the dark. Had someone made it through their heavy doors? She reached for her cell phone and a baseball bat, then tiptoed to the top of the stairs. A huge butcher knife waited in the kitchen. Ansel had tried to talk her into buying a gun to keep in her nightstand, but guns scared her. Maybe she should reconsider that. She didn't have one ounce of victim mentality in her genes. She stopped and listened. Something was scratching at the kitchen doors.

She padded down the stairs, crossed the living room, and peeked around the corner. The motion light flooded the back patio, making it easy to see a raccoon trying its darnedest to open the kitchen door. George's food bowl sat within easy sight, and the raccoon knew a good thing when it saw it.

Jazzi called the security company to tell them it was a false alarm. She turned off the noisy blasts and walked to the door to shoo the raccoon away. It shuttled a short distance from the door, then turned to wait for her to leave. The minute she went upstairs, it would be back. Not in the mood to battle a masked bandit, she raided the refrigerator and tossed a heap of deli turkey to it. Then she moved George's food bowl to the side of the refrigerator, out of sight.

She had trouble falling asleep when she got back in bed. Too much excitement. No one had tried to break into her house, but what if someone had? Who would drive to Meghan's apartment and kill her? Had the killer gone there with murder on his mind? Or had he and Meghan talked, then argued, and then the killer had acted in a fit of anger? When Miles rushed in to protect Meghan, he'd killed him, too. Probably in panic.

Scenarios rolled in her mind like a hamster wheel, bits and pieces over and over again. She wasn't sure when she fell asleep, but the alarm woke her way too early. Groaning, she got out of bed, got ready, and drove to the Anthony house.

Chapter 34

When Jazzi reached their fixer-upper, Jerod was there. When she saw him, she wished he'd stayed home. Her tall, beefy cousin looked like he'd fall over if she gave him a push.

"Why are you here?"

His shoulders drooped. "I spent most of Saturday and Sunday bowing before the porcelain throne. Yesterday, I tried to watch TV on the couch with kids crawling all over me. Franny tried to keep them away, but they kept hoping I'd get up and play with them. Franny's dragging. She's tired of all of us, so I thought I'd rather come here and put up with you than get dirty looks from her all day. My wife needs a little alone time."

Jazzi laughed. Her big, strong cousin had come here to hide. "At least you're all on the mend now. It takes a while after the flu. You don't look like you should do anything heavy, though. What if we stain the downstairs floors together? Then we can check upstairs to see how those turned out."

"I saw the bathrooms. They look great."

"We're making good progress. We don't have to push ourselves today."

He liked the idea, so that's what they did. He started at the back of the house and worked his way through the mudroom, laundry room, and kitchen. She took the front and stained the foyer, living room, and dining room. When they finished early, they went outside to prune bushes around the house. The stain had to dry. They couldn't walk on it. The yard looked tidy by the time they got ready to leave for the day.

Jazzi teased, "This place looks better than you do. Go home and go to bed."

"I'm locking the door. I need a long nap and an early bedtime."

They set off for home, but before Jazzi had even turned onto Anthony to head north, Olivia called.

"The salon's closed today since it's Monday. I went shopping, and you won't believe the beautiful kitchen stuff I found. Wanna come take a look at it?"

Jazzi loved anything kitchen-related. Plus, it was better than going home to an empty house. "Sure, I'm on my way." She drove straight instead of turning to take State to Lake Avenue, passing grand old neighborhoods and the Lakeside rose garden. A little farther and she'd drive past the house they'd flipped before they worked on Olivia and Thane's place. She slowed to get a good look at it and was happy to see wicker furniture on the porch and a flowered wreath on the door. The owners were taking good care of it.

Traffic was heavy downtown, but it was moving at a decent pace. She pulled into Olivia's drive twenty minutes later. Her sister opened the kitchen door and motioned her inside.

"You've got to see these!" She'd spread all of her new buys across the kitchen counters. First, she motioned to a set of square dishes for eight— four fire-engine red, the other four shiny black. The minute Jazzi looked at them, she thought of Olivia, bold and showy. Next came eight vivid yellow place mats, and then a set of new square-handled silverware.

Jazzi turned to her sister, surprised, when she saw the heavy, stainless-steel cookware and slow cooker. "Are you thinking of making meals at home?"

Olivia grinned. "I thought I'd start small—one meal a week. Thane said he'd help me. He's watched those TV commercials where the couple dice and stir together. His grandma was a great cook, so he wants to learn to make some of her recipes. She's promised to send them to us. We're going to try pork chops tonight."

Their mom had decided to make those once. Jazzi still remembered trying to chew them; they were so dry.

"His granny always made them with gravy. She e-mailed him a whole page of step-by-step instructions."

Good. Olivia had a chance of success. "It took me a while to learn how to make a good gravy with no lumps."

Olivia snorted. "Lumps aren't going to bother us. Gravy's gravy. I cheated and bought microwave mashed potatoes. There's no way we'd get everything done at the same time." She cocked her head and raised her eyebrows. "You wouldn't mind sharing your recipes with us, would you? It would be even better if you came over once in a while to walk us through cooking them. You and Ansel could stay and eat with us."

"That would be fun." Ansel liked to cook as much as she did. Having all four of them in the kitchen making a meal would be a good time.

"Want to stay tonight? I bought three pork chops."

"No, you and Thane can walk through his grandma's recipe as a couple." Thane would like that better, just the two of them putting their heads together. Besides, Jazzi was pretty sure Thane could easily eat two chops. "Anything else to show me?"

Olivia pointed to the corner of the counter top by the sink. "My new KitchenAid mixer."

Jazzi stared. It was bright red with all kinds of attachments. Jealousy raised its ugly head. "I still haven't bought one of those. My hand mixer does a great job."

"Thane's been wanting one, so I thought why not?" Olivia frowned at it. "It looks serious, doesn't it?"

"You could probably make your own sausages."

"Ugh. But I can mix cake mixes with it, can't I?"

"You can do that by hand if you have to." Jazzi glanced at all of Olivia's new things. "Your kitchen's ready to go. All you need is a food processor." They already had an expensive blender for mixed drinks. "Have fun breaking things in tonight."

"You don't have to leave already, do you?"

"Thane will be home soon. He's going to be excited about all of this. I'm going to take off and let you two enjoy yourselves."

Jazzi passed Thane's van on Sycamore Drive. Since she was on this end of town and was hungry, she stopped at Seth's bar to grab a burger and a beer instead of going home to deli food. Greg was working alone since it was too early for the hordes to arrive. He sauntered to stand across from her and smiled. "What can I get for you, fair lady?"

"Your number three with onion rings, bacon, and special sauce."

His gaze swept her figure. "How do you eat those and stay in such great shape?"

"You burn off a lot of calories remodeling houses."

"I'll take your word for it. It's worked wonders for you."

The man was full of great lines. Her gaze swept the restaurant. "No Seth?"

"Lunch was crazy today, I guess. On a Tuesday. Never happens. He just took off for his bank run."

The door opened, and Peyton came to plop on the stool next to her. Greg frowned.

Peyton didn't notice. "I saw your pickup in the lot. I wanted to tell you thank you. You didn't have to stop to save me from Ed. Glad you did, though. I think he meant to finish me off."

"No problem. Ed just lost his temper and went ballistic."

"Yeah, Eve says he does that a lot."

"Does she give him reason to?" Or did Ed react like that to everything?

Peyton looked surprised, then nodded. "He's usually pretty chill, but she loves to push his buttons. She thought she was marrying wealthier because he bought her lots of little presents when they dated. And he still buys her things, but she thought they'd be bigger."

Greg listened as he poured her beer. "Women like money, that's for sure." He looked at Peyton, and without being asked, Peyton showed him his ID. "Good, you're twenty-one. What'll it be?"

"A Miller and your buffalo wings." Peyton turned to study the bar. Upscale. U-shaped, upholstered booths lined the far walls. Smoky-colored glass-top tables filled the center. "I've never been in here before. Meghan used to talk about it all the time."

Greg's gaze sharpened when he heard the name. "You knew Meghan?"

"A little." Peyton grinned at him. "Were you the bartender she had the hots for?"

"How did you know her?" Greg asked.

"The hospital. We worked together. I'm almost ready to graduate as a nurse, and we were on the same floor. She was never too busy to help me, talked about you a lot."

Greg grimaced. "Yeah, she came here to flirt, but Seth—the owner—is the one who had the hots for her. Awkward."

He'd said that before, but Jazzi wondered if there was some other reason Seth doted on Meghan. Did he feel sorry for her? Had she done something that made him grateful to her? She took a sip of her beer. "I have a friend who raved about Seth's mixed drinks. Said you and Seth might start working parties together until you're ready to go out on your own."

Greg gave her a thoughtful look. "You meet a lot of people, don't you? Your friend's right. There's a lot of money in working private parties, especially if you become known as a mixologist."

She nodded. "And that's what you want? Do you know any chefs you might hook up with? Seth worked with Annabelle Burton, so they had both food and drinks covered."

"I'm looking into that. I know a chef who might be interested." He turned to Peyton. "You worked with Meghan and never hit on her? She was pretty."

Peyton rolled his eyes. "I hit on lots of women, but all Meghan talked about was you. Just like the woman sitting next to me. All she talks about is her Viking."

Greg smiled. "Sometimes you strike out."

"And it's always with the ones you really want. A life lesson, right?"

Jazzi couldn't remember whom she told what. "You both knew Meghan was pregnant when she died, right?"

Greg looked thoughtful. "That's why she ordered pop the last few times she came in here. She'd always ordered beer before."

Jazzi nodded. "She wasn't very far along."

When Greg went to get their orders and serve them, Peyton shook his head. "Meghan was so conservative, I just don't see her sleeping around. That doesn't make sense to me."

Greg returned with their food. "Guys tried to pick her up all the time, and she never hooked up with anyone. At least, as far as I could tell."

"She hooked up with someone." Jazzi bet it was only one special person, but so far, no one knew who that was. She bit into her burger, and juice ran down her palm. She'd groan with pleasure, but both of the men she was with would take that the wrong way.

Peyton looked at Greg and shrugged. "Beats me. I gave it my best and didn't get anywhere. She wasn't into me. I even asked around at work, put out feelers to see if she was with someone, but no one knew anything."

Greg shook his head in defeat. "I stayed a safe distance away. I'm not stupid enough to compete with my boss."

They were spinning their wheels again. Jazzi wiped her hands on two napkins, then reached in her purse. "If either of you remember anything that might help, you should call Detective Gaff. He's working the case." She handed them Gaff's card, then returned her concentration to her food.

A few more people entered the bar but settled in the booths, waiting for the waitresses to serve them.

Peyton picked up a wing to bite into. "You know, Meghan was so naïve, she might have thought if she got pregnant, a guy had to marry her. She didn't understand guys at all."

A cluster of girls who did *not* look innocent walked through the doors and headed to the bar. Chat time was over. Jazzi watched Greg switch into Super Bartender.

Peyton did, too. He shared a knowing smile with her. "The guy's good. He can turn it on as fast as I can."

"Fake gets you laid, that's all," she told him.

Peyton wrapped his arms around her, careful not to touch her with his fingers, covered with sauce. "You're special, you know that? I don't have a chance with you, but I'm still glad we met. I'm adopting you as my big sister. You give me plenty of advice."

She snorted. "Like you listen."

"Hey, that's what family's like, isn't it? We listen but don't pay much attention."

He had a point. She was close to Olivia, but they each did their own thing. "Okay, I adopt you. You can be my horny little brother."

He threw back his head and laughed. The girls at the bar turned to stare at him. He winked at them, and they smiled.

When Jazzi finished her burger and paid to leave, Peyton ordered another beer. Oh yeah, he was going to flirt. The boy was incorrigible.

Chapter 35

Jazzi took the back way home, down Hillegas Road, which turned into Huguenard. She wasn't looking forward to walking into her house, alone, again tonight. She'd watched too many movies and finished the book she was reading. When she reached the turn to the Animal Control building, she found herself taking it. She'd always had a thing for cats. At least, she thought she did. Mom always preferred dogs, especially little ones that barked.

The parking lot was empty, so she pulled to the front door to read the hours. It closed at five-thirty. Probably a good thing. Doing things on the spur of the moment didn't always work out well.

She got back on Huguenard to drive north again. She passed the orchard. Its parking lot was full, and she noticed people walking between the trees, picking their favorite kinds of apples. Two blocks later, she glanced at a sign in a front yard. FREE KITTENS. Too much of a coincidence. Maybe she was destined to get a kitten? She pushed on the brake and stopped at the house. A young boy, maybe ten or eleven, came to stand on the front stoop.

Jazzi walked toward him. "I saw the sign about kittens."

His lips turned up in a huge smile. "Dad says we have to find homes for them or they're going to the shelter. He says people don't adopt black cats. They get spooked. I hope you like Inky. Marmalade's not black, but she's naughty."

Were people still superstitious? And should the boy tell people that Marmalade was a troublemaker? "Can I see them?"

"Come on. They're in here." He walked toward the attached garage. He was opening the door when his father came out to greet her.

"She's here to see Inky and Marmalade," the boy said.

The dad looked relieved. "Good news. We didn't get the mother cat spayed in time. She's safe now, but we have to get rid of the last kittens."

The garage held two cars and a riding lawn mower. A cardboard box with an old blanket in it sat near the mower. Jazzi leaned to see inside the box, and her heart melted. The black kitten stretched his paws up and mewed. He wanted to be held. His orange sister quit licking her paw to stare at Jazzi. She mewed, too.

"How many were there?" Jazzi asked.

"Five." The boy picked up Inky and crushed him under his chin to rub the kitten's head. "Two more orange ones and a calico."

Marmalade tried to climb out of the box to be with her brother.

The boy looked sad. "The one left behind is going to be lonely."

"Not for long," the dad said. "She'll make lots of new friends at the shelter."

Jazzi didn't like the sound of that. She looked back and forth at them and couldn't decide. "I'll take both of them."

"Really?" The boy's eyes lit up.

"We have a big yard and a pond. Plenty of space for two cats."

The dad didn't waste any time. "We'll load the whole box into your pickup."

Jazzi moved the passenger seat back to make room for it. "Thanks so much."

"Thank *you*," the father told her. "You look like the type of person who'll give them a good home. Here." He handed her a bag of dry food for kittens. "We don't need it anymore."

She nodded and spoke to the boy. "We love our pets. We'll take good care of them."

The kittens got nervous when she started driving. They didn't like the feel of the tires moving under them. She parked by the kitchen door and carried the box into the house. She took it to the laundry room and slowly tipped it on its side. She'd seen shredded papers on the floor in the family's garage, probably in place of litter right now, so she got a low wooden box and did the same. She went to the kitchen for a paper plate and filled it with dry cat food.

The kittens took off, exploring. Inky led the way, Marmalade close behind him. They went from the kitchen to the living room and then up the stairs. She followed after them. The stairs were a challenge. The kittens were small, and the steps were high for them. But Inky was determined. After they'd been in every room, she scooped them up, one on each shoulder, and closed all of the doors upstairs except the door to the spare bedroom.

Then she escorted them back downstairs, set them loose in the laundry room, and went to plop on the couch in front of the TV.

Before she started a show, she called Gaff and told him what she'd heard from Greg and Peyton.

"We should make another round and talk to all of them."

"We?"

"People talk to you, Jazzi. They clam up when a cop knocks on their door."

She'd sure like to find out who killed Meghan, Miles, and Leo. "Okay, call me when you're ready."

"Will do."

Inky found her first. He kept attacking her foot while she watched *Dancing with the Stars*. Marmalade managed to climb the sofa and curl next to her head, at the top of the couch cushion. The show ended at ten, and Jazzi scooped them up again and got ready to carry them upstairs. She shredded more papers to put in the guest bathroom and closed the bedroom door to keep them in one place.

Ansel called. "Talk to me. Tell me interesting things. All I did was milk all morning and roof all day. I forgot that my family just eats at supper, no conversation. No one has anything to talk about except cows and farming. We work until dark and then we eat, and then people get ready for bed. I should have rejoiced when they sent me away."

She laughed. "You're going to be attacked when you get home."

She heard the smile in his voice. "Do you miss me that much?"

She realized what he was thinking. "Yes, but I'm talking about our new kittens."

There was a pause. "You got kittens?"

"I was lonely. There was a sign."

He laughed. "We have plenty of farm cats. Need them to catch mice. I like cats. So does George. He still doesn't like my family."

"Smart dog." Relief spread through her. "One's black and one's orange."

"We're ready for Halloween."

She hadn't thought of that. "They're really little—six weeks old."

"The mother had a late litter."

She hadn't thought of that either. It would never have occurred to her. "The black cat's naughty. The boy warned me about Marmalade, but it's Inky who's going to get into everything."

"Good, he'll give George a run for his money." He went on. "Before you ask, Jezebel came with chocolate cake today."

"I'm not worried about Jezebel anymore."

He sounded surprised. "You aren't?"

"I whined about her at Sunday meal, and Olivia and Thane both told me that I should give you more credit and trust you more."

"They're officially my favorite in-laws now."

"You'd never cheat. I knew that. I was just worried you might leave me, that you might want to stay and not come home."

He was quiet for a long time, then said, "I thought I'd get a Dear John phone call, telling me you'd found someone else."

"It's not going to happen," she told him. "I think we're stuck with each other."

"I vote for Super Glue so it stays."

"Me, too. We might not have rings, but for me, it's official."

"You're the best. You know that?"

"I'll keep reminding you."

He chuckled. "You don't have to. I know quality when I see it."

She yawned. Then he yawned, too. She chuckled. "I love you, Viking, but I'm going to sleep. You should, too."

"I'll be home as soon as I can."

"You're going to be jumped at the door."

"I can handle kittens."

"I meant me."

"I can handle that, too. 'Night, Jaz." And he clicked off.

She dropped her clothes where she was and climbed under the covers. Little claws dug into the comforter, and soon two little kittens curled at the end of the bed. They all slept.

Chapter 36

Jazzi and Jerod were installing new shower tiles in the bathrooms when Gaff called.

"Want to go with me to see Seth?"

"Seth? Why him?"

"Greg told you Seth picked up every tab for Meghan. I'd like to know why."

Good point. She'd meant to ask Seth about that, too. She looked at Jerod. He still looked a little green around the gills. "Care if I take off with Gaff for a while?"

"Perfect. I'll put down the paint cloths, make them comfy, and take a nap."

"On the floor?"

He layered every paint cloth they had in a corner.

Yup, her cousin wasn't up to par. "Go for it. Sleep as long as you can." She asked Gaff, "When are you coming for me?"

"Does now work?"

"Yup, but I'm messy."

"I'll be there in fifteen minutes." And he was.

Jerod was asleep before she walked out the door. Gaff drove across town to Seth's house. It made sense that it was on the south side of River Bluffs since his bar was southwest, but Jazzi stared in surprise when Gaff turned onto Old Mill Road. Prestigious, grand houses of yesteryear lined the street. The man must be swimming in money. She'd always admired the houses close to Foster Park. They were big and old and classy. Seth's was a Tudor a block from the golf course.

"Will he be home?" she asked as they went up the walk. "He's usually either at the bar or Louisa's by now."

"I called him," Gaff said, and at the same time, the door opened.

Seth motioned them inside. He smiled at Jazzi. "Hey, there."

Cocoa ran to greet her. Laughing, she ruffled the Lab's fur. "She lives with you now?"

"She loves the walking trail around the golf course."

Amy came down the staircase to greet them, too, and Jazzi tried to hide her surprise. Seth reached for Amy's hand, looking happy. "Amy moved in with me. We're at the age where we don't need to date forever to see if things work. I think we're a good fit."

"I'm happy for you." They looked good together, comfortable and easy. Seth had been alone since Annabelle moved to Florida. Amy lived alone after the father she'd cared for died three years ago. It was nice they'd found each other.

Seth motioned to Cocoa. "One of us takes Cocoa to Aunt Louisa's house when we have to work. Cocoa's not used to being alone."

"Sounds like a great plan to me." It was nice to have some happy outcomes.

Gaff reached for his notepad. "I came to ask you a few questions about Meghan."

Amy went to the foyer table and lifted Cocoa's leash. "I'll take her for her morning walk." She left them to give Seth some privacy.

Seth motioned for them to follow him to the kitchen. It had black cupboards and granite counter tops. "Coffee?"

They both nodded, and Jazzi went to help him carry mugs to the kitchen island. Once they got settled, Gaff clicked his pen, ready to work.

"Greg told us that you never made Meghan pay for any food or drinks at your bar. Is there a reason?"

His question caught Jazzi off guard. Gaff rarely mentioned who told him what when he interviewed a suspect. He must want to verify Greg's statement and let Seth know who'd said it.

Seth didn't seem upset, though. He shrugged. "The first time Meghan ever came to the bar, it was before the heavy rush of the lunch crowd. She was wearing her nursing scrubs, just wanted a quick order of chicken tenders to take to work. I asked her for advice. My head cook was totally out of it, completely confused. He didn't want me to take him to the emergency room, but I was getting worried. He loves his pot, but he doesn't smoke in the morning. Meghan came to the kitchen and talked to him. Told me to give him a glass of orange juice and a few crackers to see if that helped. It snapped him right out of it. He has low blood sugar and doesn't take care of it. I told her I owed her, and I meant it. From that day on, she had a free tab."

Gaff stared. "So you never charged her after that?"

"Feliz told me he'd quit if I dragged him to the hospital. I've never had a better cook than him. Meghan's tab would never add up to the cost of an emergency room visit."

Gaff nodded, satisfied, and looked at Jazzi.

She smiled, happy that Seth had a good answer. She didn't want him to be involved in the murders. "It was too easy, huh?"

Gaff grinned. "It only took one question. It's never that simple."

Seth understood. "Ask Feliz about it if you want to. He drinks a glass of juice when he comes to work now. I was never interested in Meghan, but she did me a favor, and I appreciated it."

Gaff finished his coffee. "Thanks, that's something I can cross off my list. I think we're done here."

He and Jazzi headed to his car. Gaff looked at her. "It's time to talk to your friend Peyton."

"No! It can't be him. He's too nice. Did you call him? He's young. He's always on the run. He's probably not home."

"I'd stay on the run, too, if I slept with so many men's wives. We're going to meet him at a coffee shop on North Anthony, close to the college."

Jazzi knew where that was. It was down the street from the house they were working on.

Peyton was sipping a latte in a booth, waiting for them, when they walked in.

He grinned when he saw Jazzi. "Hey, big sis!"

Gaff turned to her, raised his eyebrows.

"Long story," she explained under her breath. She went to the counter to order an iced coffee. "Want something?" she asked Gaff as he slid onto a seat across from Peyton.

"The same."

The girl nodded and went to make their drinks.

Gaff started. "We've hit a dead end, so we're questioning everybody again who knew Meghan, hoping to find a new starting point."

"I was going to try to catch Jazzi today and tell her what I heard. I met a girl at Seth's bar last night who knew Meghan."

Gaff flipped open his notepad and looked aggravated. "Why would you tell Jazzi instead of calling me?"

"I like her better."

The look on Gaff's face made Jazzi laugh. She slid in beside him and pushed his coffee toward him. Then she turned her attention to Peyton. "What did you hear?"

"We were talking about going to college. She's studying to be a teacher. I deliver pizzas for extra money, and she cleans businesses. One of them is the office for Meghan's apartment complex. She cleans its laundromat, too, and that's how she met Meghan. She could see her apartment from the laundry room."

Gaff swallowed his coffee. "And she saw something?"

Peyton nodded. "A navy-blue vehicle left early on Monday mornings. Jo doesn't give a fig about cars. She thought it might be an SUV or a minivan. She didn't pay attention."

Jazzi rubbed her hands together, excited. "So Meghan did have a boyfriend!"

"Looks like it." Peyton grinned, his dimples showing. "Jo even saw the guy leave once. He was too far away to see his features, but he wore a baseball cap and an orange T-shirt."

"Could she describe him?"

"Tallish, dark, and thin."

Gaff pressed his lips together. "Not much to work with."

Jazzi was hopeful. "We can rule out any guy who's blond."

Gaff rolled his eyes, drained his coffee cup, and then excused himself to head to the bathroom. Too many fluids.

Peyton glanced at his watch. "Gotta go. I have a class in twenty minutes. Did Gaff want to ask me anything else?"

"I don't think so. Thanks for the new information. Can we have Jo's number? Gaff's going to want to talk to her."

Peyton gave her the number, then hesitated. "Jo was a nice girl. Smart and cute. I'd like to see her again."

Jazzi raised an eyebrow, skeptical. "To add to your list?"

"No, she's special. I'd like to get to know her better."

"Would she say yes? Did she like you back?"

"I hope so. We hit it off awfully well." He pulled his keys out of his jeans pocket and nodded good-bye.

"Good luck!" Jazzi called after him.

When Gaff returned, he looked at Peyton's empty seat.

"His class starts soon. He had to leave. He gave me Jo's number."

Gaff took out his keys, too. "Other than that, I didn't have anything else for him."

"But we have a new clue." She had a new spring in her step as they walked to Gaff's car.

"We'll go with this for now," he told her. "I'll drive you back to Jerod. What if I call this Jo, and if we can, I'll pick you up to go talk to her when you get off work?"

Jazzi would love to meet a girl who actually interested Peyton. "Sounds good."

They were only five minutes away from the house she and Jerod were working on. Gaff dropped her at the curb, and when she went inside, Jerod hadn't moved. He was still asleep on the paint cloths. She tried to tiptoe past him into the kitchen to grab a sandwich, but he sat up, blinking. When he saw her, he said, "How did it go?"

"I'll tell you over lunch."

He followed her into the kitchen. "Breakfast for me."

She opened the refrigerator and handed him a ham sandwich, then took one for herself. They'd gutted everything so went outside to sit on a step to eat. It was one of those wonderful days when the temperature was mild, there was a blue sky, and a short-sleeved T-shirt felt good.

"Peyton gave us a new clue. A girl he met cleans at the apartments where Meghan lived."

Jerod shook his head. He was barely hanging in there, too tired to get excited about much. "Small world."

She told him what she'd learned while they ate. "Gaff and I are going to talk to her when I leave here tonight."

"Good luck. Hope it helps find our killer." Jerod wasn't as hungry as usual and passed on a beer. The aftereffects of the flu.

After lunch, they finished up the tiles and installed toilets before leaving for the day. Tomorrow, the kitchen cabinets came. They'd finish the bathrooms, then start installing those.

Before Jerod left for the day, Jazzi called Gaff. "I'm done here. Have you called Jo?"

"On my lunch break. She can meet us if we zip to her place now. She has plans for later tonight."

"Perfect, I'm ready. Where does she live?"

"Downtown, on Fairfield, in that old apartment building." He gave her directions.

Jazzi had gone through the building on a Christmas walk two years ago. The apartments were interesting and quirky. "I know the place. What if I meet you there?"

He sounded relieved. "That will save me a trip."

"Good, see you in half an hour." When she finished talking to Jo with Gaff, she'd go to the store and buy a kitty-litter box, litter, and a play area with two cat beds. Then she'd drive straight home. Inky and Marmalade would be waiting for her.

Chapter 37

Jazzi pulled next to Gaff's unmarked car in the parking lot. High, wrought-iron fences surrounded it, but the gates were open. They closed at night for security. This area of town had beautiful, old restored houses and, not far away, houses with boarded-up windows. The two areas had been this way, juxtaposed, for years.

Gaff got out of his car and motioned for her to join him. They walked into the building's expansive foyer and took the elevator to Jo's floor. The hallways were so narrow, they had to walk single-file to her door. When they knocked, she didn't answer, but the door creaked open.

Jazzi got goose bumps and stared. "I've watched too many creepy movies that start like this."

Gaff shrugged. "Maybe she's puttering around in the kitchen and expects someone."

Maybe. Jazzi pushed the door wider and called, "Jo? Are you home?"

Music blared from the back of the apartment. No answer. Maybe she didn't hear them. Gaff stepped inside the square living room and called again. "Hello. Is anyone here?"

Maybe Jo went out and forgot to lock her door?

Gaff started toward the kitchen and halted in its archway. He was a big enough man that he blocked Jazzi's way. She peeked around him and gasped. Jo lay crumpled on the floor, the back of her head bloody.

Gaff turned and led Jazzi back into the living room. Then he called for his crime scene crew. "Don't touch anything," he told her.

Her stomach rolled. She shut her eyes but still saw short brown curls soaked in blood. Why? Why would the killer come for Jo? How would he even know about her?

Unless...No! It wasn't Peyton!

Gaff put a hand on her shoulder. "Are you okay?"

"My stomach's settling. I'm going to be all right."

"You don't need to stay here for this. If we find anything, I'll call you. Why don't you go home?"

She'd observed enough techs going over a crime scene. "Thanks, I'm out of here."

She hurried down the hallway and out of the building. When she got in her pickup and closed the door, she took deep breaths. Had the killer learned that Jo saw him and his vehicle? How?

She made herself drive to the grocery store to buy cat supplies. When she got home, she carted the bags into the house, and two rowdy kittens came to greet her. They saw the gargantuan cat tree she'd bought and began climbing all over it. She poured herself a glass of wine, plopped on a stool at the kitchen island, and watched them.

She didn't want to think. She concentrated on the cats, pushing all other thoughts away. Eventually, Inky came and climbed up her jeans to stretch on her lap. She could hold him in one hand if he didn't squirm so much. Instead, she stroked his black fur. Marmalade wasn't far behind. Where Inky went, so did she. Their antics finally brought a smile to her face, and she felt herself relax a little.

After a while, Inky mewed, ready for his supper. Jazzi lowered both cats to the ground and opened a can of wet cat food to split between them. She refilled their water bowl and dry cat food dishes. She could watch their tummies expand as they ate. And then they were off again, climbing up and down the cat tree while she got their litter box ready. When they finally tired, they curled up together in one of the beds high up on the tree. They were so cute, Jazzi took a picture with her cell phone and sent it to Ansel.

She hadn't eaten yet, but her stomach still felt a little funky. She poured a can of tomato soup in a mug and went with that. She ate it in front of the TV for distraction, purposely turning to the food channel so that she wouldn't see anything serious. On *The Best Thing I Ever Ate*, Alton Brown was extolling the glories of egg salad. She loved the stuff and decided she'd make it on Saturday. To her, it was like deviled eggs between bread, and she loved those, too.

The kittens found her and clawed their way onto the sofa to join her. Before bed, she cut a long piece of kitchen twine and moved it from couch to couch while Inky and Marmalade followed and attacked it. She wondered how George would react when he came home to kittens. Would the pug like them?

When she felt safe to go to bed without having nightmares, she picked up the kittens and climbed the steps to the spare room. She'd buy a cat tree for up here, too. But for now, she lifted Inky and Marmalade onto the bed and got under the covers.

When Ansel called, she told him about Jo.

"I'm sorry, Jaz. I should have been there for you."

"Don't be silly. Who could guess we'd find another dead body?" She'd found her share. She was ready for the trend to end. "How was your day?"

"We have half the barn roof done to the peak. We start on the other side tomorrow."

"I bet you don't ever want to see another roof again. At least, not for a long time."

"You've got that right. The only nice thing that's come out of this is that I've gotten closer to Radley."

When Ansel talked about him, it sounded like Radley was as bullied by Bain and Ansel's dad as Ansel and Adda were. "That's good. Now you can enjoy your brother."

"Yeah, I'd like to invite him to visit us sometime. Is that okay?"

"He's family. We'll make him feel welcome." She'd knock herself out if he came. That meant that Ansel would be home, with her. And he'd feel like it was his home, too.

"I saw the picture you sent. The kittens are cute."

She laughed. "They think your side of the bed is theirs. You're going to have to tussle for your spot back."

"We'll all fit. Let's hope George doesn't get jealous, or he'll want to be on the bed, too."

"He's out of luck. He snores."

He gave a grunt of amusement. "Well, I'd better turn out the light. We start out early tomorrow. I'm ready to get this job done and get out of here."

"Good, because I'm ready to have you here with me."

"I love you, Jaz."

"Love you, too." And they hung up.

As she drifted to sleep, Jazzi wondered if Jo had had a boyfriend who lived with her if she'd have been safer. But there hadn't been any signs of a struggle at her apartment. She'd fallen close to the refrigerator. It made Jazzi think she'd invited someone in and offered them a drink, and when she turned to take it out of the refrigerator, her guest had hit the back of her head and cracked her skull.

Chapter 38

Jerod called to cancel work again on Tuesday. "I thought I was getting better. I was wrong."

It was probably better, because Gaff had called Jazzi and asked her to visit a few different people with him. Peyton was the first on his list.

As they drove to the hospital, where he worked, she asked, "Why Peyton? He's the one who told us about Jo. Why would he tell us if he meant to kill her? And he drives a red SUV, not something blue."

"We never got to talk to Jo," Gaff said. "Peyton could have lied and told us about a blue vehicle to mislead us. Maybe he thought it was safe to tell us about her, that it would make him look good, but then he found out she knew more than he thought, and it was incriminating."

More maybes. Jazzi didn't believe it.

When they walked into the conference room where he was waiting, Peyton was a mess. "Jo's dead?" He stared at Jazzi. "Was it my fault? I asked her about Meghan. She took your spot at the bar, but we kept our voices low."

"Was Greg working?" Gaff had his notebook out.

"Greg and Seth. Oh, the EMT and his girlfriend were there, too. I saw them at the hospital, so I recognized them, but I don't know their names."

Gaff's pen paused in midair. "Mack and Tonya were there? Do they come in often?"

Peyton spread his hands. "I don't know. I hardly ever go there. I only went to see Jazzi."

Gaff scribbled himself a note. "We'll ask about them later. It would be interesting if they started hanging out there once they knew it was one of Meghan's favorite spots."

Peyton stared. "I looked out the window and could watch the EMT walk the nurse to his car. It was a blue crossover." He ran his hands through his dark, wavy hair. "What if they heard Jo tell me that she saw a blue vehicle at Meghan's apartment on Monday mornings? What if I got Jo killed?"

Jazzi reached across the table to put her hand over his. "You didn't kill Jo. It's not your fault she's dead."

He didn't look convinced. "We were just talking, you know. I didn't think it was a big deal, but I thought you'd be interested in what she told me. I thought it would be just one more small piece of the puzzle."

Gaff leaned forward to make his point. "It *is* just a small piece. Our killer is ruthless. He's the one to blame, not you."

Peyton nodded, but still looked shaken and miserable.

Gaff cleared his throat. "Just for the record, where were you between noon and four yesterday?"

Noon and four? Jazzi took a deep breath. She and Gaff had gone to Jo's after she got off work at five. Jo's body was probably still warm. Maybe. Jazzi didn't know how fast death settled in.

The color drained from Peyton's face. "Was that when Jo died?"

"Looks like it."

"And you think I might have killed her?"

"Have to ask," Gaff said. "Part of the job. Let's hope it gives you an alibi."

"I was at the hospital on the floor, five a.m. to five p.m. When I left there, I went to deliver pizzas."

It was a good thing he was young. A schedule like that would kill Jazzi. She shook her head. Poor word choice.

Gaff laid down his pen. "That's all I've got for now. Sorry about Jo. Take care, kid. When I find who did this, I'll let you know."

Peyton left, upset, and ten minutes later, Tonya came to join them. She glared at Jazzi but folded her hands on the table and turned to Gaff.

Jazzi tried to shake it off, but Tonya irritated her. The girl had a chip on her shoulder.

Gaff studied her. "Have you heard that a young woman who knew Meghan was found murdered in her apartment recently?"

Tonya looked bored. "Mack didn't do it."

Gaff raised his eyebrows, surprised. "I didn't say he did."

"But you think it. That's why you brought me here again. Mack was with me that night."

"You don't even know when the girl died."

"Doesn't matter," she said. "Mack moved in with me. When he's not working, he's with me."

Gaff opened his notepad. "I've heard that you and Mack were at Seth's Bar and Grill a few nights ago."

She lifted her chin. "What's wrong with that? Is it against the law for Mack to take me out?"

"That was Meghan's favorite bar. Did you and Mack ever go there to spy on her?"

Tonya snorted. "Mack was over Meghan. He knows who'll give him what he needs, whatever he needs, whenever he wants it."

Pathetic. Jazzi stared, and Tonya glanced at her defiantly. "Men trip over themselves for you, just like they did for Meghan. So don't give me that look."

Darn! The girl sure had a thin skin.

Jazzi shrugged, not about to argue with her. "I think you sell yourself short, that's all."

"That's because you were never in the glory of Meghan's presence. Beauty can make men stupid."

Gaff went for the opening. "Was Mack stupid around her?"

"He practically drooled. It was pitiful. He blubbered to me about her all the time. But who got him in the end?" She squared her shoulders. "I did."

Gaff tried to head the conversation in a different direction. "The girl who was murdered saw the killer leave Meghan's apartment. He drove a blue vehicle."

Tonya rolled her eyes. "Do you know how many blue vehicles are on the road? Get a grip."

"Mack drives a blue crossover."

"My grandmother drives a blue sedan. So?"

Gaff tried again. "Could you tell me where you were yesterday between noon and four?"

"At home. By myself. I don't have another shift until Thursday."

"Can anyone vouch that you were there?"

"No, no one spies on me, but then, you can't prove that I left my apartment either."

"When did Mack get home yesterday?"

Tonya narrowed her eyes. "He worked a twelve-hour shift yesterday, seven to seven. He was home by seven-thirty. Satisfied?"

Tonya was so unpleasant. How did she become a nurse? Jazzi hoped that if she ever ended up in the hospital, she wouldn't be anywhere near her.

Gaff handed her another business card. "If you think of anything, give me a call."

She got up and threw the card in the trash on her way out the door.

Jazzi let out a long breath and looked at Gaff. "That's one seriously nasty personality disorder. She'd do almost anything to protect Mack."

Gaff nodded. "Either that, or she's the killer."

Jazzi winced. She had to admit that it was a possibility.

Chapter 39

Jazzi had no desire to be a good girl and go to the house on Anthony to work for the rest of the day. She felt like she was up to her eyebrows in dead bodies and clues. Restless, she drove to the grocery store and filled her cart with all the ingredients to make some of Ansel's favorite dishes. If she cooked for him, he'd stay in her thoughts, and she'd feel better.

She tossed a big head of cabbage, ground chuck, and ground pork into her cart. She added lots of cans of tomatoes, and everything to make a dark chocolate cake. A bag of potatoes joined a package of diced ham. She tossed in a couple of bags of salad before she paid at the register.

Once she was home, she carried the bags into the kitchen and stopped to stare. Inky was hanging on the sheer curtain at the front window.

"No!" She hurried to unhook his sharp, little claws and lower him to the ground. She shook her finger at him. "That's not allowed."

He batted at her hand.

"No!" Her voice was firm.

The kitten recognized the tone. He backed away.

She returned to her groceries and spread them on the counter top. It was only early afternoon, but she locked the screen doors anyway and turned on the security system. She'd forget later. Then she reached for her recipe file. She stashed every recipe she tore from a magazine in its different slots. pasta. soup. sandwiches. mexican. oriental. fish. pork. beef. one-dish meals, etc. She reached for the one-dish meals. She quickly found the recipe for cabbage rolls.

Ansel loved cabbage rolls served with potatoes au gratin. She only made them once a year, in January. Not for any specific reason. That's just the rhythm she'd gotten into. She knew she had a few strange fetishes with her cooking. She always made duck breasts in February. In March, she liked seafood curry with bok choy over rice with pineapple upside-down cake for dessert. She marked each month with a certain meal. Odd, she knew. But the foods she cooked helped her track the months and seasons.

She was breaking tradition. She didn't care. Inky tried to climb the kitchen towel draped over the oven door's handle and fell to the floor with it. The kitten was curious about everything. She opened the junk drawer where she tossed everything and found a small paper clip. She flipped it on the floor, and he batted it. When it zoomed across the wood, he chased after it. Soon he and Marmalade were chasing it back and forth.

Jazzi filled her stockpot with water and put it on to boil. She cored the cabbage. And then she started work on the filling. When the water boiled, she lowered the head of cabbage into it. Soon the kitchen smelled like cabbage and tomato sauce. She turned on music. Keith Urban crooned in the background. She finished the cabbage rolls and put them on the back burner to simmer.

She kept her mandolin in the bottom corner cupboard. She didn't use it often, but she wanted consistently sized slices. When she had a high enough pile of potatoes for her gratin, she buttered her casserole dish and added half of them. Onion slices covered that layer, and then the rest of the potatoes went on top. Ansel loved anything potato, but she rarely went to this much bother. She added the broth and seasonings, then covered it with foil.

After she put the potatoes in the oven, she stopped to make a sandwich and carry it into the living room to eat. The kittens took that as an invitation to attack her and beg for deli meat. She gave them each a few tiny pieces while she halfway paid attention to the TV. She'd thrown the mail on the coffee table and sorted through that. Nothing to brag about. She tossed all of it. She was beginning to lose energy. If she didn't make the chocolate cake now, it wouldn't happen.

She'd finished frosting it and was loading dirty bowls into the dishwasher when headlights flashed in the driveway. Bummer! She was ready to crash and relax. No one came here at eight at night during the week. Maybe Gaff?

She opened the front door to see who was there. Mack reached for the handle on the screen door to yank it open. Thank heavens she'd locked it. He was spotlighted on the front stoop, big and menacing, his face contorted with anger. He yelled at her through the screen.

"Tonya said you cornered her in the hospital again to drill her some more. Stay out of my business! Sniff around someplace else."

"How did you get my address?"

"You're in the phone book. I looked you up. Your pickup has your company logo. It was easy."

"Did Tonya tell you we found another body, a girl who knew Meghan?"

"I don't give a crap about Meghan. She got what she deserved, but I didn't kill her. I don't care who did. I told you I was done with her, and I don't want you pestering me about her anymore."

"If Detective Gaff asks me to come with him, I do. It's his choice. If you don't like it, talk to him."

Mack reached for the handle again, and Jazzi moved her finger to the security system. "Leave, or I'm calling for backup."

"It would take cops at least ten minutes to get here."

"It would take you longer to get through this heavy door when I slam it. And by the time you got inside, I'd have my shotgun loaded."

He stared. "Shotgun?"

"Ansel hunts." He did, but Jazzi had no idea where he kept his bullets or cartridges or whatever he used. After Mack's visit, she'd find out. "And then—if you're alive—I'd press charges, and I'd guess not many ambulance services want someone who threatens people and breaks into their houses."

"You have no right hassling me."

"You're a suspect. Detectives question suspects."

He turned on his heel and stalked to his blue crossover. "Don't tell Gaff about this."

"You've got to be kidding. You were way out of line."

He didn't answer, just got in his car and roared away.

She closed and locked the front door, then sat on the second step of the staircase. Her hands shook so much, she had trouble dialing Gaff's number. When she told him what happened, he said, "Don't worry about Mack anymore. I'm bringing him into the station tomorrow to question him, and we'll see if he likes that better. I'll make it very clear he just made his life worse, and if he ever bothers you again, he'll wish he hadn't."

Feeling better, she went to the kitchen to finish cleaning up. That settled her a little. And then she dropped in front of the TV to watch *Fixer Upper*. That's all the excitement she could stand.

Chapter 40

When she walked into the kitchen in the morning, two arms reached out and lifted her off the ground. Mack! She turned to punch him between the eyes and looked into Ansel's handsome face. She threw her arms around his neck and glued her lips to his. Too soon, something jumped on her legs, and George barked to get her attention.

She pulled away to pat the top of his head. "I've missed you, George."

Two little fur balls skittered to a stop in front of the pug. George jerked back, surprised, then stared at them. Not impressed, George went to curl up in his dog bed. He'd had a long night. The kittens pounced on him, but he lowered his head and closed his eyes.

Jazzi glared at Ansel. He was finally home! Happiness gushed through her, but he'd scared her half to death. "You almost gave me a heart attack! And you never called last night."

He grinned, unrepentant. "I went to bed early so that I could get up before dawn and drive home. We finished the barn roof, and I couldn't wait to get back."

"What about the cows?" She didn't give a crap about the poor beasts, but who was going to milk them?

He squeezed her so close, she had trouble breathing. "Bain's learned to use his crutches, and Dad can use a walker. Mom invited Jezebel to supper last night, and the four of them—Dad, Mom, Bain, and the she-demon—put pressure on me to stay. That was the last straw."

"Poor Jezebel." Sarcasm. Not her best quality, but it reared its ugly head once in a while. She hated the hussy and loved it that he called her "the she-demon." She squirmed to kiss him. "Welcome home. I've missed you."

He glanced at the kitchen island and looked guilty. She followed his gaze and saw that half of the chocolate cake was gone. Laughing, she shook her head. "I baked it for you anyway, to make you a special meal."

"A meal? What are we having? Do I smell cabbage rolls?"

"I made potato gratin, too."

He set her down. "I can wait until supper. The cake sort of filled me up."

"That's what happens when you eat half of it."

He went to pour her coffee and settled on the stool next to hers. He bumped his knees against hers. "So, what have I missed?"

She told him about Mack coming last night.

Ansel worked to find his voice. "If you hadn't locked the screen door..."

"I always do. The screen's only in the top half, and the door's made out of heavy steel. I always set the security system, too."

He scraped both hands through his blond hair. "That was too close of a call. No wonder I scared you when I grabbed you. I just meant to surprise you."

She smiled. "You did."

"I'm sorry, Jazzi."

"How would you know about Mack last night?"

"You could have called me, you know."

"When you don't call, I figure you're so tired, you sat down and fell asleep. I didn't want to wake you."

"But that was serious!"

"And it could wait. There wasn't anything else to do about it."

He was about to say more when Inky climbed up his jeans to get his attention. The black kitten narrowed his eyes at him, arched his back, and hissed.

Ansel broke out laughing. "What are you going to do to me?"

Marmalade climbed his other leg, and Ansel used a finger to pet the top of each of their heads. Purrs started. "I can't believe how little they are. I'm going to have to be careful not to step on them."

Jazzi glanced at the clock. "I'm glad you're home, but if I don't get moving pretty soon, Jerod's going to wonder what happened to me. He needs all the help he can get. The flu wiped him out. But if you want to stay home and chill out, I won't blame you. And I could call Jerod and bail out today. We could stay home and...catch up with each other."

He laughed. "Don't think we're not going upstairs early tonight! But I can wait. I'm so ready to be back on our regular routine, I can hardly stand it."

"Gaff might call me away sometime today."

"An even better reason for me to go. I can be backup for Jerod. Has your cousin missed me?" Ansel picked up George, she grabbed the cooler with their lunch, and they started for the door.

As Jazzi settled on the passenger seat of Ansel's van, she gave a small sigh of pleasure. She'd missed this, sitting next to him on the drive back and forth to work. Yakking on the way. "Jerod talked about you a lot until he got the flu. Now he just tries to make it through each day."

They turned onto Highway 37 toward town. It was a short drive to Anthony Boulevard. They passed the college campus on the way. What had started as one lonely building had sprawled into a local campus with a crosswalk that led to housing for students. Ten minutes later, they pulled into the drive for their fixer-upper. Jerod's pickup was already there.

When they walked into the house, Jerod was marking off where he wanted each kitchen cabinet and appliance to go. He turned and saw Ansel and gave a whoop of happiness. "It's about time! We almost finished this place without you. It wouldn't have felt right not to have your stamp on it, too."

Her cousin looked ten times better than yesterday. Ansel shook his head. "Here I thought I'd find you weak and sorry, but you don't look too bad."

"I've been worthless lately. Jazzi's done most of the work. Thank heavens this was an easy remodel. We've almost got it finished."

"Have you lined up the next one yet?" Ansel asked.

Jerod gave him a long stare. "Between the flu and Jazzi trying to help Gaff, we've been a little stretched."

That reminded Jazzi. "Gaff's going to grab me again today sometime."

"No problem." Jerod nodded toward Ansel. "I have the big muscles with me today. I couldn't do the cupboards by myself."

Jazzi grinned, teasing them. "If I time this right, I won't have to hold cabinets for you guys to drill into place."

Jerod pointed at her and used his fingers to make the *shame on you* motion. "Your guy just got back from slave labor on the farm, and you're already throwing extra work at him here?"

"She made me cabbage rolls and chocolate cake. I'd crawl across broken glass for her," Ansel told him.

Jerod stared at her, using his best hurt look. "Cabbage rolls? Really?"

She pointed to the cooler that held their sandwiches for lunch. "There's a storage container full of them for you and Franny."

Jerod pulled her into a bear hug. "You're the best cousin ever!"

She sniffed. "You say that now. Just wait until you feel better. You'll be giving me as much grief as ever."

"A sign of love," he said. "And we've doted on each other enough. It's time to put these cabinets up."

Yeah, the love fest had lasted long enough. None of them were comfortable with too much praise. They all got in gear and carried the cabinets to where they'd be put in place. Gaff waited too long to call her, and Jazzi had to shoulder every top cabinet in its proper spot while the guys installed them. They had half the base cabinets done when Gaff finally called. They'd have the island situated before lunch.

"What if I come pick you up about one?" he asked. "I've scheduled some time to talk to Mack's EMT partner. I've already talked to Mack, and we won't have any more problems with him."

Jazzi wouldn't want to be on the other end of a serious discussion with Gaff when he wasn't happy. Mack wasn't nearly as scary as her nice detective could be. She'd never seen that side of him, but she could tell it was there. "One is fine. See you then."

The granite counter tops were coming after lunch, but between Ansel and Jerod and the delivery team, they wouldn't need her. The white Shaker cabinets looked really good, and she couldn't wait to see how the kitchen came together.

They worked right up until Gaff came, and Jazzi carried her deli roast beef sandwich with her to eat in his car. "Do you want one? I have extra."

He shook his head. "I already grabbed a quick lunch."

She chowed down on their drive to the south side of River Bluffs. When they crossed the bridge into town, Jazzi glanced at the St. Mary's River below them. It was low this time of year. Fine with her. They'd had enough rain in spring that the three rivers that ran through town had overflowed their banks in too many locations. Farm fields south of town were flooded, looking like shallow lakes.

Gaff drove past Headwaters Park, with its beautiful landscaping and trails, past downtown proper, and kept going until he reached Rudisill Avenue. He turned, and they passed beautiful old neighborhoods to make their way to a turnoff on Engle Road. The parking spot for some of the walking trails there was so close to the wetlands and where they'd found a scrap of Leo's shirt that it took Jazzi back. She'd seen Mack's ambulance parked there often when she passed the street.

The parking lot was empty, but a few minutes later, an ambulance pulled in beside them. A tall, broad-shouldered black man with graying hair got out and walked to the gazebo overlooking a wide expanse of connecting shallow ponds. They got out to join him.

Gaff showed his badge and sat across from the man. Jazzi sat beside Gaff.

"Thanks for meeting with us," Gaff said. "We have some questions about your partner, Mack."

The man held out his hand. "I'm Cornelius. I've worked with Mack for four years now. He's sort of a mixed bag."

"How's that?" Gaff opened his notepad.

"He talks like the biggest bigot you've ever met. Doesn't have anything good to say about anyone who isn't white, but I'm the exception. So is the Hispanic who works weekends with us sometimes. If he knows you, you're all right. If he doesn't know you, it's a whole different story. Same with women."

"What do you mean?"

"If men sleep around, that's their due. If women sleep around, they're whores. Unless they're friends of his. Then he listens to them and doesn't judge. He's sort of a bipolar bigot."

Jazzi got a kick out of that, a great term. "How did he feel about Meghan?"

Cornelius took a minute to think. "She was a saint until she wouldn't sleep with him. The boy has double standards. It's wrong to sleep around, but it's fine if the girl sleeps with him."

"And if she doesn't?" Gaff asked.

"Mack doesn't handle rejection well. And he has a simmering anger issue. I still don't think he'd kill anyone." Cornelius squinched his lips together and shook his head. "No, Mack's more the type to cuss and run his mouth. He tries to intimidate, but that's about it."

"Have you met his new girlfriend, Tonya?"

"No, and I don't want to. He never stops talking about her. He thinks he's in love, but I'm telling you, that woman sounds downright scary. I told him to run, but he didn't listen."

Gaff looked up from his notes. "Tonya comes off as super jealous of Meghan."

Cornelius looked across the open fields and water of the wetlands. Ducks that Jazzi had never seen before floated on the nearest pond. Cornelius chose his words carefully. "Have you ever met one of those women who get along with every guy they meet but can't get along with any other woman? That would be Tonya."

Jazzi got it. "She views every other woman as competition."

"That's Tonya. If Mack introduced her to me, she'd be all friendly and nice."

"Was Mack with you your entire shift on Monday?" Gaff asked. "He didn't take a break in the afternoon and disappear?"

Cornelius shook his head. "It was him and me from seven to seven. We stopped and grabbed a pizza for lunch together."

Gaff rested his pen above the notepad. "Anything else you can tell us?"

Cornelius shook his head.

Gaff reached across the wooden picnic table to shake his hand. "Thanks for your input. I appreciate it." He handed him one of his business cards. "If you think of anything else, give me a call."

Cornelius pushed to his feet. "I left Mack at a Subway shop. Better go get him. He has a lot of issues, but I don't think he's a killer."

They followed him to their vehicles and parted.

On the drive back, Jazzi asked, "What do you think? Do you think Mack's all bark, no bite?"

"Anyone can be pushed too far," Gaff said. "Say Mack and Meghan had a one-night stand. If Mack found out she was pregnant with his child, and she still didn't want to get together with him, that might push him over the edge."

"Do you think Meghan would sleep with Mack?"

"Stranger things have happened. Maybe it was early on, and Mack wouldn't let it go, kept bugging her when she'd decided she didn't like him."

"He'd have told us that happened. He'd have thought it put him in the right."

"Not if he'd settled on Tonya in the meantime. If she even got a hint of that, she'd make his life a misery."

Jazzi hadn't thought of that. Detecting got too twisty and confusing. When Gaff turned north on Jefferson, he passed Seth's bar, and out of habit, Jazzi turned to look at it. From this direction, she noticed Seth's black SUV parked at the very outer edge of the lot. A blue sedan was parked next to it.

A blue sedan? Was that where the bar's employees parked? Who drove it? She pulled her cell phone out of her pocket and called Seth. "Hey, I just passed your bar and saw a blue car parked next to your SUV. Do you know who drives it?"

"Sure. It's Greg's. You interested in it? He's thinking of trading it in for a van in case he starts working private parties. He'll need something with more space for carting supplies back and forth."

"No, I was just curious. Thanks. And don't tell Greg I asked, will you?"

"It's our secret." But she heard voices in the background. If Greg was close, he'd have heard Seth's side of the conversation.

When she hung up, Gaff asked, "What was that all about?" When she told him, he shook his head. "You never mentioned that you were with me.

You should have. This way, it makes it sound as if you're the only person who noticed Greg drives a vehicle that could belong to the murder suspect."

"But he knows I tell you anything I learn," Jazzi protested.

Gaff gave her a stern look. "We're dealing with someone who's murdered four people to cover his tracks. I don't want to take any chances. From now on, you let me make the calls to get more information. Okay?"

"Okay." Her curiosity had gotten her in trouble. From now on, she'd let Gaff do all the dirty work.

She was glad when Gaff dropped her back at Anthony and she walked in to see a kitchen that was coming together. Ansel and Jerod were putting up the backsplash, and the rainbow-colored, glass tiles were beautiful.

"Nice, huh?" Jerod asked.

"I love it."

Ansel stopped to run a hand over the marble counter tops. "This kitchen should sell the place."

His words proved to be an omen. Before they finished work for the day, a car pulled to the curb in front of the house and a man walked to the front door and knocked.

Jerod went to welcome him.

"I've seen work trucks here for a while now. Is someone finally going to do something with this house?"

Jerod motioned him inside. "We're renovating it so that we can flip it. We'll be done soon."

The man seemed to like what he saw. A big archway opened the living room to the dining room and kitchen area. "How much do you want for it? I like this area, and this is one of the bigger houses available."

Jazzi and Ansel let Jerod haggle. He was better at it than they were. The three of them had already decided on what they thought would be a fair price. By the time she and Ansel finished the last trim and the kitchen was complete, Jerod had taken the man to tour the upstairs and returned. When the man left, the house was sold.

The three of them stared at each other.

"I could get used to this," Jerod said. "I told the guy he could have the house at the end of next week, once his money cleared. He's paying cash, has to get it together. His parents are helping him."

Ansel nodded. "We'll have it done by then, but we don't have the next house in mind yet."

"Let's all look for something tonight," Jerod said. "We've done enough for today. Let's talk about it tomorrow."

They locked up together and left. Ansel put George on the back seat of his van, and the dog stretched out, happy. Things were back to the way they should be.

The kittens attacked them when they got home, and George let them climb all over him. Jazzi reheated the cabbage rolls and potatoes. She knew Ansel liked the food, because he took seconds at supper.

He leaned back in his chair and stretched his long legs. "I never realized what good cooking was until I met you. My mom put a supper on the table every night, but it was nothing to brag about."

Cooking for Ansel made Jazzi happy. She loved it when he enjoyed her meals. "This is your first night home. I mean to make it memorable."

His blue eyes glittered. "What have you got in mind?"

"I went shopping while you were gone."

He arched a blond brow. "I should mark that on our calendar. It's a rare event."

"Let the dishes soak. Give me ten minutes, then come upstairs."

When she headed up the steps, Inky and Marmalade started after her. "Not this time," she said.

Ansel picked them up and locked them in the laundry room. They weren't happy about it, but they'd learn the routine. George had.

When Ansel finally climbed the steps, she was waiting for him in their bedroom, wearing her new Victoria's Secret purchase. To say that he liked it was an understatement.

The dishes never got rinsed, but Ansel came down much later to bring the pets up with them. Exhausted, they all cuddled and slept. No search had taken place to find a new house for a fixer-upper, but that could wait.

Chapter 41

When they walked into the house on Anthony, Jerod shook his head at them. "I'm guessing no research got done last night. You both look too happy."

Jazzi grinned, unrepentant. "Guilty as charged."

"It's a good thing," her cousin told her. "Because I found a place I'd like to try."

Ansel frowned. "This sounds like you're giving us a sales job. What's the rub?"

"It has more issues than any place we've taken on before, but if we fix them, I think we'll get a great return." They'd gotten a great return for the house on Anthony, and the new owner had still bought it for a good price. The work had been easy. Jerod spread a sheet of newspaper out for them to see. The house was listed under local auctions.

"Really?" Jazzi stared at the picture. The roof had missing shingles. The front porch sagged. So did the back corner of the house. That meant the foundation had issues. It was in a nice neighborhood off Rudisill Avenue on the south side of town. It wasn't that far from Seth's house, but in an area that wasn't nearly as expensive as his. All of the houses around it looked like they were in good shape.

Ansel counted off problems on his fingers. "Foundation. Roof. Exterior. Front porch."

Jerod defended his decision. "It's been on the market a long time. The owners kept lowering their price. They finally put it up for auction. I think we can get it for a low price."

Ansel and Jazzi exchanged glances. Finally, Ansel said, "If the price is right, why not?"

It was a big, solid old house that had been neglected. If they could restore it to what it had been, they'd have done a good thing. The house deserved some TLC.

They'd have to invest some serious money to fix it. "How high do you want to bid on it?"

"I'd like to get it for close to sixty thousand, but I won't go over seventy. It's not just money we'd have to invest in the house. It's going to take more time than usual, too. Our time's worth something."

Ansel nodded. "I'm sold. We'll give it a try."

Jazzi agreed, and Jerod grinned with pleasure.

"The auction's this Saturday," he told them. "Want to come with me when I bid on it?"

"Can we pass this time?" Ansel glanced out the front window at the small front yard. "We're behind on everything. I'd like to work to get the yard and projects caught up."

Projects? Jazzi didn't want to know. But she knew her Viking would be chomping at the bit to work on the yard.

Jerod looked almost happy they weren't going to make the auction. "I think I'll take Franny with me, and she can bid on the antiques the couple owned."

Jerod loved spending time with his Franny. That put him higher up on the ladder rungs for Jazzi. She looked around the house, trying to decide what they still needed to do. "What now?"

"Finishing details," Jerod said. "Then when the guy has his money, we can give him his keys."

They got to work, and even if they took their time, they'd be finished when they left tomorrow night. A wondrous thing. That meant they could take Friday off. They took a longer lunch break than usual and still left before three-thirty.

Thursday was an even shorter day, and when Ansel pulled out of the driveway, they wouldn't be coming back. The house was done.

Jazzi had more time to get ready for Sisters' Night Out. When she left to meet Olivia later that night, she was wearing one of the new outfits she'd bought while Ansel was out of town, her hair cascaded past her shoulders, and her makeup was flawless.

Ansel looked at her as they both walked to their vehicles. "You look hot. I feel like I should stay with you to beat men away. Want to make it a foursome tonight?"

"Against the rules," she told him. "But when I get home, you'll get to help me *out* of these clothes."

He grinned. "A boyfriend's bonus. Worth a short wait. Have fun, Jaz. Thane and I are going to the Tower Bar tonight. Their special's prime rib. See you later."

Did all men love beef as much as Ansel and Thane? Wings ranked right up there, too. Come to think of it, they liked everything meat. She and Olivia were going to their beloved Henry's. Jazzi had to laugh at herself, but going out with her sister and leaving Ansel to spend time with Thane restored her sense of balance. At the end of the day, when she went home, Ansel would be there for her.

On the drive across town, she remembered she was supposed to let Reuben know when Ansel got back, so she gave him a quick call.

"Thank the heavens! We were beginning to worry. Isabelle and I wanted Ansel here for our wedding. It's coming up, you know. The twenty-ninth's not that far away."

Jazzi realized with surprise that their wedding was closer than she'd thought. They'd been adamant they didn't want any presents, other than their friends' company. But Jazzi wanted to buy a special dress for the occasion. It would mean a lot to Reuben and especially Isabelle. They'd realize she went to more effort than usual for them.

Olivia was waiting at the door when Jazzi pulled into her drive and ran out to jump in the pickup. "Your man's home. I'm so happy for you! When you go home tonight, he'll be waiting for you."

They gossiped nonstop all through supper. By the time Jazzi drove home, her mood soared, and it only got better when Ansel met her at the kitchen door.

"We've both had a good night," he told her, "but it's only going to get better."

George huffed when Ansel left him at the base of the stairs and said, "Later." The kittens knew the routine when Ansel locked them in the laundry room, but at the end of the night, they all settled in the bedroom and fell asleep.

Chapter 42

She and Ansel slept in on Friday. When they woke, Ansel shooed all the pets out of the room and closed the door for a little privacy. An hour later, they finally got up and moving. George looked relieved when they headed downstairs to the kitchen. The pug went straight to his food dish.

Ansel chuckled. "George knows his priorities, but at least he's eating like usual again. He hardly ate at the farm."

Jazzi rolled her eyes. "I find that hard to believe."

"Really. He didn't touch anything until I put his food dish in my old bedroom. He ate before we went downstairs in the morning and when I went upstairs to sleep. He didn't like being around my family."

Jazzi stared at the pug. She didn't realize his feelings were so sensitive. After all, he'd lived with Ansel's last girlfriend, Emily, and she did things on purpose to annoy him because she knew it would bother Ansel.

While Ansel fed his pug, Jazzi fed the kittens.

"The pets get babied before we even drink our first cup of coffee." Ansel didn't really mind. He patted the top of George's head before he put pumpernickel bread in the toaster.

"What do you want to do today?" Jazzi couldn't remember the last time they had had a free day, a day when they could do whatever they pleased.

"I want to drive past the house Jerod found."

"Good. I do, too." They had good intentions for an early start, but the kittens pestered them for attention during breakfast, and before they realized it, they'd lost a good chunk of time dragging strings across the kitchen floor.

Oh, well, what were bonus days for if not enjoying some extras? The kittens had frolicked enough that once Jazzi gave them small portions of wet cat food, they climbed their luxury cat tree and curled up together to nap.

Ansel stood next to her and stared down at them. "I never realized how cute kittens are. We didn't pay much attention to them on the farm. I'd always squirt milk into their mouths when they came around when we were milking."

"But you have machines."

"When we lined the cows up to connect them to the machines, I'd shoot a few squirts first. Radley does that, too."

"Let me guess. Your dad and Bain don't bother."

"Dad and Bain wouldn't bother putting out dry cat food, either, but Radley and I do. We think it keeps the farm cats healthier."

She leaned into him and gave him a hug. "You're a nice person."

"Bain says I'm a sucker."

"Bain should marry Jezebel. They'd be perfect for each other. They're both selfish."

He chuckled. "Let's go take a look at this house. Then maybe we'll drive downtown and eat lunch at Coney Island."

Now he was speaking her language. She'd only eaten one piece of toast, and she'd be hungry again soon. Coney dogs were close to gourmet for her. They loaded into his work van, with George on the back seat, and drove south.

When they pulled to the curb in front of the house, Jazzi was glad they'd voted yes before they saw it. The porch looked like it would crash down if someone kicked one of its columns. It was empty, so they went to peek in a window, and the steps creaked when they climbed them. They'd have to replace them. They could see through the living room into a small kitchen with worn linoleum—a hideous pattern that must have dated back to prehistoric days.

"A gut job," Ansel said.

"Worse. The inside and outside need to be redone." Jazzi glanced at the sagging fence that surrounded the backyard. "*Everything* needs to be repaired."

They walked back to the van and turned to study the house from the street.

"It's big," Ansel said. "Three stories."

Jazzi's mind went to the novel *Little Women*. "Maybe there's a writing garret in an oversized attic."

His brows rose in surprise. "Is that something you've always wanted?"

"No, but I've always thought an artist's garret sounded romantic."

He laughed. "If you say so. It sounds cold and drafty to me."

They tramped around a little more, then decided to drive to Main Street to grab their hot dogs. Ansel ran in to buy a half dozen of them—two for Jazzi, three for him, plus a plain one for George—then they drove to Headwaters Park to eat them. That way, George could join them. They were enjoying the nice day when someone came to stand by their bench. Jazzi looked up and flinched at the look on Tonya's face.

"See!" Tonya shifted the bag of Coney dogs in her hand to point to Ansel. "Girls like you can have any man you want, and then you look down at someone like me who has to work hard to attract Mack."

If Jazzi had a violin, she'd play a sad tune for Tonya. A victim. Misunderstood. The girl needed to get over herself.

Ansel, however, stood, his stance intimidating. "Don't talk to her like that. You don't know a thing about her."

"Pretty girls always get the guys, whether they're nice or not."

"Jazzi *is* nice. You're the one who isn't, so go away."

"Or? What are you going to do about it?"

Jazzi shook her head. Tonya was messing with the wrong person.

He took out his cell phone. "I'm going to report you as harassing us." He jerked his head toward the city-county building. "I can have help here in a few minutes."

Tonya took a step backward. Ansel didn't bluster like Mack did. "No need for that. I'll leave." But she hesitated.

Jazzi was tired of her. She wadded up their dirty food wrappers and motioned for her to move on. "Gaff's already talked to Mack. Do you need a lecture, too?"

Ansel's brows furrowed into a frown. "She obviously does, but if she gets out of here, I'll put my phone back in my pocket."

Tonya turned and hurried away.

Ansel shook his head in wonder. "Is Mack as bad as she is?"

"They're a perfect pair."

He sat down next to her to finish his last hot dog. "You shouldn't have to deal with those two anymore. If she bothers you again, I'll ask Gaff to deal with it."

"You won't have to. I'm out of patience with them, and they know it. They won't come around again." Tonya would be stuck with Mack for as long as she could hold him, but that's exactly what she deserved.

* * * *

They loaded back into the van a short time later, and Ansel drove home. It didn't surprise Jazzi when he climbed onto his riding lawn mower half an hour later to mow around the house.

"That way, I can take extra time to bag all the clippings today, then I can mow around the pond tomorrow."

"If you're going to work, I'm running to the store to get that out of the way. I want to deep clean the house tomorrow. I've rushed things lately."

"Don't buy anything to cook for supper tonight," he told her. "I'll run to get Chinese so you don't have to cook. This is a goof-off Friday. It's special."

"A freebie. I love it." Ansel started his mower, and she headed to the store. The weather was so nice, and Ansel loved to grill so much, she decided to buy sirloins and chicken breasts for Sunday. She'd marinate both. She grabbed corn on the cob, because soon she wouldn't be able to get it, and three bags of coleslaw. She decided to make cream pies for dessert.

Ansel was still bagging the clippings when she got back, so she carried all of the groceries into the kitchen herself and put them away. When she emptied the brown paper grocery bags, she tossed them on the floor for the kittens to run in and out of. She only had a few. The rest of the bags were plastic. When the kittens got bored with the bags, she also tossed down two felt mice filled with catnip she'd bought in the pet aisle. The kittens pounced to attack them and batted them around the kitchen. George waited until she got to the bag with his favorite doggie bones. She tossed him one, and he carried it to his dog bed to guard it.

She'd lost more time shopping and putting things away than she expected and had just finished when Ansel walked back in the house. He glanced at the clock. "It's later than I thought. Let's clean up, then I'll go grab us Chinese."

They both headed up to the shower. It was a while before they came back downstairs, and if a dog could roll its eyes, George did. Jazzi had changed back into her T-shirt and shorts. Ansel ogled her legs. "No matter which part of you I look at, it's a treat."

"You're prejudiced." He was. Some men zoned in on breasts. Some liked legs. Ansel even liked her back. He had eclectic tastes. "Want me to come with you?"

"No, I'll be back as fast as I can."

She started to the living room. He'd be gone about fifteen minutes, no longer. Not enough time to bother with anything. "I'm planting myself in front of the TV. I'm going to be lazy."

Forty minutes later, she glanced at the clock. What was taking Ansel so long? Ten minutes later, she started to get worried. Had he been in an accident? Then she heard his van pull into the drive and park near the kitchen. She got up to open the door for him in case his hands were full.

He carried in a big bag of Chinese food, a tiny sack, and a bottle of champagne. He went to the kitchen island and dropped the food and bubbly there. Then he came to her and removed a small square velvet box from the tiny bag, went down on one knee, and flipped the box open. A white-gold braided band nestled there, embedded with small diamonds.

"I think we make a pretty good pair," he said. "We can fix anything if we work together. I know you said you didn't want diamonds, but you can't snag these on anything. Marry me?"

He fit the ring on her finger, and she threw her arms around his neck.

"Is that a yes?"

"Yes!" She knew she'd said they needed more time, but she'd never meet anyone she wanted more than Ansel.

He scooped her into his arms and started for the stairs. George didn't even bother to follow them. The Chinese food needed to be reheated by the time they got back to it, but the champagne was still cold.

Chapter 43

Nothing had really changed, but everything felt different when Jazzi started cleaning the house on Saturday. She was wearing Ansel's ring. They were official. It was almost awkward at breakfast. What did you do when you declared yourself taken?

Ansel kept glancing at the ring on her finger, and he looked proud of himself. "You're the best thing that ever happened to me," he told her.

Silly man. He could probably do better, but she wasn't about to tell him that. "It's mutual, but I like things just the way they are. I don't want anything to change."

"Agreed. We're perfect as is, so I'm going to do what I always do." He glanced outside with a gleam in his eyes.

She had to laugh at him. She might be able to compete with other women, but she was no match for the riding lawn mower. "Big Green's calling to you." His name for it. "The grass is at least a half inch too high around the pond."

He acknowledged his fixation with a grin. She didn't need to tell him he was a bit obsessive about the lawn. Besides, the man loved being outside, and this was a perfect day. An artist could have painted the blue sky filled with puffy white clouds. The perennials in her flower beds were just about done, only the sedum and mums blooming, but they were still attractive. When she looked out the back windows, beauty greeted her.

When he went out to tackle the yard, she got busy scrubbing toilets, tubs, and sinks. Not nearly as glamorous. She dusted the upstairs, swept the floors, and changed the sheets on both beds before starting on the living room. She'd finished dusting it when the doorbell rang. She glanced at her reflection in the living room window. Hair a mess. Ratty T-shirt and mid-thigh shorts. Not good. But it was Saturday. What did anyone expect?

The front door was open, and she saw Greg standing at the screen. It was locked, as usual. But the big door was wide, so he'd know someone was home. Still, at this angle, he couldn't see her. Jazzi didn't scare easily, but Jo had opened her door to someone she knew and ended up dead. Greg drove a blue car. Ansel was mowing around the pond and wouldn't hear if she screamed for help. She moved closer to the wall, out of sight, and didn't answer the door.

He pushed the doorbell again, waited, then started to walk around the house to the back. She should be safe if she met him outside. She scrambled through the kitchen, grabbed her cell phone, and pushed Ansel's number, then rushed to the back patio and bent to deadhead a few flowers, as if she'd been working there and didn't hear him.

When he saw her, he gave her his best smile. "I thought you might be out here. Hey, I found this cell phone at the bar, and I've been carrying it around for a while. Wondered if it might be yours."

She glanced at it and shook her head. "Nope, I have mine, but thanks for thinking of me."

A light gray van was parked in the drive. It surprised her. "Did you get a new car?"

A swift look that she couldn't define passed over his face. "I'm going to start working mixed-drink parties with a friend who's a chef. I needed something big enough to haul food and supplies."

She wanted to kick herself. She shouldn't have mentioned the van. It had alerted him that she knew he drove a blue car. She put on a happy face for him. "Good for you! You get to start your mixology business. Is Seth going to teach you his secret recipes?"

"He's even going to show up at the first few parties to give me a good start."

Jazzi looked him up and down. He was looking particularly snazzy today in light jeans, a white button-down shirt with the sleeves rolled up, and a red tie hanging loosely for a pop of color. "Are you doing a party tonight?"

"No, just testing things out." Greg wiped his forehead with his arm. "The sun's got some heat to it today. I don't suppose you have a beer?"

She didn't want him in the house with her. She motioned for him to take a seat at the patio table. "Sure, wait here. I'll grab one for each of us."

He pulled out a chair but didn't use it. Instead, he followed her into the kitchen and gave a low whistle. "You've turned your house into something special." He looked at the heavy Dutch oven on the six-burner stove. "That looks serious."

"It is. When you fill it, it takes some muscle to lift it." Did he use a heavy pan to bash in the back of Jo's head?

He went to try it out. "I see what you mean. You couldn't swing this thing."

She wanted him out of here. The sooner she gave him a beer, the sooner she could lead him back to the patio. She opened the refrigerator. "Is Stella all right?"

"Perfect."

When she bent to reach for one, she heard him move. She gripped the beer bottle so that she could use it as a weapon if she had to, but the back door opened at the same time, and Ansel stepped into the house.

He frowned at Greg. "Didn't know you were here."

"I didn't know you were back in town." Greg took a few steps back toward the kitchen island.

"Got back just in time to put a ring on Jazzi's finger. Did you notice it?"

Greg's expression turned sour. "Not really. I came to return her cell phone, but it's not hers. Someone else must have left it at the bar." Jazzi slid the Stella across the island toward Greg, but he shook his head. "I think I'll take a rain check, but thanks anyway. I have a few things to do before I work tonight."

Jazzi went to stand beside Ansel. Greg had been coming up behind her. What for? With a visible effort, Greg tried to turn on the charm. He looked frustrated but started toward the front door. "I hope I'll still see you at the bar sometimes."

Ansel nodded. "We'll be there."

Greg winced at the *we*. Had she misread things? Had he come to flirt with her? Was he going to grab her and kiss her at the refrigerator?

Jazzi watched him walk to his van and drive away. She couldn't relax until he was gone.

Ansel crossed his arms over his chest and glared at her. "What the heck were you thinking—letting Greg in here when you were alone?"

"I called you and met him on the back patio. He followed me in the house when he asked for a beer."

"I wouldn't be any help when I'm working by the pond. I can't even see the house over the rise. If something happened, I wouldn't know you needed me."

She blinked. "That's why I called you."

"You didn't leave a message."

"I didn't have time." Her arguments sounded hollow, even to her own ears.

"He was four steps behind you at the refrigerator when I walked in. He was starting to take off his tie."

His tie. She could feel the color drain from her face. She'd never seen him wear one before. A perfect noose. A perfect way to strangle someone. Meghan had been strangled. She went to a barstool. She suddenly needed to sit down.

Had he worn the same outfit when he went to Meghan's apartment?

She was getting ahead of herself.

Ansel came to stand behind her, to wrap his arms around her. "I never want to lose you. You have to be more careful."

"You could be right. What if you are?"

"We'll let Gaff decide." He kept one arm cradled around her as he made the call. When he hung up, he said, "Gaff took it seriously. He's going to look into Greg more."

They let the subject drop for the moment. Jazzi didn't want to dwell on it. Apparently, neither did Ansel. He locked the front door and grabbed a bottle of water to take with him to finish the lawn.

He stopped at the door. "We need some kind of system so you can call me to the house when you need me."

"You can't be there for me every minute of every day." She was a strong woman. If Greg had slipped a tie around her neck, she'd have given him a run for his money, starting with a broken beer bottle across his face. He'd have scratches and bruises, for sure. Meghan was a nurse, though. Nurses lifted patients when they needed to. They were strong, too. But Meghan was nice. How much of a fight did she put up? Jazzi was nice, too, but she'd grown up around Jerod. She could tussle with the best of them.

Ansel looked solemn. "I know I can't always be there for you, but I can be there as much as possible."

She loved him. She waved him away, too choked up to talk about it anymore. When he went back to the yard, she cleaned with a vengeance, concentrating on eliminating any trace of dirt rather than thinking about what-ifs.

When the house was spotless, she turned on music and started cooking for the Sunday meal with her family. She started with the desserts—chocolate cream pie, butterscotch pie—then moved to Jerod's favorites, coconut cream and pecan cream. Cooking calmed her. Then she made the coleslaw. If it sat for a while, it would be better. Everything else could wait until tomorrow.

Ansel glanced at the desserts when he finished for the day.

"Not even a nibble," Jazzi told him. "They're for tomorrow."

He made a face but didn't argue. "What's for tonight?"

"Carry-in fried chicken. The works."

He raised his eyes to the heavens. "That's the way it always works. Put a ring on a girl's finger, and she stops cooking for you."

She tamped down a smile. Thank heavens, they were back to normal. "You get gruel for breakfast."

He laughed. "George and I love fried chicken. I'm buying every side to go with it."

"Just remember you're grilling steaks tomorrow. Save room for them."

He looked offended. "I can always eat a steak."

Come to think of it, he could. So could Jerod.

Gaff called later that night. "Just wanted to let you know that we traced where Greg traded in his car for the newer van. The dealership's already cleaned it, but my techs are going to go over it anyway. If Greg stuffed Leo's body in the trunk, we should find something."

Jazzi wasn't sure if she wanted the killer to be Greg or not. If it was him, she'd had a close call today. She thought back on his visit, and she remembered how his expression had changed when she'd asked him about his new van. Had he driven it here as a test? To see if she knew about his blue sedan? She had to get better at this detecting stuff. No, she had to avoid it. From now on.

Chapter 44

The kittens disappeared when people started filling the house on Sunday. The talk was all about Ansel's return and the ring he'd given Jazzi. She and Ansel had agreed not to mention a word about Greg's visit yesterday. It would only upset people.

While Ansel and Jerod grilled, Jazzi's dad and Eli—Jerod's dad—went out to join them. The women stayed in the kitchen, and Mom and Gran oohed and aahed over Ansel asking Jazzi to marry him.

"Do you have a date?" Mom asked.

"We haven't gotten to that." Jazzi carried dips to the table for Franny's vegetable tray. She added pita and bagel chips. Everyone stood around the kitchen island, yakking and snacking. Jerod came in to grab some food to take outside.

Gran raised her hand to her throat, beaming. "Our Lynda gave such a beautiful engagement party here. Remember it, hon? You should give one, too."

Joy flooded Jazzi. Gran remembered that long-ago party when Lynda was going to marry Cal and she could still stay grounded in the present. When she wasn't stressed, Gran didn't retreat to the far past.

"We should give *you* an engagement party," Olivia said. "Thane and I will buy the drinks if you do all the cooking."

Franny laughed. "That's the majority of the work."

"But I can't cook!" Olivia protested.

"I thought you and Thane were going to make recipes his grandma gave you." That's what Olivia had told her.

Olivia blushed, embarrassed. "We tried a few of them."

"And?"

"It takes time to cook. There's always something to chop or dice. And then it takes more time, cleaning everything up."

Jazzi raised an eyebrow. "What about the new KitchenAid you bought?"

"I still have it."

Talk about dodging the issue. Jazzi gave a frustrated sigh. "Have you used it?"

"It has even more parts that need to be cleaned."

"Exactly," Mom said, rushing to Olivia's defense. "Cooking is overrated."

Jazzi shook her head, dismissing them. "I like to cook. We'll have to plan a party, but it has to wait a while until Ansel and I decide what we want to do."

Talk turned to the armoire Franny was close to finishing. Her shed was full of pieces to strip and stain. She was trying to get them done before her due date. Her stomach moved, and she put a hand on it. "This baby moves a lot."

She looked uncomfortable, and Jazzi felt sorry for her.

When the men carried in the food, people gathered around the table, and talking dropped off as they ate. Conversation returned over pie and coffee.

Jerod's dad said, "Jerod told us you finished your last house and sold it already, then he bid on a wreck on the south side of town and got it."

Jazzi looked up, surprised.

"Sorry, I told Ansel while we grilled together," Jerod said.

"A good price?" Jazzi asked.

"Right in the zone."

They'd still have to restore the big three-story to dazzling to make a decent profit on it, but when the three of them put their heads together, they always came up with something good.

The men talked about the house and restoring it until people began to drift away. When the last person left, Jazzi and Ansel got busy cleaning up, and the kittens got brave enough to scamper underfoot.

George went to the back door to go out, and when Ansel opened the door for him, Inky dashed out with the pug. Ansel hurried in pursuit, holding him in one hand and scolding him as he carried him inside.

"These cats should never go outside," he told Jazzi. "There's a woods at the back of the field. I've heard a coyote before. Coyotes hunt small pets."

Jazzi glanced out the window at George. "We don't have to worry about one carrying off our pug."

"Owls hunt cats, too," Ansel said.

He didn't have to convince her. "I'd rather keep Inky and Marmalade as house cats. I've seen strays go through our yard. Some of the dogs don't look friendly."

Ansel rubbed his chin, gazing at their property. "We should build a privacy fence around the small yard."

"And ruin our view?" Jazzi loved the open space around their house.

"The cats would be safer. We could keep them closer to home."

She didn't want a fence. "An owl could sit in our tree and swoop down in the yard."

"Maybe we should cut down the tree."

She stared at him. "No. No fence, and the tree stays."

"What about the cats?"

"We'll buy shocker collars for them so they get zapped every time they run out a door."

"Do those really exist?"

"I don't know, but we'll have to find out. What about a buried invisible fence? We could install one at the end of the patio. Then when the kittens are old enough, we could let them go outside to sit on the cement." She knew Ansel took his pets seriously, but this was ridiculous. He was a little obsessed about keeping her safe, too. She thought about Greg. Maybe that was a good thing...as long as he didn't push it too far.

Chapter 45

Jazzi, Jerod, and Ansel were sitting in the front room of their new fixer-upper when Gaff called. They'd brought four lawn chairs and a card table with them since there was no furniture.

"Can I stop by and talk to the three of you?" Gaff asked. "I have news."

Was it good or bad? He wouldn't tell her if she asked. He'd make her wait. "I brought extra sandwiches if you want to come for lunch."

"What kind?"

Sheez! Everyone was getting picky these days, but she was ready for them. She'd made a pork roast with lots of garlic and citrus juices in the slow cooker last night. "Cubanos with pork and ham. I'm bored with plain old deli right now."

"Never had one. I'll be there. Twelve-thirty." And Gaff clicked off.

She made a face when she turned off her phone.

Jerod had enjoyed the exchange, his expression downright ornery. "Have I told you that you need to step up your side dishes? We always get chips of some kind."

She tossed him an evil look. "You're right. I'll start bringing fresh vegetables. We'll be healthier."

He groaned. "Please. No veggie tray. I love my Franny, but whenever she has to carry in a dish, that's what we take."

Jazzi took mercy on him. She had no desire to trash Franny's offering. "We'll stick with chips. We need the salt since we sweat so much."

"I'm using that line," he told her. "A defense of salt."

They went back to drawing up plans for what they wanted to do, and in what order, to the house. First, the foundation.

"We'll call Darby," Jerod said. They'd worked with him more times than not when they needed someone who drove a cement truck. "We'll see how soon he can get here."

They were going to have to jack up the back corner of the house and repour that part of the foundation. They'd done it before, building forms and reinforcing them. Once they finished, the house would be on a solid footing again.

"We haven't seen the old coot for a while now," Ansel said. "Haven't needed him for any cement work."

"We might get lucky since it's late in the season. He won't be as busy since some of the builders have quit knocking up new houses."

Jazzi couldn't believe how many new subdivisions had gone up around River Bluffs this year. The city kept growing.

They turned back to their planning sheet. "Then the roof," Jerod said.

"We should do the front porch after that," Ansel said. "And the fence. Once we get all of the outside work done, then we can dig into the interior. That's going to take the longest."

Every room was small and poorly designed. They started listing the materials they thought they'd need to get started. They were still working on that when Gaff arrived.

He gave a quick knock and came to find them. He turned to look the house over and shook his head. "Did you guys get bored because the last house was too easy?"

Jerod snorted. "Make fun of it now, but wait till you see how it turns out."

Gaff dropped into the extra chair. "I don't have any doubts about that, but you've sure got your work cut out for you."

"Talking about work, what did you find out about Greg?" Ansel glanced at Jazzi. He wanted answers.

"Let's eat while we talk." She got up, came back with the cooler, and handed a sandwich to each person.

The minute she was finished, Ansel said, "Is Greg the killer?"

"We arrested him at his apartment last night. I talked to Seth on Sunday afternoon, and he told me that Greg never got married. He was a serial monogamist but wouldn't even move in with a girl. He didn't want anything to tie him down. His last girlfriend was on the pill but went off it without telling him. When she got pregnant, she thought he'd marry her. He hated her for it, and now he's stuck paying child support for a kid he never sees. Doesn't want to."

Seth had told Jazzi about that a long time ago, when she first asked him about Greg, but she'd lost track of it. Meghan was pregnant when she died. Had Greg snapped when she'd confessed that to him?

Jerod looked disgusted. "If he didn't want kids, he should have bought a box of his own protection."

"Greg didn't see it that way," Gaff said. "Precaution was the girl's responsibility."

"So all he did was show up and have fun."

"Pretty much." Gaff unwrapped his sandwich and took a bite. "Boy, this is good!"

Ansel scowled. "So Greg got Meghan pregnant and then strangled her because she was going to have his baby?"

Gaff took a swig of water before answering. "He denied everything until we got the results from the trunk of his car. He'd cleaned it. The dealership cleaned it, but we still found evidence. Then he broke down. He said it wasn't fair. Meghan had faithfully taken her pills. He even used protection, but she still got pregnant. He said it was like the heavens were laughing at him."

Jerod leaned forward, aggravated. "Then it wasn't Meghan's fault. What more did he want her to do?"

"He didn't blame her, but he wanted her to abort it. They had a big fight. She refused. She said she'd raise the baby by herself, that he could just walk away."

"Then what was his problem?" Jerod reached for a beer and another sandwich.

"He said that any time she wanted to, she could ask for a paternity test, and then he'd be stuck. He was gearing up to start working as a mixologist, and a chef had agreed to partner with him. He had visions of big bucks. A baby could mess everything up. He said he just snapped. The next thing he knew, he was strangling Meghan with his tie, and Miles slammed through the door to stop him. He punched Miles down and finished killing Meghan, then grabbed a heavy skillet and smashed it into the back of Miles's head."

Ansel shook his head. "I'm not buying his story."

Gaff looked surprised.

"Greg wore a tie when he came to see Jazzi. He never wears ties. When she asked him about his new car, he was ready to strangle her. If he wore a tie to see Meghan, he meant to kill her."

"It was premeditated." Gaff sat back in his chair, his expression serious.

Ansel reached for Jazzi's hand. She thought it was more to assure himself than her. "He killed anyone who got in his way."

Looks sure could be deceiving. All those girls who vied for his attention at the bar saw him as a good-looking, fun-loving guy. Jazzi thought about Leo. "Poor Leo died because his dog led him to the shallow graves where Greg had buried Miles and Meghan."

Gaff nodded. "Greg must have used the binoculars when he took a break at work and seen Leo. He knew if the dog got close to the wetlands, he'd sniff out the bodies. It was easy enough for him to disappear for a while and kill Leo. Then later he tossed his body in the restaurant's dumpster to make Seth look bad. Meghan died because, even though she was careful, she'd gotten pregnant by him. And Miles died trying to defend her."

"How many people would Greg have killed to protect himself?" Surely, he'd worry that the more bodies that stacked up, the more Gaff would become suspicious of him.

Ansel's voice had an edge to it. "As many as it took."

Gaff let out a long breath. He wrapped up his sandwich to take with him and stood. "Well, as usual, thanks for your help."

"We hope it's the last time." Ansel smiled to soften his words.

"Hey, I get it." Gaff gave them a wave and let himself out.

They sat at the table a while longer, a little stunned. It took a while to shift back into work mode.

Jerod pointed at the list he'd written of materials that they needed. "I hope Greg rots in prison, but I don't want his vibes anywhere near this house. Let's figure out how to make it beautiful."

A perfect sentiment.

Talk returned to crown molding, woodwork, and colors of paint. They might not be able to fix warped human beings, but they could fix houses. And they'd do a good job on this one.

Chapter 46

Ansel and Jazzi attended Isabelle and Reuben's wedding the next Sunday. She'd bought a new hot-pink dress to wear. Ansel wore a tan suit and a pink dress shirt. Jazzi never thought she'd be one of those couples who dressed to match, but she had to admit that she and her Norseman looked pretty good together.

She didn't think she'd ever be a weeper, either, someone who teared up at weddings, but she was so happy for Isabelle and Reuben, she misted up when they were finally officially married. The Oyster Bar couldn't hold another person, but it felt good to be surrounded by people who'd come to celebrate with her friends.

Once the ceremony ended, the chef carried out trays of hot and cold oysters. Shrimp cocktail, smoked salmon, and crab cakes followed. Tenderloin sliders provided something for non-seafood lovers. Isabelle and Reuben circulated from one knot of friends to the next until they finally reached them.

"Congratulations! I'm so happy for you!" Jazzi reached out to hug Isabelle, but her friend grabbed her arm and yanked her hand toward her.

"Is this an engagement ring?" Isabelle stretched Jazzi's hand toward Reuben. "Look, hon. What do you think?"

Reuben's face lit up. "Is this official?"

Ansel jammed his hands in his pockets. "We were going to tell you later, but we wanted today to be about you two."

Isabelle tugged Jazzi into a fierce hug. "You're engaged! When's the wedding?"

Ansel almost spilled his drink when Reuben slapped him on the back. "We haven't picked a date yet. We're keeping it simple. Justice of the peace. The reception at our house."

"You have to invite us!" Isabelle went to slide her arm through Reuben's.

"Will your family be there?" Reuben asked Ansel. "If your brothers come, can I be rude to them?"

Ansel shook his head. "We haven't gotten that far. When we do, we'll tell you, but for today, we're here to celebrate *you*."

"But this makes it perfect, doesn't it?" Reuben turned to see Isabelle's reaction. "It's a doubly happy day."

"*You* two are perfect together," Jazzi told them.

"That's how we feel about you. We'll have to stay friends for forever." Isabelle hugged Jazzi one last time, then said, "We'd better finish seeing more friends, but this is"—she paused with a smile—"the icing on our wedding cake."

And as soon as the words left Isabelle's lips, the cake was carried out—a three-tiered wonder. But no one was in a rush. People went back for seconds of food, more wine, and more laughter.

When Isabelle and Reuben left to chat with the next group of people, Ansel slid his arm around Jazzi's waist. "I can't wait until we're official. The sooner, the better."

Jazzi turned a thoughtful gaze on Isabelle and Reuben. They looked so happy. Any doubts she'd had about Ansel were gone. She smiled up at him. "Early November?"

His blue eyes glinted. "Are you serious?"

"Why not?"

He lifted her off her feet for a bear hug and smashed his lips against hers. That kiss lingered for the rest of the reception.

On the drive home, Jazzi tried to contain the giddy feeling that bubbled inside her. Life was blossoming around her. Their fixer-upper business was good, and she and Ansel were spectacular. How much better could things get? And no more dead bodies, she told herself. Just work, play, and Ansel. A perfect trifecta.

Please turn the page for some recipes from Jazzi's kitchen!

Cabbage Rolls

To begin, core one head of cabbage as deep as you can to get out most of the core.

Boil water in a soup pot or deep Dutch oven. Carefully lower the head of cabbage into it. When the outer leaves get soft and curl outward, peel each one back with tongs and put each leaf on paper towels to drain, being careful not to tear the leaves. Do this until you have enough leaves and only small ones remain.

For the filling:

In a mixing bowl, combine:

> 2 lbs. Bob Evans regular-flavored ground sausage
> 2 lbs. ground chuck
> 3 cups cooked rice
> 1 chopped onion
> 4 tablespoons Worcestershire sauce
> 2 tablespoons parsley
> 2 teaspoons salt
> ½ teaspoon Tabasco

For the sauce:

> 1 lb. Bob Evans regular-flavored ground sausage
> 1 lb. ground chuck
> 1 chopped onion
> 1 teaspoon salt
> 2 large cans of diced tomatoes
> 4 cans (8 oz.) tomato sauce
> 4 teaspoons dill seed
> 2 teaspoons sugar
> 4 tablespoons Worcestershire sauce

Brown the ground chuck and the sausage, then add the other ingredients.

To assemble:

In a large Dutch oven: Place leftover, small cabbage leaves on bottom of Dutch oven. Place heaping tablespoon of meat mix in center of each cabbage leaf. Fold two sides over filling, then roll up. Lay filled cabbage leaves on top to form a layer, add sauce, another layer, more sauce, etc. Bring to a boil. Partially cover and reduce to a simmer for 2½ hours.

Chicken Salad

Prepare the dressing first. It will be even better if you allow it to chill and "steep" overnight.

For one whole, baked chicken, mix together ½ cup each of mayonnaise, Miracle Whip, and sour cream.

Stir in:

> 1 tablespoon vinegar
> 1 tablespoon sugar or Stevia to taste
> ¼ cup finely chopped onion
> salt and white pepper to taste

Dice the chicken. Add ½ cup finely chopped celery and a generous dash of Lawry's Seasoned Salt.

Add dressing and toss. Chill until time to serve. If salad looks dry, add ¼ to ½ cup of Miracle Whip.

Note: This basic recipe is meant to be altered to fit your taste. The ingredients should stay the same unless substitutes are needed due to allergies. Grapes and walnuts are possible additions. Any leftover dressing makes a great cucumber salad; just slice cucumbers and onions and add dressing.